to C

THE COLLATION UNIT

Happy reading

THE COLLATION UNIT

DAVID JARVIS

Matador
9 Priory Business Park,
Wistow Road, Kibworth Beauchamp,
Leicestershire. LE8 0RX
Tel: 0116 279 2299
Email: books@troubador.co.uk
Web: www.troubador.co.uk/matador
Twitter: @matadorbooks

ISBN 978 1800462 083

British Library Cataloguing in Publication Data.
A catalogue record for this book is available from the British Library.

Printed and bound by CPI Group (UK) Ltd, Croydon, CR0 4YY
Typeset in 11pt Adobe Garamond Pro by Troubador Publishing Ltd, Leicester, UK

Matador is an imprint of Troubador Publishing Ltd

CHAPTER ONE

This was no ordinary burial.

Children were chasing each other around the grassy graves and the vicar was sharing a joke with the formidable Mrs Harker. Rooks wheeled overhead, while others brayed from the misshapen horse chestnuts which now served as their much-reduced nesting site. The avenue of majestic elms was long gone, consigned to the collective corvid memory through twenty generations. A hundred precarious, untidy heaps of sticks that had formed the largest rookery in England; the Mother of all Parliaments. Gone forever.

Master of Ceremonies at the interment was a white-haired man. He had retired to the village seven years previously in 1992, but had remained something of an enigma. His smile was disarming but his frown could freeze delinquent children to the spot. Still, it was good to have a man of distinction presiding over affairs; a knight of the realm; a man with connections … and Sir Cecil certainly had those.

He had decided to offer his services several months earlier on a sunny morning in March. That day had begun normally enough, even if everything seemed to take a little longer. With arthritis in his knees since his fifties, the daily routine of carrying his breakfast tray into the lounge had degenerated into a painful shuffle. Slumped in the winged armchair, he had savoured the first real shafts of sunlight that year. His days had begun with a pot of orange pekoe tea and a copy of the *Times* since long before his retirement, long before the death of his wife four years ago and long before he had joined the Foreign Office in 1951. The tea always brought back memories of the Hill Club, of Nuwara Eliya, and of Mountbatten. As he poured his first cup that spring day, the sun began to roll like a cheese (a rather pallid Wensleydale) up the hip tiles of the Cotswold stone roof opposite. That wonderful first sip took away the taste of the night and he started to scan the headlines on the front page. At some point around the letters page he poured his second cup, but he would never drink it. An hour later he would throw it away stone cold. It was not only the tea that would remain unfinished that morning; the crossword would not even be started.

It was the face of his old friend Robin Mills, frozen by some 1960s photographer, that stared out at him from the obituaries page. Transfixed by that face, waves of … waves of something or other swept over Cecil. He had not realised that they now put the Head of the Secret Service in the obituaries; did that mean that they would put Cecil himself in? Who would tell the newspapers? Why?

But worst of all by a long chalk was the realisation that he was the last of the six who had shared a somewhat special secret; the Big Six, as he had called them after Arthur Ransome's novel.

Good God, he was used to secrets. Where MI6 purchased its paper clips was a secret. But this was a secret that could not be written down, a secret which had literally changed the world, and a secret which would now die with him.

There was a stillness. Barely a mote of dust dared enter the shafts of sunlight now streaming in through his windows. The village was silent.

Even after a life in the Secret Services, where his agile mind had constantly to think of every possible scenario, Cecil had never once thought that it would be him left carrying the baton … surely he had been one of the oldest? Robin had been his junior, his Deputy, his successor. Robin would outlive him – not that Cecil had ever consciously gone through this thought process before.

Rereading the obituary, it seemed to concentrate on Robin's university days and sporting record for at least three-quarters of the piece. His time at the Foreign Office only occupied a couple of lines. Cecil raised his eyes, but did not focus. So it would not be Robin who took the decision. It would not be Robin who would have to judge the political and social climate of the time and decide if any good would come from revealing the truth. Maybe it was Cecil's own impending death after seven years of retirement that now gave the matter added weight? If he dropped dead tomorrow, it would be lost forever. At that moment he had a strange urge to commit it to paper; a spontaneous feeling so at odds with his previous life where as little as possible was documented (normally the number of words was inversely proportional to the importance; the purchase of paper clips warranting reams).

He had become aware of the silence. Normally, he loved silence. Since his wife had died, his retirement to a quiet village on the banks of the River Avon had almost turned him into a recluse. He loved the peace and isolation … even his garden was not overlooked. However, to the villagers he was an unknown quantity; a charming, white-haired retired diplomat with sharp blue eyes. They (the villagers, that is) had all tried to find out more. It had become a bit of a game for a while, but to no avail.

Jocelyn, the Conservative Party agent, had tried a few times (after all, Cecil looked like one of theirs). "Want a ticket for the cocktail party at Hanbury's Farm? Kingston, our MEP, will be there. Super chap."

Whether it was Mr Hanbury, Mr Kingston or Cecil who was the super chap was not explained.

"Don't suppose you want a ticket for the House of Commons terrace next month? A hundred pounds? As a diplomat, expect you've had it up to here with politicians?"

"Yes, I have" did not advance the search for details of Cecil's past, or sell many tickets.

Peg, the down-to-earth organiser of the Christmas parcels for the elderly in the village, had no success either, although she had received a warmer welcome. "We've had a disco and a jumble sale, and we give all of our OAPs a parcel," she told Cecil on his doorstep that first December.

He almost took the proffered package as the easiest way out, but his conscience got the better of him and he asked that it be given to someone more deserving … and could he give a bottle of Chablis to the cause? "The best thing to come out of France," he said, handing the bottle over at the door.

"Seems to know a lot about France," Peg had said in all innocence down at The Feathers that evening, and so another rumour had started. By Christmas, Cecil had been our Ambassador in Paris, Ambassador to Canada, and Head of every company from Perrier to Peugeot. Of course, no one had the guts to ask him outright, so the rumours continued to mutate.

It had therefore been a surprise when, one March day in 1999, Cecil turned the tables and appeared on Peg's doorstep.

"I understand from the parish magazine that you are trying to organise the schoolchildren into burying a time capsule to celebrate the Millennium?"

"That's right."

"I think it's an excellent idea. I wondered if you needed someone to help fund it, organise the competition to select the contents; you know, act as general factotum?"

Peg did not know what the last bit meant, but having Sir Cecil on board would be marvellous. "Of course. Why don't you come to the first meeting? Perhaps you could chair it?"

"I would be delighted."

And so it happened. Under Cecil's steady control, the project went smoothly from concept to construction. Funds were raised, the local newspaper was involved, a site in the graveyard at the base of the east tower was chosen, and the capsule's contents were debated and selected. Cecil himself had arranged for the waterproof canister to be made by local craftsmen.

Almost nine months after his conversation with Peg, Cecil was standing as Master of Ceremonies with the whole village watching from every vantage point in and around the churchyard.

"So," he said, "let us mark the year 2050 in our minds, so that the time capsule might then be lifted and its contents examined and discussed. This will enable our children and our children's children to watch the objects of today become the relics of the past."

He smiled for the camera and waited while the man from the *Gazette* took the photograph of the lucky child who had won the honour of burying the canister.

"Can I just ask a couple of questions?" the journalist pressed Sir Cecil. "When did you have the idea of burying this time capsule?"

"It wasn't my idea. I read about it in the parish magazine and thought that it was an excellent idea. Coincidentally, I had just read of the death of a close friend in the *Times* that day, and that made me think about the passing of time."

"And what do you think the villagers will make of the contents when they dig them up?"

"I think we all take for granted aspects and artefacts of our daily lives. I am sure that everyone will be greatly surprised, greatly surprised … they may even look at their lives and those of their forefathers in quite a different light."

* * *

"Randall, what a surprise."

"Hello, Sir … Cecil."

"It must be seven years? Come on in."

The uncomfortable visitor with the bald head stepped into the cool, dark interior of Cecil's hall. "I was shocked to read about Robin."

"Yes, an aneurism of some sort … whatever they are."

Randall sank into the armchair indicated by his host. This was the schoolboy, now successful in middle age, meeting his retired headmaster once again.

"Fancy a Scotch, or are you driving?"

"I have a driver … yes, please." How Randall wished that he had just said, 'Yes, please. I am not driving.' It had sounded like he was now allowed to wear long trousers.

"So, who's taken over?"

"A … good chap."

They both smiled and the tension evaporated; their past relationship forgotten, the new confirmed. Randall not needing to reveal the identity of the incomer and not insulting Cecil by reeling off the name promoted by the media.

"Either you have achieved no promotion in ten years and, through your incompetency, have mistaken the date of my annual visit, or you now have the key to the executive lavatory, and this is related to Robin's death."

"In a way it is related to his death, and I'm sorry the questioning on these occasions is one-way … this is not easy."

Randall was looking for some acknowledgement from Cecil of the awkwardness of the situation. Something like, 'I also had to deal with my retired boss once, so I understand', or, 'I know that I once knew all of the country's secrets, so how can I help?' He had another problem, too. He did not know exactly why he was there or what he should be asking.

At the last meeting that he had chaired, Robin had suggested that an annual visit to key personnel who had retired was not enough. It did not protect the Service adequately or provide the correct level of welfare. One could not rely on long-suffering wives to make contact if their husbands went doolally and started to regale locals down the village pub with tales of one-time pads and derring-do. Anyway, most wives knew little of their husband's past, while others might be reluctant to telephone Whitehall and admit that dear Johnny was going senile.

There was yet another reason for the visits. Few of us lead wholly secret lives. The pressure of being able to say nothing and not discussing matters is relieved by spending one's day with others in the same boat. On retirement, even this avenue is closed. At a time when one is reflecting on one's life, deprived of the unspoken camaraderie, and missing being in a position of power, one is left alone in a Cotswold or Norfolk village with a cat for company and the onset of Alzheimer's. Unlike Prime Ministers or Secretaries of State for Northern Ireland, Heads of the Secret Services do not get lifetime protection; they do not even have a Special Branch officer with whom to talk about Leyton Orient's chances of promotion.

Randall knew full well that he was playing chess without being able to see his opponent's pieces but, from Robin's last meeting, there had been a clear inference that it was Sir Cecil he had in mind for the additional visit. But why? Cecil had done nothing wrong in the seven years since his retirement. He had lost his wife, but clearly had coped with that.

So what could it be? Internal intrigue in the Service? Unlikely. After seven years, who would care? Why would Cecil be holding secrets? External intrigue by the Service? Cecil had a reputation for ruthlessness, for being cantankerous, but also for being fiercely loyal and patriotic. If something had not bothered him seven years ago, why now? Had he acquired some new conscience as he mellowed into old age? Had he been contacted by someone?

Whatever it was, it could not be written down. Randall had checked the main files and the personnel reports. It must be unwritten and involve Robin. It must be something that could compromise both Cecil and Robin. Here Randall went slightly awry. He was not to know that Cecil and Robin had shared the secret about actions which had absolutely and fundamentally changed world politics in the last decades of the twentieth century. Randall could also not know that, since Robin's death, Cecil was revisiting the whole issue in his own mind. It would be a strange meeting, therefore. A strange meeting that would go nowhere without delicate probing and provoking by Randall.

Surprisingly, it was Cecil who sacrificed the first pawn. "You will not, perhaps, realise the several significances of today's date?"

There was no reaction. Cecil had revealed that there was something significant. Randall had revealed that he did not know about the dates. Stalemate.

"Was this the Zugdidi affair?" Randall asked.

"No, that was a minor distraction during the Falklands War ... which ended on this day in June, seventeen years ago in 1982."

"So it did. What else happened today?"

It was Cecil's turn to explore how much Randall knew or had been told by Robin. "The Zugdidi affair did almost mess up something else ... of which one of the key dates was, or is, today." He paused. "Seventeen years ago there was an important funeral in the Soviet Union, I recall."

He watched Randall's eyes for the merest hint of recognition. None.

"Anyway," Cecil continued, "have some tea. I am sure that you didn't come down here to talk about the irrelevant coincidence of a few dates over the last twenty years and ... burials."

CHAPTER TWO

It was far too early in the year to have a barbecue, even if it was a warm March evening. Still, it was his forty-fifth birthday.

It was March 1982, and the garden had not recovered from the winter. Gnats zigzagged within their imagined confines under a lime tree. There was a dampness in the evening air, in the charcoal and on proceedings, generally. Charcoal – was ever a substance more ill-fitted to its task? Highly water absorbent and, having been burnt once, less than enthusiastic about a return match. The round-shouldered men, in a loose ruck, clutched at greasy glasses of Hirondelle and poked the matt black briquettes with Taiwanese spatulas, tongs and prongs. The word 'napalm' had been heard.

On the distaff side of the kitchen window, frustration was being kept in check. The word 'microwave' had been heard. Serried rows of meat on grey marble platters resembled the leftovers from some hideous transplant experiment. Rump steak and lamb chops were losing their acrylic sheen, and the air was developing a metallic edge. Adding to the assault on the senses, the telephones sounded throughout the house and garden with an unsynchronised ringing and trilling.

"Jack!" Sarah shouted unnecessarily through the open window. "The phone!"

Jack swapped his tongs for a Taiwanese-made phone handed to him through the kitchen window. He pulled the long cable to its full extent while backing into the gnats. They reformed their holding position three yards to the left, flying back and forth with added passion.

"Jack?"

"Speaking."

"Jack, it's Harry. Aunt Mary is not too good, I'm afraid. She's in hospital."

"Do you want me to come up?"

"I think that would be a good idea. Bring some clothes. You can always stay here if you need to stop over."

"Have you been trying to contact Ross? Only, he is here. We're having a barbecue."

"I was just about to. Ask him if he'd like to come as well. I don't think that she is going to make it."

Jack Pennington replaced the handset onto the dial pad in his left hand. His eyes betrayed no emotion. They rarely did. His facial expressions ranged from 'politely concerned vicar' to 'politely unconcerned vicar'. He turned to Ross, who was to be found cursing behind clouds of acrid steam, the product of lighter fuel on barely glowing charcoal.

"That was Harry. We have to go in. I'll tell Sarah. Where's Margaret?"

"Stabbing sausages in the kitchen. I'll tell her when she comes over."

Jack turned to look at the children, who were playing their own version of *633 Squadron*. Arms outstretched, they were streaming across the lawn carrying footballs. These were launched at the base of the bird table in an attempt to topple a Coke tin perched on the rim. Jack handed the phone back through the window and walked into the kitchen to be met by the resigned faces of both Sarah, his wife, and Margaret.

"Let's guess."

"Afraid so."

"Can you finish eating?"

There was no reply.

"I don't care if the Russian Navy is halfway up the Thames; Ross is not leaving until that barbecue is lit."

Jack turned to the open kitchen door. No one was within earshot, and he let the flippant indiscretion ride.

* * *

Ten minutes later, Jack was driving his Volvo estate through the tree-lined roads of suburban Cheltenham. Ross would follow in a further quarter of an hour; not to ensure that the charcoal was glowing red-grey, but to put some distance between them. In any event, Ross would have to drive home to collect his overnight bag. The air in the car was cold from the confines of the garage, and Jack shivered. Perhaps it was a bit early for a barbecue? He ran his hand up into his unmanageable shock of wavy greying hair. His brown wool jacket began to slide off the front seat as he negotiated his way around the roundabouts that mark the boundaries of Cheltenham before climbing Birdlip Hill towards Cirencester.

In the unlikely event that anyone would want to delve deeper into the nondescript world of Jack Pennington, a series of defences had been devised for him. In twenty years the need to use even the second defence had only arisen on a handful of occasions, and then for genuine and innocent reasons. He was a civil servant. He had a wife called Sarah, two children, and a Labrador. He knew a little about archaeology and a lot about Middle Eastern stamps, of which he had a reasonable collection. All of this was true.

If asked, he was an office administrator, the grown-up ink monitor, the man who made sure that no one ran out of biros. This was not true. If pressed, perhaps by neighbours or by relatives, he would reveal that this office administration was at GCHQ – the Government Communications Headquarters at Cheltenham. Consequently, he would say, he couldn't talk too much about his job even though it was low-key. None of this was true. Although he had worked at GCHQ for a period, this was no longer the case. Whereas people had heard of GCHQ and knew roughly what was undertaken there, they had never heard of his real workplace or his real job.

Cheltenham was so full of secretaries, cleaners, security guards, ground maintenance staff, you name it, from GCHQ that Jack's cover was unlikely to be questioned, and remained of little interest. If you want to hide a worker in a small very secret establishment, put him in a town with a large secret establishment.

After a quarter of an hour the Volvo was slowed by a series of right-angled bends reflecting field patterns long ago rendered irrelevant by arable farming methods. Jack accelerated along the next long straight, a consequence of the Roman influence on the Cotswolds. The grassed hangars of RAF Mannington appeared above the low oolitic limestone walls. One of several Second World War airfields in the vicinity, it sat on a broad ridge with an old runway now quiet except for the occasional Land Rover patrol. The barley crop, which was growing right up to the expanse of tarmac, was a sea of green. The insecticide spraying was about to begin. The blue sign at the gate warranted barely a glance from the Cotswold caravanners or the Cheltenham racegoers rumbling along the old Roman route. To anyone interested, it pronounced the ongoing presence of the 36th Postal Communications Division and the Administration Supplies Depot (Western). Nowhere had a sign so understated the truth, putting the 'lie' into 'litotes'.

Jack Pennington turned off the main road, drawing up at the token guardroom with its barrier and concrete-filled oil drums. The vast acres of runway tarmac and barley fields were given counterpoint by the neat flower beds, bare except for clumps of daffodils which surrounded an incongruous metal post. The Spitfire which had perched atop this had graced the entrance for many years, but was now to be found in crates at the new Imperial War Museum Duxford. The metal post on its concrete plinth added to the feeling of relegation from vital and active airfield to a forgotten and neglected relic of the past.

Given his fictitious job as an office administrator at GCHQ, it was not surprising that Jack should be seen visiting the stores at Mannington. Presumably this was where he would come to count boxes of photocopy paper and audit mountains of tables, chairs, drawing boards and filing cabinets which now occupied the hangars behind their giant sliding doors. Not that anyone was interested.

Out of sight of the main road, he approached a second control near one of the main collection of hangars. Not only was he expected, but he had been followed by discreet cameras from the first gate. Entry beyond this second point was 'by recognition only'. There were none of the standard mechanisms for entry; even the maintenance staff who visited infrequently had to establish recognition codes on a one-to-one basis after the most exhaustive vetting process.

He drove through a vehicle-sized aperture cut into the main sliding door of a hangar which served as a car park, passing a few dozen cars that barely filled a tenth of the space. At the far corner he approached two guards in a bombproof security box. He waved at the occupants. One of them passed Jack his security card through a small window. No security cards left the site. From the moment he swiped his card in the slot, his movements in the complex were tracked by the security computer.

He entered a lift, descending to the third floor below ground level. Excavated as a secret bomb store in 1940, it had been extended in 1964 to provide a six-floor underground complex. Jack needed his card to both get out of the lift at the third floor and to enter his section. The view that faced him always struck him as unreal; a vast, windowless room, with subdued lighting and packed with eighteen computer stations. The 'Babbage Patch', it was nicknamed. These were no ordinary computer terminals; each consisted of two large, deep monitors to the front, two to the left and a single larger version to the right. The operator was surrounded by more keyboards than Rick Wakeman and more screens than ... well, a Currys shop window. A long shelf made of angle iron was attached to the end wall, where six additional screens appeared to teeter precariously, seemingly held in position by the bundles of grey cables that came through the wall and interconnected them. The background buzz was overridden by an occasional electronic bleep, and the heat generated by the system was barely countered by the crude air-conditioning system which further added to the noise.

There were six similar floors. This was Floor C; 'C' was for Middle East – the logic behind this had long been lost. Floor A was for South and Central America; Floor B was for the Soviet Union sphere of influence, and so on. Floor F stood for 'friendly' (this at least had some logic to it), and covered the USA among others. Jack Pennington was Head of his team of almost forty Middle East experts. Twelve men and women were on station at any one time; seven monitored the most important countries, and the other five covered the minor countries and had a parallel responsibility for liaison with each of the other five floors. In times of emergency, the remaining six terminals were occupied.

RAF Mannington was given over to Collation; the Big Yawn, as it was known affectionately to a very small section of the Secret Squirrel community. It is probable that the blue sign at the gateway could have been replaced by an illuminated sign saying, 'CENTRE FOR INFORMATION COLLATION (THE WORLD)' and no one would have batted an eyelid. There is something about the word 'collation' that is both anodyne and soporific.

Pre-Second World War, the obsession among the governments of all countries had been the acquisition of information. Who was doing what, when, where and with whom? There was so little data; a spy here, an embassy dispatch there. It took a man from the Foreign Office two minutes over a kümmel on ice at his club to work out the implications; then 1939 changed all that. Getting information became easier. Local phone tapping, aerial photography and radio soon overloaded the system. When worldwide phone tapping, satellite photography and early computers reinforced this, the system broke down. There was too much information. The answer was in there somewhere … but where? The silicon chip and artificial intelligence had tested to breaking point the very intelligence of their creator.

To cope with this problem, the Collation Unit was established. It was manned by former staff from GCHQ, and normally one had to work on the collection and/or translation of data before being moved to Mannington. Once there, the information from all sources, almost however sensitive, was fed to the relevant floors, the relevant sections. Over eighty per cent of all information collected in a 'sphere of influence' was only relevant to that area. The remaining information had to be collated by the five operators who had a liaison role with the other floors.

Jack Pennington sat down on his chair, swiped his card and keyed in his security code. While the start-up sequences flicked across his seven screens, the Head of the Collation Unit, Marcus Billingham, appeared at his side.

"Sorry to phone you at home, Jack."

"No problem."

"Hope it didn't ruin the barbecue?"

"It's impossible to ruin a barbecue. You start with all of the elements against you and try to produce edible food despite them."

The screens settled down to constant pictures.

"I've put the relevant pages on the network. Call up MB320."

Jack tapped in the necessary commands. With that, two letters from a Georgian working at the Russian Embassy in

London came up on the left screens, a record of a telephone conversation between Saudi Arabia and an unknown individual came up on one of the central screens, and a close-up satellite photograph wiped down on the large single screen to his right.

"They may be about to move."

Jack read all of the text and looked at the aerial photograph. A forested hillside was fretted with a series of tracks which ended abruptly against a wall or a door. "There's no sign of activity yet, is there?"

"Try MB321."

The view of the mountain roads was replaced by a much-speeded-up video sequence of a small ship. Its name, its location in the Black Sea and the passing of real time were all displayed at the top of the screen.

"Watch this … there."

At a time specified in the text on the other screens, the small ship changed course and moved eastwards towards the Adzharsk coast.

Ross walked into the room, scratching his ginger beard and with his corduroy jacket over his shoulder. He stood behind Jack. "Are they on the move?" he asked.

"Yes … and it looks like to Saudi Arabia."

CHAPTER THREE

Ibrahim sat behind a big desk; he needed to, he was a big man. A curl of cigarette smoke caressed his cheek but avoided his hooded eyes. He was Egyptian. An office administrator. The man who made sure that you ran out of biros.

This was Saudi Arabia.

Of course, his brother knew a business acquaintance who had a pen franchise but, alas, there was a cost. How urgent were these pens? Really? That urgent?

The glistening mahogany dome of his head would shake from side to side, gradually tilting forwards. His chins would concertina until they overwhelmed his white shirt collar, threatening the double Windsor knot of his black-and-white striped tie. More than enough time to calculate his percentage, so that as his head came back up the eyelids would lift, the long lashes flick away any of your doubts, and the dark tourmaline eyes would reflect all of your hopes and desires.

"Right-On! Come in! Sit down! How are you?"

Basil closed the pair of doors behind him. Ibrahim stubbed out his cigarette, rising to shake hands in one enthusiastic movement.

"Take a seat. Not literally; I only have a few hundred. Though my brother has a franchise. Hah! How are things, Right-On?" Ibrahim asked. (He was also Head of Personnel.)

"I was hoping that you would tell me," the Honourable Basil Wynne inquired. He had given up reminding Ibrahim that it was his brother who was the Right Honourable.

"Spiffing! Is that right? Spiffing?"

"Exactly."

"Spiffing. It sounds like something we dirty Arabs do on the pavement."

"Hardly." Basil Wynne squirmed inside at Ibrahim's rather direct style.

"Would you like some coffee?"

"Thanks."

"Turkish? Just joking. Nescafé with milk. I know you aristocratic English." Ibrahim managed to press a switch on his telephone with one of his large fingers. "Abdullah, Nescafé … *shukran.*"

Basil placed his leather handbag on his lap in anticipation. Ibrahim, for his part, reached into a drawer and placed a folder on his desktop.

"Basil."

He had never been called Basil by Ibrahim before, just 'Right-On'.

"Basil, Sheikh Abdullatif has big plans for you."

This did not sound like good news. Basil foresaw impending doom. What he actually saw was a snake strangling three ice-cream cornets, but this proved to be the bizarre ceiling light reflected in the vast expanse of Ibrahim's shiny desktop.

"Sheikh Abdullatif would like to honour you with promotion."

Basil rotated his cufflinks. This served to remind him that he was in a land of short-sleeved shirts. He was a fish out of water; a fish in the desert.

In an action reminiscent of a fat lady walking, Ibrahim rotated the paper on his desk using two of his stubby fingers.

"What does this promotion entail?"

"Sheikh Abdullatif would like you to combine a new role as 'reviewer' with your duties as Professor of Desert Engineering at the university."

Basil did not like the sound of the role titled 'reviewer'. It was not specific. Reviewing what? He moved lamely on to the offensive. "I may find it difficult to combine the two tasks. The university work can be quite demanding."

In poker, Basil would have shown his opponent his hand and asked his advice. He was not a thinker-through of consequences. He spoke as a response to the last thing said, not in anticipation of the next. University work to Basil meant a rather gentle nine hours' teaching each week in a rather vague subject to students operating in a foreign language – English. Nine hours was not demanding.

"You are right, Right-On", Ibrahim chuckled, and Basil relaxed, even smiling at Ibrahim's surprising mastery of English. "Sheikh Abdullatif said that if you found it all too much he would respect your decision and relieve you of your university duties – much as you have been appreciated."

Basil found himself (not for the first time, teaching desert engineering) between a rock and a hard place. He wanted to stay at the university. It was easy, protected, lucrative, and his wife Gaynor had settled into the dinner-party regimen. It would be better to undertake this 'reviewing' in the comfortable chair of his study on campus than … where? He had come to the correct conclusion but, as always, a bit late.

"I'm sure I could combine the reviewing with the professorship."

"No, Basil," they were back to Basil, "Sheikh Abdullatif has the interests of you and your lovely wife Gaynor firmly in his heart. He asks that you undertake the job of reviewer which is of particular importance to him, and in recognition he will increase your salary by sixty thousand riyals per year and give you a Ministry Mercedes."

"Thank you. Sheikh Abdullatif is very generous."

The word 'Ministry' was just beginning to register with Basil.

"… and I am to find you a villa of the very highest quality." Ibrahim beamed and raised his heavy hand not too high above the desk as an indication of quality.

The Honourable Basil le Strange Wynne, the second son of the Earl of Mallow and Blackwater, could see his world falling apart. This was a shame. It had taken him forty-seven years to get his world together, and that was mostly over the last six months. When he was seven years old he couldn't wait to leave Wellbeck House and the family estate for boarding school. The old house was vast and cold. The antiquated heating system leaked and the radiators were furred up from years of chalkland water. The rooms were ill-lit and depressing. It was a gilt-edged deprivation. He was prevented from kicking a football indoors because of the stretched silk which lined most of the walls; the shiny blue fabric was a temptation akin to a still pool begging for a tossed pebble. When he hit the silk, ripples radiated around the room or down the hall, passing behind the dark countenances of ancestors captured in ever-crazed oils. For his twelfth birthday his father had given him a folly, a sixty-foot-high brick tower on the estate, when all he wanted was a bicycle. His only company comprised dogs; supercilious salukis who coiled in front of any log fire, soaking up the heat. He was lonely, seeking comfort in the shadow of his elder brother's countless sporting and academic successes.

For Basil, the Royal Agricultural College at Cirencester followed boarding school; while his elder brother, Ralph, left Oxford for a life in the Diplomatic Service, finding himself in Mexico City and then Madrid. His first full ambassadorial posting to the Philippines was not a month old when he became the fifteenth Earl of Mallow and Blackwater. Basil was the obvious choice to run the Wellbeck Estate given his experience.

"To which Ministry am I to be attached?" Basil asked with as little interest as he could conceal.

"The Ministry of Foreign Affairs. We call it MOFA."

"And what exactly will I be reviewing?"

"Construction plans." Ibrahim glanced at one of the two air-conditioning units that had temporarily joined phase to produce a hypnotic rhythm. "In the desert," he added somewhat gratuitously.

Basil desperately needed clarification of the last point. Were the projects in the desert? Or, more importantly, was he to live in a villa in the desert? The latter did not bear thinking about. Gaynor would divorce him.

It was at the Summer Ball in what became his last year at Cirencester that Gaynor had stepped on his toes and into his life. All the Usher dresses and Valentino jackets in the world could not hide the fact that this was a cattle market, if not an upmarket market. A glitzy occasion where the wealthy met the even wealthier; where girls from Cheltenham Ladies' College trapped their lords and masters. A rich canvas where the rich canvassed and, later, upstairs, money made money.

Gaynor had not really noticed the slightly stooping young man with the drawn face but strong chin. He was uncomfortable in his black tie and was having trouble drinking out of a glass following a visit earlier that afternoon to the dentist. He had been politely answering, with a paralysed rather than stiff upper lip, the banal, barked questions of an American girl. She was a frequent visitor to the college and was nicknamed 'Hackenbush' after the character from the Marx Brothers film (by way of 'hacking cough', 'hacking jacket' and 'cracking bush').

Only when Gaynor heard the five words 'Earl of Mallow and Blackwater' did she make her move. "Are those high cheekbones a family trait?" she asked.

"Lack of food for generations and a recent visit to the dentist," was the embarrassed reply.

But Basil was caught; Gaynor's victim; a trap devised over seven years camouflaged by the deceptively muted eau de Nil uniform of the Cheltenham Ladies'. Even when it transpired that he was the new earl's brother and not the earl himself, she did not miss a beat. After all, Ralph was in the Philippines and Basil would live with her in Wellbeck House.

Things had gone almost entirely to plan for this machine-tool manufacturer's daughter from Coventry. The sale of three small oil paintings of young girls with bulging eyes and long, pale necks had paid for a new heating system and her participation on the active social circuit. Basil had used some of the money to install a comprehensive irrigation system which upgraded part of the estate on clay lowland into a profitable farming venture. Two children followed, and everything was rosy in the several gardens.

It never made the British press but Ralph had been found in a sufficiently compromising position in Manila, such that his future in the Diplomatic Service would probably lie in Sierra Leone or Riga rather than Paris or Washington. He took the honourable way out and threw his brother, the Honourable, out of Wellbeck, reaping the rewards of a newly profitable estate.

"How much?!" Gaynor had screamed, with just a hint of the West Midlands.

"Twelve thousand pounds a year." Basil repeated the sum payable to him from the family trust – now his only source of income.

"You'll have to get a job."

But Basil was, at best, a farm manager with an interest in irrigation systems. No such position in Britain was going to enhance the twelve thousand a year to a level acceptable to Gaynor. She came up with the answer. The Middle East. He could go abroad and earn the money. She would stay in Wiltshire; a place where her raspberry coulis was appreciated and there were committees to chair. After all, he spoke English, he knew about irrigation and he was aristocratic. The Saudis would love him. She was right. Three months later he was at the Sheikh Abdullatif Al-Rahman University in Riyadh, teaching irrigation techniques and earning twenty thousand pounds a year tax-free. *That is better*, Gaynor thought.

She hadn't realised that Basil was not the only son of an old British title to have found himself in a similar position. They were also in Riyadh, teaching, advising or supervising. They had brought their wives, many from Cheltenham Ladies'

College, and there was a burgeoning dinner-party circuit behind the walls of the various university, oil company or hospital compounds. She soon joined him, albeit hesitantly, becoming a convert to the cause; a key actress in the play which set the Cotswolds inside the rendered compound walls to the exclusion of the desert and Islam, whatever they were. The Arabs, for their part, assumed that Gaynor, Bumble and Loveday were the usual names of British wives.

"Nefud-al-aan," Ibrahim said.

"That's fifty miles into the desert." Basil released his leather handbag, which was now wet from his grip.

"Basil, you are already three thousand miles from home – what is fifty more?"

Basil couldn't contain it any longer. "Gaynor will not be happy. She will not fit happily into life on a building site."

Ibrahim's hooded eyes were at their most reassuring. "This is *the* building site. This is the largest military city being built in the Middle East. She will be on a compound just like the one at the university."

Basil shuffled on the leather chair.

"You will be Sheikh Abdullatif's personal representative, in charge of reviewing all external works. You will be his eyes and ears. It is a great honour. Gaynor will love the Ministry Mercedes. Take her to Cyprus more often on holiday."

These were good points, Basil had to concede. Knowing that there was no alternative also made it easier … for him. Gaynor would take time, but she would see the many advantages in the end.

"Basil, Gaynor will love it. Trust me. She will enjoy herself with all of those American wives."

Oh dear.

CHAPTER FOUR

It was the morning after the curtailed barbecue and Jack Pennington was still underground. He was fiddling with the loop of string that controlled the thin venetian blind in a room several floors below the Gloucestershire countryside. The view beyond was of yet more dumpy monitors sat on grey desks; a reason why the blind was permanently down, perhaps giving the vainest of hope that if it were raised there would be a sunny panorama of Leckhampton Hill. Little disguised the 'bunker' effect. There were no pictures on the walls, no photos of family members on the desks. Instead there were frequent reminders of institutionalisation: Government-issue fire extinguishers, cups and saucers with the letters 'E:R' in royal blue, and grey linoleum tiles that encouraged everyone to walk in straight lines. Only a solitary phallic cactus sat in a small pot on one desk; its owner convinced that it would help absorb the radiation from the computer system, having been given this idea by a visiting American software engineer.

Jack was in Room 401, which belonged to Marcus Billingham.

"Who are 'they' and where is 'it' going?" Jack asked.

"If we knew the answer to one, we could probably work out the other." Marcus was unable to remove his eyes from the alarming slant that the slats of the venetian blind had now attained.

"My best guess is that this is being paid for from Saudi but the destination is off Saudi soil."

Marcus visibly relaxed as the blind clicked down to a series of more usual horizons.

"We know every Saudi site backwards," Jack continued, as if reassuring himself. "We either designed it, built it, equipped it or helped man it."

Marcus raised a white eyebrow but said nothing.

"They are using Western technology. They're our friends. No, they are paying for it and possibly organising it, but I need convincing that they want them on Saudi soil."

"If they want to keep it secret from their friends, perhaps they are going to build somewhere new and separate?" Marcus pushed up his bottom lip and waggled his head, asking for an answer.

"They must have somewhere waiting already. You don't buy cows and then think about building a barn."

"OK, but you haven't been looking for your barn in Saudi Arabia. Not only have you not been looking for one, but they may have disguised it as something else."

Jack didn't answer.

"While you have been scanning every inch of Iran and Iraq for new military facilities, perhaps the Saudis have been building one?"

Jack pinched his upper lip between thumb and forefinger abstractedly, leaving his gaze on his boss.

"And where better to hide a barn than on a farm?" Marcus picked up his theory and developed it.

Jack, for his part, had already passed this point a few seconds earlier and was now back at the beginning, taking stock. "Let's assume the sources to date are genuine. That we haven't been set up," he began. "The Saudis want to go nuclear. They are reliant on the West, who won't equip them either openly or tacitly. If asked, we would say no. They don't ask. They get a trusted individual to organise it. They fund it. If it fails, they deny all knowledge of it and blame Israel or Saddam in a prepared press strategy." He paused and shifted his gaze up to the ceiling, where the white soundproofing tiles blurred into one as his mind explored the possibilities. "So they won't want them based on their land … I would suggest Syria."

Marcus was not convinced. "The bigger the secret, the fewer people must be in the know. I'm having enough trouble believing that a few individuals in Saudi are trying this believing that they can hide it from us, without involving Syria or anywhere else."

"Never underestimate how vulnerable Syria feels."

"Shall I call Ross, Prib and Paula across for a meeting in an hour?"

"Yes."

"What about Simon if you are convinced that Syria may be involved?"

"Why not?"

* * *

At ten o'clock in Meeting Room 409, the five men and one woman met to discuss the possibilities, what they knew and what they needed to know. Several other meetings were taking place in the other meeting rooms because a bunch of scrap-metal merchants had landed on some islands in the South Atlantic called South Georgia and claimed them for Argentina. The things people do for media coverage. They would probably be acclaimed as heroes when they got back to Santa Cruz.

Ross Smith, Jack's co-conspirator in the barbecue fiasco, arrived last, still chewing the remains of a cheese roll, much of which seemed to be stuck in his beard. He was responsible for Saudi Arabia. He had told his colleagues that his problems sounded a little more serious than a bunch of drunk Argentinian sailors frightening a few walruses on an ice-covered island eight thousand miles away. It was pointed out to him that walruses were northern hemisphere creatures and he should concentrate on deserts where he (hopefully) had a better grasp of the situation. Teddy Przybylski, 'Prib' to everyone on station, wore an open-necked shirt which made no attempt to conceal a tuft of curly black hair. By contrast, a tight black crew cut gave his head a square appearance. A third-generation Pole, he covered parts of Eastern Europe. His boss, Paula, was talking to Simon Burroughs about some Croatian basketball team when Marcus called the meeting to order.

"As with the proverbial London bus, we get nothing of interest for a few days and then two pieces come along at once. This meeting concerns the Saudi-Soviet problem; we shall leave the Argentinian pirates to another floor." He paused. "You will have seen the first assumptions posted by Jack on the board. The purpose of this meeting under the protocol is to establish the veracity and relevance of this data, any consequences which may arise and, finally, any shortfall in intelligence. At the end of this meeting we shall establish the interest and programme for each floor." Marcus sipped the dark coffee that was his addiction and continued. "Followed to its obvious and logical extreme, this 'event' could be the most important this year. Jack will introduce the three pieces of intelligence seen on the board."

Jack, in his smoky grey shirt, began with the telephone conversation of an individual in Jeddah. This was a routine (if 'routine' was the right word) computer check of telephone calls which searched for up to 1,200 keywords worldwide – or, at least, everywhere that had a telephone exchange. The word 'Zugdidi' had appeared in the call from Jeddah. This was a theoretically non-existent place in Georgia below the Caucasus Mountains which was a prime location for Soviet nuclear missiles; the furthest south-west. The individual, Nabil, was a Jordanian who had married a Saudi princess. He had a fifty-one per cent stake in a series of 'franchises' in Saudi Arabia – indeed, across the Arabian Peninsula – which included German car manufacturers and Japanese computer companies. The telephone call, made to Madrid, had been received via the monitoring station at Gibraltar and transmitted onwards to Morwenstow in Cornwall.

The two letters from a Georgian at the Soviet Embassy in London had been monitored out of Heathrow by CI9. The computer system COLINT had thrown these two sources up on the screens in Mannington; this would have been enough. However, three hours later, a satellite photograph of the Ingur Valley in Georgia was given 'A' priority by SATINT in Cyprus and sent to Mannington. This aerial view appeared to show large agricultural vehicles leaving the mountainside at the known underground site at Zugdidi.

It was the automatic combination of these three varied pieces of information that had led to the summoning of Jack and Ross from their barbecue. By the time they had reached Mannington, a series of systems had picked up the satellite view of the ship in the Black Sea, monitored on behalf of C-in-C fleet an equivalent number of floors below ground at Northwood in a sleepy London suburb. The Georgian letters had mentioned a Turkish ship, the *Ikiz*, which was picked up in the Black Sea en route to the eastern coast of Turkey just below Sukhumi.

This was the scenario presented to Jack that Thursday evening at 8.30pm. At the meeting he gave his clinical evaluation of the likely reliability of the various pieces of intelligence; he explained his own interpretation of events and possibilities. Three areas would need enhanced monitoring, he suggested, in the immediate future.

Marcus stood up to pour coffee from the Cona jugs placed on a table just inside the door. "Now," he carved up the silence, "this is where we consider the shortfall in intelligence. Anyone?"

Whether this was an invitation for coffee or for an opinion was not specified. Prib declined more coffee but offered his and his colleagues' acceptance that the source of the letters in the Soviet Embassy must be followed. The satellite coverage of the ship and the Zugdidi site must be given a higher priority even though it was still months before a series of satellites would be launched to boost the current limited number.

Half an hour later, they were still scheduling the information required. This proactive, prescriptive approach represented a fundamental change in the Secret Services, precipitated by the emergence and evolution of Mannington to its cutting-edge state today in 1982.

Mannington had begun by receiving information and collating it, and within a week had begun leading the demand for the next tranche of information. It was a subtle and unnoticed transference of power from London to the Cotswolds. Knowledge is power. Eton, the club lunch and the London and Provincial Lodge were superseded in less than five years by the County Treasurer's son who had read Spanish at Birmingham University. 'Being in the right place at the right time' is always a match for 'It's not what you know, it's who you know.'

CHAPTER FIVE

The Secret Intelligence Service, under its Chief, Sir Cecil Mackay, had for so long been content to let GCHQ collect all relevant transmitted information and send it up to London. It did all of the donkey work and allowed Century House in London to perform its 'managerial' function. It was no threat. It was a servant. When intelligence from all sources grew exponentially, the SIS was equally happy to have the boring task of collation carried out by the new unit at Mannington. The SIS did not foresee that the Collation Unit was effectively taking over an ever-increasing percentage of its workload; the most important parts. Mannington was now receiving all intelligence, analysing it and forming a clearer, broader picture than London. Tensions built up, and by 1982 the servant was perceived as having exceeded his responsibilities. It was after a cool telephone conversation with Sir Cecil that Marcus Billingham had convened the meetings with Jack, Ross and the others. With the South Atlantic and Middle East active, the relationship between Mannington and London was about to be tested.

The meeting in Room 409 had established that the blatant shortfall in intelligence fell in the destination of the warheads, or whatever the materiel was. Where were they going (if something really was being transported)? The general consensus was either to Saudi or Syria, Ross Smith or Simon Burroughs; either way, under Jack Pennington's ultimate control. The shortfall problem appeared to be worse in the case of Saudi Arabia. A combination of satellite photography backing up the details provided by an American project-management company working for the Saudi Arabian National Guard on all of their key military cities should have been giving Mannington all it needed. Clearly not. The only satellite in the area was, unhelpfully, over Israel where any trouble was likely to occur, rather than the vast expanses of desert further to the South.

Mannington was humming, and not just as a consequence of electronic overload. At his station, however, Jack had switched from work mode to domestic. The strategy for the next forty-eight hours was in place, with both Simon and Ross staying on site. Jack could, therefore, disappear for twelve hours and see his family. It sounded plausible. It needed to. If you are going to sneak off to see another woman you have enough problems. When you work at one of the most sensitive intelligence sites in the world, you have serious problems. If it seemed incredible that Jack worked in the Secret Squirrel community, it was equally unbelievable that he was being unfaithful.

Driving back to Cheltenham, he cut off the corner at The Air Balloon public house by taking a shortcut down the local rat run. The lane zigzagged down Birdlip Hill. The Birdlip Run.

Birdlip Time. Birdlip Space. The one occasion when Jack was free; free to think. Between work and home. Between Victoria and Sarah. Between the devil and the deep blue sea.

The young Jack had been average; never picked for the first team, never winning any school prizes. He had a good memory and a natural awareness of the structure of languages. His collection of O and A Levels were as expected, and French at Leicester or Exeter beckoned. His father had missed out on university not because of money but because of minutes; his application had not been received in time. Now at the top of his trade, he wanted John (he didn't become Jack until university) to go to Oxford – to Wadham. Jack would never get to Oxford, let alone Wadham, reading pure French. He needed a niche. It's not who you know, it's when you know them. Jack got into Oxford during his Third Year Sixth to read Arabic and French; the year that his art master's brother took up the chair in Middle Eastern Studies. Oxford fitted Jack like a glove, and he excelled there. His studies came easily to him. He did a master's at Cairo University, where he met one of the chief Arabists at GCHQ who was visiting the Cultural Attaché to Egypt. The rest, as they say, is history. By the age of forty he was Head of Arabic at Cheltenham and married with a pigeon pair.

One of the problems at GCHQ had been the recruitment and retention of secretaries; they grew bored of the restrictions on their lives, and disappeared to work in building societies where they could get cheap mortgages. Victoria had appeared aged twenty-three; she was uninteresting in the extreme. During the vetting process, investigators almost became suspicious because of the mind-numbing averageness of her family and interests. She must be hiding something. As it turned out, she was not. She was keen and attractive in a boyish sort of way, with a complete lack of dress sense, and straw-blonde hair that looked as if it had been cut with shears. Jack began to use her more and more. AQT, a form of in-house training, provided secretaries with the opportunity to progress and increase their salaries. Jack pulled out the stops to get Victoria on the course; she stayed and their paths crossed more frequently.

He could never remember the day when he went from not noticing her to finding lame excuses to bump into her, but by the time he was forty-two and she was twenty-seven they were in a relationship. Out of the blue he was moved to Mannington – a rogue thread in the rich tapestry of life. They had never lived together and now they weren't working together. Jack had been vetted all of his professional life. Vetting was part of his life; he had had nothing to hide. Now he did. As Head of Arabic at GCHQ he was vetted. As Head of Middle East at Mannington, even the people who vetted him were vetted as they did it. Jack knew that his telephone calls from work, from home, from call boxes near work and home were monitored; they were listening to the listeners, watching the watchers. How could he stay in contact (especially physical contact) with Victoria?

He saw her occasionally at GCHQ. He saw her even less frequently when he called in discreetly at her rented cottage in Great Witcombe at the bottom of the Birdlip Run. If she wasn't at home, he left a message by adjusting the arrow on the disused, rusting milk-bottle carrier by the doorstep; a simple code of '1' meaning 'tomorrow', '2' meaning 'the day after', etc. The relationship was not going to last if something didn't change soon. She wanted some permanency, to be able to hold hands in public. He wanted his kids to grow up and leave home. She wanted his kids *and* him to leave home.

As he slowed at the bottom of Birdlip Hill, Jack looked at his rear-view mirror. He turned into the village and pulled up alongside Victoria's cottage. How he envied other men their affairs. All they had to do was deceive their wives. Jack's wife expected him to be deceitful, not to come home and not to answer questions about work. His problem was that he had to deceive the whole Secret Squirrel fraternity.

Unknown to him, his problems were about to increase, and these didn't concern whatever was being transported across the Black Sea in the Turkish trawler *Ikiz*.

CHAPTER SIX

The window gave onto a square of grass enclosed by tall Georgian buildings. This was one of the most expensive yet useless pieces of turf in England, located, as it was, just an IRA mortar's flight from Downing Street.

The Foreign Secretary pressed a hand against the pulled burgundy velvet curtain in a subconscious attempt to throw more light on the proceedings. "You see my dilemma, Marcus?" he asked.

There was no reply, but the leather chair exhaled pointedly as Marcus shifted his weight. Sir Cecil Mackay, also seated, seemingly gazed abstractedly towards the clouds. His ears were scanning for every nuance in the Foreign Secretary's voice. He was sat with both arms stretched out along the back of the chesterfield. In contrast to his dark grey suit, his striped shirt, striped tie and spotted handkerchief produced a visual nightmare reminiscent of the test card.

"We've been caught napping … all of us, I mean," the Foreign Secretary continued. "We've been watching pigeons on the roof of the Kremlin when we should have been watching penguins on South Georgia."

"I think that's my point. We don't want to be caught again. We need to watch Zugdidi." Marcus appeared to be losing the argument.

"Perhaps we should put a satellite over everywhere called Georgia?" Sir Cecil quipped in quiet confidence. His staff had seen photographs of Zugdidi frequently over the past five years. With so few satellites, he wanted them where things were actually happening, preferably over the South Atlantic. The Prime Minister had just decided to send a task force of six thousand to the Falklands and she needed a geostationary satellite over Port Stanley, not over the Caucasus.

"Marcus, we need communications and intelligence, you know that. We cannot fight a war down there without a satellite. I am as conscious as you are that we are using up one of its nine lives by moving it."

Sir Cecil kept quiet. The Foreign Secretary was arguing his case for him.

Marcus decided to try one last time. "We must follow anything that leaves Zugdidi. A nuclear threat in the Middle East is a damned sight more worrying than a few Argentinians on the Falklands."

"You are right, but all of this is on the basis of two letters and a telephone conversation." The Foreign Secretary had clearly made up his mind.

"OK," Marcus conceded, "but we must have high plane surveillance of the Black Sea and some people on the ground."

"Are you happy with that, Cecil?"

"Of course, of course. Marcus has done a fine job collating all of the various sources."

Marcus almost fainted with damn praise.

"However," Sir Cecil began again, "the satellite needs to begin moving now. Mannington will, no doubt, let us know where the warheads are going in due course. If Mannington is right and Saudi is the final resting place, we have just recruited someone perfectly placed to update us on the current military construction sites."

Both the Foreign Secretary and Marcus looked across at him.

"We up here," Sir Cecil nodded towards the window to indicate London, "are quite capable of acting speedily on information collected from the various sources and collated by Mannington."

Marcus had noted the obvious need for the Head of MI6 to defend his position in front of the Foreign Secretary. Now it was Marcus's turn to keep quiet.

"So I can tell the Prime Minister that she has nothing to worry about from Zugdidi? She can concentrate on the Falklands?"

"You can tell her that within twenty-four hours of Mannington telling us that the warheads are definitely on a ship in international waters, the SBS will send the lot to the bottom of the sea," Sir Cecil replied, pushing his handkerchief into his top pocket with his finger. "And, in parallel, we shall establish where they were meant to be going in Saudi or elsewhere in the Middle East."

"Good. I hope that your man in Saudi is up to the job?"

"He's the younger brother of the Earl of Mallow and Blackwater. He's just been appointed construction reviewer to the new military cities. He's the right man in the right place … and of the right material."

There seemed to be an element of criticism in this last remark that went beyond Marcus to include the Foreign Secretary. Sir Cecil seemed oblivious to it.

"Well, thank you, Cecil. I'm late for lunch."

Sir Cecil stood up without betraying a hint of self-satisfaction on his face. He had put Mannington back in its box and taken firm control of the Zugdidi affair. He could concentrate on the Argentinians, who had been the main reason for the meeting.

"Goodbye, Cecil." Marcus extended his hand, making it clear that he was staying behind. While Sir Cecil's face kept control, his body language betrayed his annoyance that he was not included in their lunch arrangements. His left hand, which was poised to press Marcus out of the room in front of him in mock deference, remained at a foppish angle as he pirouetted. The solid soundproofed door clicked shut.

"Where does he find these people?" the Foreign Secretary asked. "Does he phone up the matron at his old school and ask if she's had a postcard from anyone in Saudi Arabia?" He pulled the stopper from a decanter, flicking it invitingly at two glasses.

"Yes please." Marcus nodded. "You know my thoughts on the old boy network. It's one of the reasons I wanted to ask for a wider remit for Mannington. Cecil needs us but we no longer really need everything that he does."

"It's a huge step, Marcus."

"I'm not advocating shutting down London, but look at the advantages of allowing us to direct intelligence gathering in immediate response to a piece of collation. Six years ago the SIS had five divisions. In that time we have fully replaced the Intelligence Analysis wing. I know Cecil doesn't like it but he's a dying breed."

"Unfortunately, they are not. They seem to put disproportionate weight on producing sons and heirs."

"All the more reason to act."

"Your main reason to act now is that you have a Prime Minister who is not old school, not on the square and not a man. She respects merit and success."

"If she gave us some operational capacity it would make perfect sense. We get pieces of intelligence from a satellite or embassy, we collate them, analyse them and immediately direct the satellite or embassy to follow it up. I'm not interested in Technical, Administration or Counter-Intelligence. Cecil can keep them."

"I don't think Cecil would stay if any of Operations went to you."

Marcus took a long sip of whisky to avoid having to comment.

* * *

Back in Century House, Sir Cecil was joined by his Deputy Chief, Robin Mills.

"How did it go with the Foreign Secretary?"

"Fine. There's nothing like a war to increase the importance of the SIS in a Foreign Secretary's eyes. The satellite can be moved, the SAS can go to South Georgia as suggested, and we can trade with France over the Exocets."

"Excellent."

"Not everything in the garden is rosy, however."

"You don't mean Mannington and this Zugdidi thing?"

"Not exactly. Having gained agreement on the satellite, I conceded that if Mannington found the ship in international waters, we should send it to the bottom of the ocean. It wasn't much of a concession given that we have the SBS in Cyprus. I told them about Basil in Riyadh and I thought that that was probably an end to the matter."

Sir Cecil stood up to relieve his arthritic knee. The pause had an incidental dramatic effect.

"As I was about to leave, the Foreign Secretary made it clear that he was seeing Marcus separately afterwards."

"Both of them know that their line of communication is through you?" Robin rubbed his own knee out of subconscious solidarity.

"At best he is giving Marcus a sympathetic hearing and intends to do nothing. At worst they are conspiring." Cecil paused. "Either way, you and I must nip this in the bud."

"Unfortunately, the Argentinians have given Mannington their first real war to show off their skills."

"Exactly, Robin, so we must perform our functions to the same level or better … and I mean *all* of our functions." Cecil sat down. He had not lowered his voice. If the Chief of the SIS could not speak freely in one of his offices, who could?

After about fifteen minutes, Hamish Dawes, the Head of Vetting, entered the room, having been summoned from the lower floor. He was an ex-Army intelligence man with pockmarked skin and a thin neck that was lost inside his shirt collar like some Galapagos tortoise. He stood jingling coins in his twill trouser pocket, eyeing his two superiors suspiciously. His job was to be suspicious.

"Hamish, we have a job for your people," Sir Cecil began. "We are led to believe by a very highly placed source, which I cannot reveal at this time, that someone at Mannington is breaking a few rules." He smiled and continued. "Now that we have the Argentinians to worry about, we cannot have any weak links, can we?"

"Ah, no. Definitely not. Who is the weak link? D'ya have any idea?"

"All I can say is that we think that he is in the Middle East section."

"There's more than forty of them."

"Quite."

"We're a wee bit pushed just now. I cannot watch forty people." Hamish's mild Scottish lilt was a refreshing change from the clipped tones of everyone around him.

Sir Cecil needed some dirt on Mannington. He couldn't ask Hamish just to go out fishing for it; that might backfire later. He needed a credible reason so that Hamish would search and find something (anything) that could be used to halt the rise of Mannington. He needed to give Hamish a target big enough to have a chance of finding something, yet small enough for him to believe that he had a real source. The Middle East section sounded about right, if a little big.

"We think it is at the higher levels, Hamish," Robin added helpfully.

"That's still a dozen people. I've got one team permanently watching Mannington. They concentrate on telephone calls, bank accounts and spot checks. They haven't reported anything."

"How many teams do you have at GCHQ?"

"Three."

"Couldn't you move one team over for a couple of weeks to follow a few people?"

"If you are that confident that something is up?"

"I think we should," Sir Cecil reassured him, "and if they come up with nothing, so be it. They can return to GCHQ."

"Thanks, Hamish." Robin put an end to the meeting and the Scot left somewhat perplexed.

"Let's hope he damn well finds something."

"If not, we will use Basil to cock it up for them."

* * *

"Do you think that they are taking this Turkish episode, if I can call it that, seriously?" Marcus asked the Foreign Secretary. The two had established an easy relationship from the first time that they had met; two grammar-school lads, one from the Shires and one from the Home Counties.

"I think that they are under pressure because of the Falklands. They are very nervous about the ascendancy of … your place … and rightly so. You caught them napping – or, to be fairer, they were caught napping. They underestimated Collation. They thought that you were another Cheltenham; a servant. You are now more powerful than them … potentially." The Foreign Secretary savoured the smoked duck with kumquat marmalade – a special at the Goring Hotel off Grosvenor Gardens. They had chosen their hotel (and their words) carefully.

Marcus was controlling his intake of a delicious Rully 1978. After all, this was the first time that he had had the Foreign Secretary entirely to himself for an hour. It was a welcome break because they would both be working long into the night thanks to Leopoldo Galtieri and the 'Malvinas'.

"Please don't get me wrong," Marcus said, "we have nearly thirty-five of the South American Group on overtime at my place. We don't underestimate the Argentinians; it's just that this other matter typifies what's wrong with the system. Sending the seaborne lot out to deal with the matter retrospectively, and asking a Hooray who is three-hundredth in line for the throne to watch out for people buying high-octane rocket fuel isn't what's necessary."

"I can't see the framework changing until the South Atlantic is sorted out. She is preoccupied … and not surprisingly," Marcus continued. "I accept the loss of the aerial pictures; in fact, it may help me in the South Atlantic. If I come up with a better method of monitoring the product en route or nearer its destination, would you support, or tacitly ignore, what I was up to?"

The Foreign Secretary took an inordinately long time to stack his fork with a sliver of duck and marmalade. He took even longer to chew, savour and digest them.

"I understand that the Goring was the first hotel in London to have radiators in every room," was what the Foreign Secretary eventually said.

* * *

Marcus declined the waiting taxi outside the hotel and walked along Grosvenor Gardens. Selecting a red public phone box, he dialled, concealed by the montage of prostitutes' cards stuck to the small glass panes; 'montage' being the operative word.

"Hello? Jack?"

"Yes, hello."

"It's Harry.

"Hello, Harry. How's London?"

"Warm, and going to get hotter."

"Did our client agree to the proposal?"

"He didn't say no."

"Looks like I had better look for our own sales rep?"

"That's it … cut out the middleman."

Unbeknownst to them or him, their most unlikely sales rep was, at that moment, travelling to Riyadh.

Marcus put down the receiver and hailed a cab for Paddington.

CHAPTER SEVEN

The peregrine falcon was at thirty-five thousand feet, a picture of controlled power and beauty. Mark Tanner was also at thirty-five thousand feet, looking across the aisle of the Saudia Boeing 747. The peregrine had a hood over its eyes; it didn't know where it was … and neither did Mark. Fifteen hundred pounds to send one of the most evolved flyers in the animal kingdom by aeroplane, perched on a bar clipped to a seat near the back of the plane next to Mark Tanner. Had the peregrine chosen to sit in Smoking next to the toilets? Mark had also not chosen to sit there; he hadn't chosen Smoking and, more importantly, he hadn't chosen to be on a 747 going to Riyadh. Alicante was the limit of his flying in the past, so this was turning out to be a very different experience, beginning with a peregrine sat next to him. *Thank God I'm in an aisle seat*, he thought to himself.

"Please?"

Mark looked up at the stewardess with an exaggerated nervousness. He used this startled innocence to conceal his startled innocence. She was offering him a small handleless cup on a tray.

"Thank you," he stammered, accepting the thimble. "Where's the needle and thread?"

Startled innocence can wear very thin. Ask Dawn, his long-suffering wife.

"Cardamom … it's a digestif," the Egyptian stewardess encouraged him.

"Not like our digestives at home."

She poured the liquid and progressed up the aisle. He swallowed it in one gulp.

"It'll never catch on in High Wycombe," he muttered, but even the peregrine had had enough of Mark Tanner.

"Those dark brown eyes drive me wild." The scruffy man with a face like a turkey suddenly spoke for the first time. The falcon shook its head, and the bells on its yellow feet tinkled. Mark, remembering that he had brown eyes, felt somewhat concerned. He couldn't see the colour of the peregrine's eyes.

"That stewardess is a stunner," the man in the window seat on the other side of the falcon continued. He had been so pissed getting on the plane that he had been unaware of take-off despite having his face smeared against the window. "Christ! You're not drinking that cardamom crap, are you? You'll be farting all night."

Mark instinctively let go of the tiny cup resting on the tray before him. "Isn't it meant to help the food through your system?"

"You mean like lager and a curry?"

"I think so," Mark replied.

The drunk now had more than enough to occupy his brain for another few hundred miles. He slumped back against the window, blocking the view of the snow-covered Alps in evening shadow.

Mark watched *For Your Eyes Only* on the big video screen at the front of the cabin through a haze of smoke while flicking gratuitously between the audio channels. Everyone else appeared to be asleep; it really was for his eyes only. Even the peregrine couldn't see the parrot talking to Margaret Thatcher as James Bond sailed off into the sunset. Neither 'Easy Listening' nor 'Country Classics' had improved the film as Mark swapped music channels to release his nervous tension. He looked around at his fellow travellers, who were mostly Arabs, male and female, in their various scarves and headdresses. The world of James Bond may have been fantasy but was his own any weirder? He wasn't sure.

He thought of Dawn and of the fire. Dawn and the children were safe; the rest didn't matter and he clung on to that thought like a lifebelt. More than most, he knew how thin the line was between reality and unreality. In his epilepsy-ridden childhood he had fought to stay behind the paper-thin wall separating consciousness and unconsciousness; to stay in the world of smiling children – fitting and not fitting. A lot of his childhood seemed to have been spent staring at the wallpaper. It had become a symbol to him. A defence, however thin, against whatever was beyond it. He resisted all attempts to peek behind a peeling corner in case it revealed a more savage reality. The patterns on the wallpaper always lulled him back into a world of false security. That's what the pattern was for – to hide the joins.

How quickly the pattern had broken up. The individual strips of wallpaper were obvious once again, the gaps becoming wider than the paper. The happy illusion gone.

One telephone call from a neighbour while he was staying with his brother in Lincoln. "Mark, is that you? I've got some bad news. Your house has burnt down."

Just like that. His first thought had been that he had his family with him so everything would be OK … in the end. He just had to hang up some more wallpaper; put up a new pattern and keep smelling those imaginary swirling roses.

Dolly Parton working nine to five accompanied Nigel Havers around the track in *Chariots of Fire*. Mark adjusted his headset. It was losing the battle with his thick, springy black hair – a legacy, together with his dark brown eyes and olive skin, of some Romany blood in his gene pool. He was listening to country music while watching a crap film, sat in a large plastic tube decorated with a palm motif. The plastic tube was, presumably, inside a metal tube that was flying at thirty-five thousand feet. Mark's company in these tubes consisted of a peregrine falcon and a drunk. Sometimes it really is best to ignore reality and stare at the wallpaper.

His world had been shattered not so much by the fire but by the failure of the insurance company to pay out the full amount. He had been paying the premiums by standing order and had even annually indexed them for inflation; unfortunately, the original figure was wrong. Whose fault? His? Probably. Nothing could be proved and he couldn't afford a lawyer. They didn't have enough to pay off all of the outstanding mortgage; they were twenty thousand pounds short. The building society was obliging in that it had allowed Mark and Dawn to go on paying the same amount monthly as before, even though they did not have any security. The small matters of where they were going to live for the next twenty years, how they were going to pay for rent as well and how they were meant to bring up two small children seemed not to register. How easily wallpaper burns.

And they had argued. Mark and Dawn Tanner had argued for the first time, taking out their frustration on each other.

"I'm not paying a mortgage for the next twenty years while we rent a bedsit in poverty!" She had a point. "Rob a bank! Do something!" This then translated itself into the more equitable, "Rob a building society! Or even better, rob an insurance company!"

Days later, Dawn had decided that Mark must go off, sacrifice a couple of years of family life and earn the money. Hence, he was sat at thirty-five thousand feet over Egypt en route for Saudi Arabia.

Yesterday he had stood in a long bunker: ninety yards of finest Berkshire sand; three hundred acres of fairways cut into pine forest edged with rhododendrons now in full red bloom. He had been making sure that the irrigation system did not spray into the hazard. Golfers prefer dry sand. Dry sand!

Mark did not have a lot of options open to him. However, there wasn't much about pop-up sprinklers and solenoid valves that he didn't know. His employer, Croton Engineering of Basingstoke, kept more golf courses green than anyone, and it didn't have a better, or odder, worker than 'Empty', as Mark was known to them. Mr Richards (Senior) was looking to expand the business outside of the UK and was keen on the possibilities and money of Saudi Arabia. He had been reading several articles and adverts in the trade magazines. Unfortunately none of his staff wanted to go, so he just supplied equipment via a dubious character called Mervyn who had to pay in sterling, in cash and up front. Mr Richards (Senior) may have been Baptist, sixty-seven years old and the last person in Pangbourne to wear moleskin waistcoats, but he understood how to make money.

And now Empty was stepping out into the hot desert evening. His jacket and tie seemed inappropriate but Dawn had insisted. He swayed down the steps from the aircraft straight onto a waiting bus. Clinging to a stainless-steel pole, he was whisked across the tarmac to the terminal building. The heat of the marble hall could have been produced by the desert sun or the thousands of sweating bodies queuing, sitting or milling around. All the blood had left the finger which held his jacket over his shoulder, and his other hand was wet from gripping his passport immigration card. The queues were moving forward slowly in a series of staccato kangaroo jumps, which involved the kicking of hand luggage along the floor. He had filled in the immigration card on the plane using his new fountain pen with its brown ink cartridge; this leaving present from Dawn was a reminder to write frequently, assuming that they shouldn't waste money on long and expensive you-say-goodbye-first phone calls.

It took over a half an hour to reach the front of the queue. A hand protruding from an Army uniform reached across the desk without a word. Empty offered his card and passport, the latter opened helpfully at his photograph.

"No good."

"I didn't have the seat adjusted properly—"

"It's no good."

"—or the blue curtain pulled across behind me."

"It must be black."

"No, there's only a choice of blue or orange curtains in the booths at Woolworths."

"The pen must be black."

Empty looked at his immigration card, written in neat brown almost italic writing. "I haven't got a black pen."

"Next!"

"What?"

"Next!"

A friendly hand patted his shoulder from behind. "There are some more forms back there. If he won't accept brown ink, he won't accept it."

"Oh."

"Is this your first trip?" the soft Irish voice inquired.

"Yes."

"Take my word for it. Just go and fill in a new form with a black biro."

"Oh. OK. Thanks."

Empty made his way back across the vast hall to a single wooden desk strewn with immigration forms. It took him five minutes to find someone with a black pen, five minutes to complete the new form and twenty minutes to reach the front of the queue again.

By the time that he walked to the baggage reclaim area, his two battered blue suitcases were ploughing a lonely furrow on the carousel. He managed to perform the difficult task of carrying them and his hand luggage towards the customs officers, who were standing behind their stainless-steel-topped tables.

"Open."

"Which one?"

"All."

The thin brown lieutenant with skin like the surface of the moon rummaged around in the first case. If Dawn could have seen what he had done to the neatly folded short-sleeved shirts she had so painstakingly ironed the evening before.

"No food."

"What?"

A large packet of peanuts, Empty's favourite, had been secreted by Dawn amongst the clothes. The spotty youth in the green uniform was now holding the packet upside down at arm's length while snipping the corner with a pair of scissors. The nuts cascaded down into a plastic dustbin, while the lieutenant's eyes bored into Empty's soul. It was only the presence of the officer's gun in its holster, a long and tiring day, and a desire to get out of the airport that prevented the normally garrulous Empty from making some innocent quip which would have put him on the next plane home.

"Open!"

"Oh … yes."

He had forgotten to open the second suitcase. Fired up by the smuggling of peanuts, the lieutenant searched it with even less care for Dawn's packing. He pulled out two paperbacks and flicked through the first. Could he read English? Could he read that fast?

"The butler did it." Empty tried to put him out of his misery in the hope of relieving his own.

The book was thrown back on top of the heap of clothes. Attention was turned to the second book.

"No good."

"Have you read it, then?" But Empty had heard the words 'no good' from the first officer he had met in Saudi Arabia, and he was learning that it did not bode well.

"No good." And with that, the front cover was ripped off. The flapping core of the book was flipped back into the suitcase. The cover, with its depiction in oils of a lady with minimal décolletage revealed, joined the peanuts in the dustbin.

"Those Penguin Classic covers are pretty boring, aren't they?"

The perusal of the hand luggage thankfully revealed nothing of the calibre of Charles Dickens or KP nuts. It was disturbed only enough to make it difficult to close again.

Empty half expected to be shot in the back as he staggered the last twenty paces across the hall towards the tiny door out into … into what? He had never seen so many nationalities, heard so many languages or seen so many headdresses. One great sea of humanity – or should that have been desert of humanity? So many things had struck him as extraordinary and he wasn't out of the airport yet: the heat, the smells, the separation of women and children, the rules … he must learn them. Startled innocence may work on High Wycombe traffic wardens, but it didn't look like a sure-fire technique out here.

He was not prepared for the deafening wall of sound and faces that confronted him on squeezing through the door. Had he peeled back the wallpaper? He straightened himself, took a deep breath, quickly regretted it and pushed through the nearest thing to a gap in the throng. Short (were they Yemeni?) porters and taxi drivers in dirty white or grey dishdashas fought to carry bags. At the main door he swapped the hot, sweaty air of the terminal for the overpowering stink of sewage which is never far away in Riyadh; in fact, about one metre below the surface, formed by fetid groundwater. Shouts fought against car horns, the throbbing diesel engines of buses, and the background roar of planes taking off and landing.

Mr Richards (Senior) had told him to wait outside the main door and to look for a man with his name written on a card.

"Do you mean 'Mr Richards (Senior)'?" Empty had asked, and Mr Richards (Senior) had laughed. If Empty was prepared to go to Saudi Arabia, he would put up with his stupid jokes for another few days.

Looking for his name was not easy as there was a wide selection of cards held at unhelpful angles by grinning Arabs. Dismissing half the names that were written in spidery scrawls of Arabic, Empty scanned the remainder – Johannson, Weibring, Kwan … did that say Tot? Smith, Markovitz … Tanner. At last he had found Tanner. He established eye contact with the old man proudly waving his name.

"Hi. I'm Mr Tanner." Why did he say 'Mister'? It had sounded wrong.

"*Marhaba*."

"No, my name's Mark. Do you speak English?"

The grubby white rag wrapped with seeming nonchalance around the man's head did not fall off when he indicated that he did not.

Empty carried his hand luggage, following Basem (at least he had established his name, although he wasn't completely sure) across the red, dusty car park to an old Datsun. The interior reminded him of a tart's boudoir; a very dirty tart's boudoir. *I've never been in a tart's boudoir*, he thought to himself. The seats were covered in brown nylon fur. Boxes of tissues in ornate brass covers perched precariously on the dashboard, which was also covered in fur. There was a very narrow band of visibility out through the cracked windscreen between the tissue boxes, framed photographs of family, scent bottles, and a selection of worry beads which hung down ominously together with a gaudy tapestry along the sun visor. This clearly (or, perhaps, not clearly) did not concern Basem, who was so short that he couldn't see much over the wheel, despite the orange cushion which gave out a puff of dust as he jumped in. Empty began to worry about the worry beads.

They bumped out onto the tarmac road and Empty saw Riyadh at night through his permanently lowered passenger window. He was struck by the walls. All the villas and Ministry buildings were surrounded by high walls. This sequence was only broken by the skywards projection of some glass office tower rising from a marble plinth. He noticed palm trees; down the middle of the dual carriageway and along either side of the road in that strip of compacted earth between kerb and the villa walls that no hot country seems bothered about. He noticed all of this despite the mesmeric effect of so many objects swinging back and forth before his eyes. He was in a mad parrot's cage.

Basem pulled up outside the wall which tightly enclosed a small brown apartment block – four flats downstairs with four above. A man dressed in long blue-grey robes and reeking of paraffin emerged from what appeared to be a dustbin store but proved to be the doorman's room. Basem shared a few pleasantries in a mutual, guttural throat-clearing exchange. The doorman retreated into his cubbyhole to continue cooking on his small stove. Empty followed his escort into the lift for the short journey from one echoing marble hall to the one above. Basem found the dimmer switch, which was hanging like an eye from a socket. Four heavy, shiny wooden doors in each corner of the hall were revealed, together with a rusty iron one which gave onto the roof.

The flat explained where Basem had found the nylon fur for his car. The whole floor was covered in a brown carpet that incongruously managed to glint and at the same time explode with dust as you walked on it. A general lack of furniture emphasised the expanse of carpet. Basem flicked on the air-conditioning units which had been punched through the wall of each room; any gaps filled with bits of cloth. The noise was deafening. Empty opened his wallet to give Basem a tip, but this was met with a genuine embarrassed refusal. Instead he directed Empty to the kitchen, where a note was prominent on the worktop next to a cardboard box of provisions. It read:

Dear Mr Tanner,

I hope that your journey this far has not been too stressful. Basem, who is one of my drivers, will pick you up tomorrow morning at ten o'clock. He will bring you to Nefud-el-aan, which is the main site on which you will be working.

Please bring the attached letter and your passport with you tomorrow. The letter explains, to anyone who asks, who you are and that you work for me. It will gain you access to the site, which is of high security status.

I look forward to meeting you.
Sheikh Faisal Al-Shaqra

Empty had an ominous feeling growing in the pit of his stomach; something much more than the obvious culture shock. He was under the impression that he was to work on providing irrigation to new hospitals. What was 'high security status' about that?

Basem grinned, pointed at the letter, gestured at his watch and was gone.

CHAPTER EIGHT

If collation was the unglamorous aspect of the Security Services on the ascendancy in the early '80s, logistics was the equivalent in the armed forces. From the 19th March 1982, when Señor Davidoff and his soldiers, disguised as scrap-metal merchants, stuck the pale-blue-and-white flag of Argentina on South Georgia, one fact was self-evident – any fighting would take place eight thousand miles from the UK on small islands with virtually no infrastructure. To compound matters, these islands were in a freezing cold sea miles from any friendly ex-colonial country that could act as a base. By the time that the Argentinians had extended their presence to the Falklands on the 2nd April, London had realised that the UK was entirely geared up for wars in a zone that was defined by the range of a Hercules C-130 transport plane from RAF Lyneham. Europe, North Africa and the Middle East were all fine. The heathlands of East Germany, the Balkans, or Israel and her neighbours were all covered; a quick mission in Libya was well rehearsed, but defending an archipelago of tiny islands virtually in Antarctica was not.

Further afield (i.e. beyond the aegis of NATO and the European Union), it was assumed that we would only be involved in conflicts under the United Nations' banner; we would be part of a UN task force made up of many countries including the USA. Our obligations would stretch to a couple of frigates, a token presence by the SAS, and a peacekeeping force of the Royal Welsh Fusiliers at the end.

However, in that late March of 1982 it was not the high-profile Tornado pilots or Army tank majors who were at the top of the shopping list. Instead, it was three distinct and widely different groups under the heading 'logistics' who were called in. The first group consisted of the likes of Cunard and P&O. The requests were simple – we need your ships. The second was a previously ignored naval group in Portsmouth called space planners. They maximised the packing of everything into containers, making sure that the first items required on arrival were not at the back. They made sure that explosives were separate from food, for example, and that there were tractor units, forklift trucks and Chinooks to move the stuff. Finally, they tried to avoid having all of one type of egg in the same basket. They were to fail in the latter, especially when the *Atlantic Conveyor* was hit by an Exocet missile and all but one of the Chinooks was lost. The final group in early demand were the engineers from each service who needed, say, to put helicopter landing decks on the *Canberra* and air-to-air refuelling systems on the Hercules transport planes.

On Monday 5th April, the aircraft carriers *Hermes* and *Invincible* left Portsmouth carrying Sea Harriers and Sea King helicopters. The following day, HMS *Fearless* set sail with her four landing craft. On Good Friday the *Canberra* made an emotional departure from Southampton carrying three thousand troops and with half of the customisation of the ship unfinished.

It was also a busy Easter at Mannington. Almost all the floors were fully staffed, and none was busier than Floor A – South America. The task-force planners and commanders in London needed to know what the Argentinians were going to do, when they were going to do it and with what force. Suddenly, phone calls from factories in San Nicolás de los Arroyos were being monitored, daily satellite photographs of lorry movements from Rosario were eagerly awaited, and international gossip from embassies in friendly countries was given a higher importance. The geostationary satellite would not be in place until the 9th April in advance of the task force's arrival, when it would provide rapid, safe communication and some more strategic photography.

The other floors were just as involved. Mannington had established at an early stage that the Super Étendard and Mirage aircraft of the Argentinian Air Force were equipped with Exocet missiles, and were based at the Río Grande and Río Gallegos airfields. How many Exocets did they have? Could they get any more? The answers to these questions would be found around the world in places like France where they were manufactured, or, it was rumoured, Ta'if in Saudi Arabia where they were a defence against any attack from Israel. Every arms dealer across the globe was being offered huge sums by the Argentinians to provide them with Exocets. These same arms dealers were also being monitored by Mannington, whether in Havana or Vienna, Singapore or Johannesburg. False requests were 'advertised' to flush out the world supply of these lethal missiles.

Despite the impending war, Mannington had other areas

demanding close attention, including events in El Salvador. For Jack and his staff it was the Zugdidi affair that dominated. Not only did he not have the answers, he didn't know half of the questions. All he knew was that a rich Jordanian/Saudi was in communication with a Georgian at the Russian Embassy in London about moving something from the nuclear site in the south-western USSR using a Turkish trawler – the *Ikiz*. Whether the Soviet authorities or the Saudi royal family were aware of this was not known. Perhaps most important of all, Jack did not know where they were going.

Although he was underground on Good Friday, it was a buoyant Jack Pennington who walked into Marcus Billingham's Room 401 just before midday.

"Good news!"

"Don't tell me. You've discovered that all Exocets are being recalled because of a design fault?"

"No … but that's not a bad idea." Jack smiled and added, "Or, even better, we could send in some lads to halt production at the French factory."

"That wouldn't do a lot for Anglo-French relations."

"Nor will the outcry if one of their missiles hits one of our ships."

They both went into reflective mood. So often in a crazy idea there's a seed of brilliance.

Marcus broke the silence first. "What if we established their stock of key components for Exocet assembly in France? And what if we could discover if they are running short of some small widget or special wire? What if the factory manufacturing this was to have an unfortunate fire?"

"Getting better. The further removed from the main factory, the better."

"I'll have a word with John. It might be worth pursuing. Anyway, what was your piece of good news?"

"We've been examining telephone calls from expats in Riyadh to the UK, and we've found a new Brit who's working at Nefud-al-aan; in particular on external works."

"What's so important about Nefud-al-aan? Is that where you think the warheads are going?"

"No, not necessarily. It is a very big new military city under construction. From his conversation with his wife, he appears to be working on several military sites."

"Fine."

"We've started reading his letters and discovered that he is a bit strapped for cash. He had a bit of bad luck. His house burnt down, apparently, so he sounds a prime target."

"What do you want to do next?"

"Monitor him for a few more days, establish his routine and his next planned trip out of Saudi," Jack explained. Then, remembering one more thing, he added, "Oh, out of interest, Lord Basil What's-His-Name is supposed to be reviewing his work!"

"Excellent."

Later that afternoon a telephone conversation was picked up by GCHQ and fed to Mannington. A certain 'Gregory', the Georgian at the Russian Embassy in London, was telephoning 'Nabil', the Jordanian in Jeddah. Gregory was again travelling from London to Madrid. He was using the time out of the embassy to contact his friend. Zugdidi and other specifics were not mentioned. However, the 'goods' at the 'factory' had now been 'updated'. The old 'goods' were now available as they were surplus. Had transport arrangements progressed? Nabil had replied to the effect that the 'boat' was on its way and 'not too far away'. It was awaiting instructions. How long would it take for the 'goods' to reach the 'port'? Gregory had replied that it would take two weeks. They had agreed that Gregory would telephone again one week later.

A few days before its new spiralling orbit would take it over the South Atlantic, the satellite had shown the *Ikiz* moored in the port of Trabzon on the north Turkish coast close to the Soviet border.

* * *

"Why don't we call the Foreign Secretary's bluff?" Robin Mills asked of his somewhat subdued boss.

"I never ask the Foreign Secretary a question unless I already know the answer," Sir Cecil replied.

"What if he sees Marcus Billingham alone again?"

"Let's cross that bridge when we come to it. Let's wait to see what the Foreign Secretary's new protection officer reports to us about his movements."

"I think that Mannington is looking for more independence, reporting directly to the Foreign Secretary, and," Robin added, "a status equal to us."

"That doesn't make sense."

"What if GCHQ was also independent and reported directly? What if the other three functions were the same?"

"I think that you are taking – or is it making? – a quantum leap."

"What else would Marcus and the Foreign Secretary discuss?"

"Stamps. First Day Covers? They both collect stamps." Sir Cecil's lips barely broke into a wry smile.

Robin knitted his brow. The absurd popularity of philately was not the problem; it was the nightmare scenario of the SIS devolved into five separate functions. "Could we put a unit of our people into Mannington to act as liaison? That could muddy the waters, and we would know what was going on." He was thinking aloud.

"And they turn native? Then we really are up Shit Creek. We could end up a bloody personnel department."

"I just feel that we need to be a bit more proactive."

"We are being proactive, Robin. We will know if they meet again, and we have Hamish looking for a crack in their armour. I personally think that this Falklands thing will soon blow over and the Zugdidi warheads are a red herring. It's some Georgian trying to con a couple of million out of a rich Arab. That's it. Anything from Basil?"

"A few plans of Nefud-al-aan came today via Jeddah. At a first look we cannot see anything odd. Basil is going to try to get all of the plans and those of the other sites, but that will be more difficult for him."

"Don't worry, Robin. All this other stuff is a distraction. You and I need to keep an eye on our agricultural friend in Moscow now that we have cleared the way for him to join the Politburo; done well for a combine-harvester driver, has our Mr Gorbachev, don't you think?"

Robin knew that to be true … but he was only one of six worldwide who did.

* * *

The dark blue Ford Escort and the maroon Rover were parked in the huge layby near The Air Balloon pub on Birdlip Hill. The cars' occupants were not there to enjoy the panoramic view of the Severn Valley laid out beneath them. The men in the passenger seats were listening to communications via their earpieces; the drivers were scanning the road behind in their mirrors.

At Mannington, in the hangar which served as a car park, Jack had handed in his security pass and was about to start his engine. He was going to call in on Victoria to try and keep their relationship alive. To his alarm, he saw Ross emerge from the security doors and offer his pass to the guards. If they drove back to Cheltenham in convoy Jack would not be able to stop at Great Witcombe. He waited until Ross was halfway to his car and got back out.

"See you tomorrow," he called.

Back at the security box, he said that he had remembered that his Volvo was being serviced tomorrow, and that he would be driving his wife's VW Golf. He checked that they had the correct licence plate number. Yes, they would inform the guards at the gate and program the security camera monitors. He drove out of the base in no great hurry, allowing Ross time to disappear.

In the layby, the car engines started. The action would have been triggered by any one of the twelve cars belonging to owners under suspicion leaving Mannington. It was Ross's Audi that slowed to negotiate the roundabout at The Air Balloon. It was Ross whom Hamish's men followed into Cheltenham and for the next forty-eight hours.

Jack Pennington was quietly cursing Ross, without knowing that his friend had done him a favour by unwittingly volunteering himself as the first of the twelve senior Middle East experts to be watched clandestinely. Jack, oblivious, turned down the rat run to Great Witcombe.

Victoria's rented cottage was not a chocolate-box picture of golden stone and mullioned windows. It was more a characterless box of peeling pebbledash with a porch of blue corrugated plastic. He parked alongside the asbestos garage, tucking the car against the untidy blackthorn hedgerow. Walking around the back, he could see a mobile of seashells suspended from half a coconut shell in its place on a nail – this meant 'all clear'. He rat-a-tat-tatted on the back door and walked in. She was stood at the sink drainer, chopping carrots on a warped breadboard. A red apron protected the pastel-coloured trouser suit that she had worn to work. Usually, she would have changed into a jumper and jeans before cooking. Her cheeks were flushed. There was a magnetism in the air that was both attractive and repelling. Jack was about to tell her about Ross delaying his departure, but swallowed the thought when he realised that it only emphasised the problems associated with their affair.

"Did you get in late?" he asked.

"No, not particularly."

He stayed on the strip of hall carpet, not stepping onto the cushioned linoleum of the cooking area.

"Would you like to stay for tea? There's plenty," she asked.

"No … uh, no."

She knew that he would have his tea waiting at home but wouldn't mention the subject. It was at this point that he became aware of the strong smell of perfume.

"Don't I get a kiss?" she asked, knowing that he couldn't go home smelling of another woman.

As she stepped forward to kiss him, he turned and their lips never met. He swivelled and sat down on the nearest chair.

"What's up?" he asked, allowing her to vent her spleen.

"I've been thinking."

He waited for the usual demands.

"I accept that we cannot be together in this country … yet," she continued as he relaxed, thinking that he may have misread the signs, "but we could be together abroad."

No, he hadn't misread.

"What do you mean, abroad?"

"Cyprus."

There was only the sound of water gushing into a saucepan as he contemplated the minefield of responses.

"Where exactly in Cyprus?" was a good delaying tactic.

"The Greek side," was an equally good reply.

"For how long?" He was raising his head over the parapet.

"Two or three weeks?"

"A holiday?" He had thought that she meant permanently.

"Why not? You can justify a few weeks at Ayios Nikolaos for work, and I can book a harmless few weeks' holiday on a Mediterranean island."

Ayios Nikolaos was the principal listening post for the Middle East, and Jack was an occasional visitor, having spent many months there (and in Tehran before it was closed) when he was working at GCHQ.

"Would you like to think about it for a few days?" she asked with pointed reasonableness.

"Well, yes … definitely."

"Perhaps you would like to think about sex, as well?" she asked with a rehearsed confidence. "Because that's when you're going to get it again … in a hotel in Cyprus."

She over-salted the saucepan, but didn't care.

CHAPTER NINE

The Honourable Basil Wynne was cool, verging on cold. The air conditioning in his Ministry Mercedes was on full, with the temperature outside close to forty degrees centigrade. He was wearing sunglasses. The car had tinted windows, and yet the sun, reflecting off the blue mirror glass of the nearest office block, was blinding. He was sitting at the front of a queue on an urban dual carriageway in the inside lane, waiting for the lights to change. Basil was miles away, musing on the TV weatherman who had used the same 'sun' symbol every day since he had been in Saudi Arabia. Actually, there had been one day when he had used an obscure symbol which proved the following day to mean 'dust storm'. Through the glass, Basil watched someone using the escalator down to the underpass; there was no cover to the moving stairs – open to the elements, it still looked odd to him.

The lights changed and a sleek brown Chevrolet in the outside lane cut across in front of him to do a U-turn back down the other carriageway before the oncoming traffic had set off. A horn blared behind Basil, and he pressed the accelerator, letting the automatic pull forward. On the seat beside him he had a full set of the 'as-built' drawings for Nefud-al-aan, as he was fully entitled to have but, somehow, he still felt guilty. The turning that he was looking for on Sitteen Street was next to a German-built pewter-coloured shopping complex. It resembled a sinking battleship just as the bow is perpendicular to the waves. Bouncing off the tarmac onto the compacted sand, he scattered a pack of feral dogs who were several evolutionary light years away from the salukis of his youth.

The villa was surrounded by a stuccoed wall. The entrance was via a rusting metal door whose ornamentation consisted of curlicues of reinforcing rod welded to a sheet of iron. Little could be seen of the building save for its flat roof (not a problem in a climate without rain or snow) and its water tank. A couple of Phoenix date palms poked up above the plot and a Delonix flame tree spread its layers of fine multipinnate leaves to give some feathery shade; it had just begun to flower with splashes of red.

Basil pressed the buzzer under a small, cracked plastic plate proclaiming in English and Arabic, 'RATCO OIL'.

A large bolt was heard being scraped back with difficulty. The final release was accompanied by a cry of "Oh, bugger!" as the fleshy part of a first finger was pinched between unforgiving metal. The door opened to reveal a man giving a passable imitation of a sheep. He was short and round with a greasy thatch of golden hair, and appeared to have several stomachs, the largest of which was hanging over his trouser belt. He was sucking his injured finger.

"Julian, have you cut yourself?"

"Hullo, Basil, come in. Caught my bastard finger pulling back the bolt. God knows what bastard diseases you can get opening up your arteries to the atmosphere out here. Bastard of a place."

Basil closed the door behind him with a loud clang. Treating the bolt with great respect, it slid with ridiculous ease back into place. He followed Julian the ten paces to the shade of the villa porch.

It could have been the lounge of any villa in Riyadh: opaque glass in every window to keep out the bleaching sun; enormous, ugly furniture; smoked-glass tables with chunky ashtrays; and air-conditioning units crudely forced through the external walls as if fired from a powerful howitzer.

"G&T? Sun's over the yardarm. Well, I expect it is. Sun's always over the bastard yardarm out here. One of its fucking good points."

Basil unrolled the plans on the coffee table while Julian Prior-Jones poured drinks on a sideboard of plastic mahogany veneer. He returned to the armchairs.

"Here's mud in your eye … well, sand anyway." Julian toasted Basil and knocked back a mouthful of the clear liquid. "I'm not sure," he continued, "whether it's the gin in my bastard bloodstream or the quinine in the tonic which has kept me free from malaria all of these years. Mind you, poisoning looks odds on, don't you think?" He indicated his finger cooling against the ice-filled glass.

"This is the final set of plans, Julian, and I have seen nothing built that is not as per the contract."

"Great. Well, you did your best, old chap. I'll send them to London, anyway. It'll give them something to paw over."

Julian Prior-Jones was attached to the British Embassy in

Jeddah where he was listed under the Trade section, but in reality spent half of his time in Riyadh. His job was to meet as many British businessmen as possible and to use them as directed by London. Julian may not know the answers but for certain he knew someone who did. He was one of those self-effacing, put-upon types who socialise with ease, never threatening, always liked. Having spent so long playing the gin-and-tonic-soaked slob, he couldn't tell where the act stopped and reality started any more. Basil had gone to Eton a few years after Julian, and their meeting in Riyadh had reassured the former hugely after the culture shock of the move from 'Yookay'. Julian knew everyone, including all of the old boys. He had founded the Masonic lodge in Jeddah, which was illegal but invaluable in a culture where drink, churches, and all theatres, cinemas and usual meeting places were banned. It was technically illegal for more than a handful of people other than Saudis to meet together, even in private. Where Freemasonry as a source of business contacts was waning back home, in Saudi it gave the British businessmen a very useful 'club'. To Julian, it was an even more useful network.

"What's happening on the Falklands front?" Basil asked.

"The *Canberra*'s halfway to Ascension Island, and anyone with an Exocet missile in their attic is dusting the bastard off and flogging it to the Argies for crazy amounts of corned beef, or whatever the currency is down there."

Basil sipped his gin and tonic gingerly. Saudi, with its strict laws and 'eye for an eye' revenge open to the victim's family, is not the place to get caught drink-driving after knocking down a child who has run out into the road.

"Never trusted the Argies myself." Julian screwed up his eyes and shook his head. "They are mostly Italians and, like

74

their crap wine, they don't travel well. Italians like to argue, and down there you've got no one to argue with. Your nearest neighbour is a thousand miles away across the Pampas … and then he might prove to be Welsh! Imagine an economy based on corned beef! The best thing about corned beef is the euphoria from getting the bastard stuff out of the tin without cutting your finger – which reminds me, I had better let Doc Fleming give me a tetanus jab. Thanks for the drawings."

Julian tipped the rest of the ice into his mouth and crunched it.

* * *

Later that week in London, Sir Cecil was having one of his regular briefing meetings with the Foreign Secretary. They were sat in a book-lined room on the north side of the building while the Foreign Secretary's room was being upgraded by the introduction of a further series of secure landlines. Sir Cecil had explained the current difficulties they were having with the satellite over the South Atlantic. He outlined the tacit agreement with the Americans over the use of Ascension Island, which is British-owned but leased to the USA principally as a link in the worldwide communications network. He gave an assessment of the deployment of Argentinian troops (mostly from a conversation with a settler on the Falklands who couldn't believe the telephone lines were still operating). The fact that the SAS were now on the islands ended his briefing.

"What about this Zugdidi business that Mannington is so keen about?" the Foreign Secretary asked.

"With the greatest respect, they should concentrate on collating information, not making wild guesses. Undoubtedly, the boat exists and is probably picking up carpets for the Saudi market. Similarly, it looks like a smart Georgian is trying to con a Jordanian living in Saudi out of a couple of million pounds by promising him some missiles or missile parts. But all of our checking of possible military sites has thrown up a complete blank. I suggest that we have enough to worry about in the South Atlantic. I know that Mannington has proved better than expected in its collation function, but I do urge you not to confuse collation with decision-making and control. Mannington really should be collating the huge amount of material relevant to the Falklands, not dabbling in some speculation game around the Black Sea."

"I'm sure you are right, Cecil. One thing that has come out of this affair is the shortfall in our knowledge about the new Saudi military cities. We really should have all that; you never know when those bases may play an important role."

"You are right, and Basil Wynne has given us all of the plans we need, so they're filed and ready for use."

* * *

At Mannington, Jack could not believe his luck. Actually, he was even luckier than he knew, for Hamish's men were now following Simon Burroughs for forty-eight hours, having given Ross Smith a clean bill of health. Marcus had decided to progress the idea he had floated in front of the Foreign Secretary, which would be a precursor to expanding Mannington's role. As a first step he was going to send some of his staff to a couple of the main overseas listening posts under the guise of improving efficiency in communication with Mannington via GCHQ. He wanted to leave the areas fundamentally affected by the looming Falklands

War to concentrate on the matter in hand. He therefore decided to send someone senior from the Middle East Group to Cyprus, someone senior from the Oriental Group to Hong Kong, and someone else from the African Group to Pretoria.

Jack had volunteered with contained eagerness and agreed to coordinate with his counterparts to devise a programme for educating the collectors of intelligence on how to make it 'Collation friendly'. He had suggested flying out a week later to be back in time for Sarah's birthday, and Marcus had consented.

"While I am there, I shall keep an eye on our friends 'Gregory' and 'Nabil' … and the good ship *Ikiz*. Maybe we can teach London a lesson."

Sarah Pennington described herself to Ross's wife Margaret as a Gulf widow, so it was no surprise to her when she received the call from Jack to say that he would not be home that night because he was very busy at the office. She was used to these clinical, sanitised conversations, and she played her part well. While Jack was getting into his car, she was taking the kids out in her Golf to the video hire shop so that they could settle down that evening to a good film while they ate a Chinese meal off trays in the lounge.

Jack reversed alongside Victoria's garage, unaware that a blue Escort and a maroon Rover were following Simon Burroughs along the Golden Valley bypass between Cheltenham and Gloucester. He scouted around the field and hedgerow next to Victoria's house for a few daisies, dandelions and some blackthorn to make a home-grown posy. With the all-clear signal of the seashell mobile tinkling in the light evening breeze, he tapped the kitchen door. She answered it, her face not revealing whether she was happy or annoyed or both.

"I trawled the flower shops of Gloucestershire to get you these … they are a peace offering."

"They're hardly appropriate. Blackthorn has fierce spines and dandelions make you pee."

"What do daisies do?"

"The washing, the ironing, and put up with prats like you." She backed against the wall to let him in. "At least you didn't pick hawthorn, because it's unlucky to bring it in the house … and it stinks of cat's pee."

He pecked her on the cheek and made his way into the kitchen. "I thought that I'd sleep tonight if that's all right with you?"

She looked surprised but stood her ground. "Fine. I'll make up the spare bed."

"I was hoping that I could sleep with you?"

"Do you think that you could take a night sleeping together but with no sex?"

"I have absolutely no doubt."

That Friday night he found himself tucking into her body under the covers, but separated by a long and furry winceyette nightdress that she had never worn before.

"Vicky, if I promise to book a holiday to Cyprus with you tomorrow morning at nine o'clock when the travel agents open, can we make love now?" he whispered in her ear.

"I don't believe you. Go to sleep."

"Vicky, if I swear on my mother's grave that I will keep my word, can we?"

"Your mother's not dead."

"No. OK. If I promise never to have sex with you ever again if I fail to book the holiday with you, will you believe me?"

She turned over. "Scout's honour?"

"You mean that?"

"Stop saying stupid things and just say yes."

"Yes."

"You'd better enjoy it, because if you are stringing me along it'll be the last time."

"Can the condemned man have a last request?"

"You don't smoke."

"Will you take that nightdress off?"

"No."

Getting up the next morning involved much reassuring on Jack's part and many cynical stares from Victoria. She sat rather pointedly in her nightdress at her small kitchen table. There was hardly room for cereal packets, breakfast cups of tea, and the *Yellow Pages* open at 'Travel Agents'. At one minute to nine, Jack reached across and handed her the telephone from the small dresser; the cable barely reached. She still looked at him suspiciously.

"So, I'm just checking flight availability, am I? Or cheap package holidays?"

He took a bite of toast. "Actually, I shouldn't phone just yet—"

"I knew it!" she screamed, standing up. "I knew you'd bloody slime your way out of it."

"—because you'll need your credit-card number—"

"What?"

"—to pay for the flight."

"Which flight?"

"The flight I reserved in your name yesterday."

She stood staring at him. "How dare you commit me to 227 pounds on my credit card?!" she shouted.

"Look, we're going to Cyprus together for a couple of weeks … what? How did you know it was 227 pounds?"

"The travel agent phoned yesterday, just before you arrived, for my credit-card details."

"You … you … cow! You knew last night! I'll kill you!" He started to edge around the table.

"Can the condemned woman have a last request?"

"You don't smoke!" he shouted while beaming at her.

"Will you take my nightdress off?"

CHAPTER TEN

Mark 'Empty' Tanner had been in Saudi Arabia for three-and-a-half weeks. It had been one long culture shock, to which could be added another unavoidable shock; namely, static. Has anything ever been so misnamed? It sent Empty flying every time he touched plastic, and the unique combination of bone-dry air, vibrant nylon carpets and his plastic-soled shoes conspired to produce electrostatic displays which could have saved Van de Graaff a lot of research time.

He was driving along a dual carriageway out of Riyadh towards Nefud-al-aan. His white Toyota pickup with orange flashes down the side was indistinguishable from the thousands of others on the road. The air-conditioning system was competing with Steely Dan, who were desperately reeling in the eels, or that's what it sounded like on the distorted cassette. The car in front stopped without warning; the driver had decided to park on the inside lane of the dual carriageway. This was less surprising than it may appear at first and there was a perfect logic behind it. The driver was going to the new eye hospital, it was forty degrees centigrade outside, and the nearest point to the entrance where you could drive your car was not the carefully laid out car park with its palms and lamp standards, but the hard shoulder of the dual carriageway. This was where people parked in a short line until joining the end of this row was too far from the entrance; in which case, one started a new line in the next lane. Empty had yet to see anyone park in the fast lane and completely block the road, despite the number of Saudis with pebble glasses who not-so-clearly needed the eye hospital. The irony was not wasted on Empty.

He passed the lorry park where the rows of Mercedes trucks, all ornately decorated with chrome fretwork and oil paintings of alpine scenes, waited to be hired. Further on, he drove by the camel souk where the foul-smelling air was enough to turn the desert green, and passed the last service station, where the chocolate cost more than the petrol. The villas thinned out until there appeared to be no reason for locating one precisely at that exact spot in the middle of nowhere. He followed the car in front as it left the tarmac, bouncing onto a dusty track which could be told apart from the desert only because there were fewer stones. He bumped off one track and onto another near the rusting wreckage of two petrol tankers that had collided, setting fire to the desert. Two hundred and fifty thousand square miles of nothing and two lorries crashed into each other? It was now a ten-mile straight run to the start of a craggy ridge past a lonely road sign that had a black spot in a red triangle. 'Beware Accident Black Spot' had seemed good advice, but that was not its purpose. It was actually a 'Beware of the Camels' sign, but Islamic fundamentalists had defaced the schematic silhouette of the camel; only Allah can create life, whatever the form. Why, in all of the 250,000 square miles, this spot should be selected to warn of camels was never explained.

Don't peel back the wallpaper. Do not peek beyond. Empty repeated these mantras to himself time and time again. *Just earn the money.* Could this ever become a routine journey to work?

The best was yet to come. On the last leg of his route the track zigzagged for no apparent reason through a half-dozen villas and a row of empty concrete-block units that should have been shops; that would work out at one shop per villa. He slowed, wound down the window and waved to a group of Saudis who were sitting in the shade of one of the unfinished units like actors on a stage. They couldn't sit under the three date palms owing to a distinct lack of shade. The fronds that did exist were brown and crispy, hanging down forlornly.

"*Marhaba!*" he shouted.

Their gap-toothed replies were lost in the cab of the pickup between the roar of the air conditioning and some song about a hotel in California from which, apparently, it was difficult to leave; that line had started to give Empty an uneasy feeling for some reason.

He had been flagged down by this motley crew on his first trip to the building site, watched over eagerly by the old sheikh who was reluctant or unable to get up from his plastic garden chair. Communication had proved impossible until they had read the open letter from Sheikh Faisal Al-Shaqra. Since then, they had waved him through without jumping down from the concrete ledge surrounding the units. You have to give them credit. Well, actually, they didn't take credit ... just cash; just Saudi riyals. If you wanted to drive from Riyadh to the site at Nefud-al-aan you had to pass through their 'village'. Whether you worked for the billion-dollar French main contractor or you were just delivering a parcel, you had to grease their palms (and not the ones with the brown fronds above their heads). This had to be done not too overtly so that sensibilities were not offended. Cunning ruses were devised. Conversations would go along the lines of:

"Can my son come and work for your company?"

"We don't need anyone, thank you."

"Oh, it's OK, he won't actually turn up for work."

So, his 'son' is put onto your payroll and all of your wagons and vans can pass by unhindered.

"Why don't you tell the old git to fuck off?" had been Empty's simple reaction back in the office.

"He's a Bedouin sheikh," they had said.

"And?" Empty had asked.

"He's a Bedouin sheikh," they had replied.

"Oh, thanks, that's a lot clearer."

And Empty had watched as every week the old sheikhs would turn up opposite his flat in the centre of Riyadh in yet more white Toyota pickups. In the back, typically, would be a goat or two tied to the metal bars, and large plastic sacks full of Saudi riyals. The old sheikhs would carry them one at a time into the Exchange House, where the money was counted and turned into a cheque to be put in the bank later. Sometimes there were three sacks left unguarded, if you exclude the goats, as there is no theft in Saudi.

The building site at Nefud-al-aan resembled a wood-ant colony. Scale disappeared in the desert; you only saw the industry. Huge tractor units criss-crossed the site, delivering each of the thirty-three different panels of concrete which comprised each new villa. Each panel was made in its own 'factory'; huge, temporary hangars of corrugated steel. The crude structure of four villas was completed every day from the bolting together of these thirty-three concrete panels. Teams of Rajasthanis in loose brown pyjama suits and ragged turbans would brave the heat and dust to manoeuvre the panels into place and drive in the bolts, all under the watchful supervision of the French supervisory team. The bathrooms came from Germany – already tiled and fully finished. They were lifted up by huge cranes and pushed into place like closing a cutlery drawer. Only the temporary steel security door on the bathroom unit had to be removed and replaced with a wooden one matching the rest of the villa. Heiner and Helmut, with cropped blond hair and frayed denim shorts, connected up the pipework as well as the electricity, and replaced any cracked mirrors or chipped basins. They worked non-stop, saving money to afford a holiday home. At this rate they should be able to buy Menorca.

Empty pulled up alongside the Portakabin that over his first three weeks he had come to regard affectionately as … a Portakabin.

"Stand by your beds!" he shouted as he stepped through the door. It had been funny three weeks ago.

He greeted his dedicated team who were hard at work: 'M' and 'K', his two draughtsmen, were sat at drawing boards meticulously transferring irrigation pipe runs onto two of the 150 very large plans that covered the whole site. M and K were actually South Koreans with PhDs in Marine Engineering, but they could earn more money drawing pipework in Saudi Arabia. How many ships did Korea design and build, anyway? Stood next to them was Francis, a tall, blond Jehovah's Witness from Little Chalfont who patently had not read the job description. Ashiq, the print-machine operator from Pakistan, completed the team. He worked at the far end of the room, printing all of the drawings on a beast of a blueprint machine that used ultraviolet light and ammonium hydroxide in some arcane way. All day he stood feeding large tracing-paper sheets between rollers, cursing as they creased and tore beneath the roar of the extractor fan. He had been a boxer in a previous life but a severe electric shock had ended his career, so that he now fought a print machine, stammering abusive epithets that not a soul on earth could understand even without the noisy fan. Through all of this, he managed to have a smile on his face.

"We have to send Sector 8 to Basil by Thursday night, so we should aim to have it finished by Wednesday. The meeting is not until Saturday anyway," Francis informed the room. Empty, for all of his shortcomings, had spotted Francis's potential from day one. He let him organise the drawing production, order the supplies and attend the weekly meetings; thirty years on the doorstep as a Jehovah's Witness made brusque American reviewers, explosive French main contractors and a succession of inconsistent Arab clients seem like a garden party.

Like life itself, the project had started with an umbilicus; a long, twenty-four-inch-diameter pipe from the desalination plant miles away. The water of the Arabian Gulf turned at mind-boggling cost into potable, pure water and pumped across the desert to … where? To a few thousand acres of stony sand which looked remarkably similar to the hundreds of thousands of acres of stony sand that surrounded it. After the pipe was installed came the miles of boundary security fence that defined the site of the new military city. Next came the Bedouin, the Bedu, who set up camp just outside the line of chain-link fence. They were the power base that sustained the Saudi system and they provided the men for the National Guard who would occupy the city, bizarrely moving from tents into cavernous villas. They had put the royal family into power in Saudi Arabia. Oil wealth may buy F-15s and Tornados, but it was these few thousand men who were the true defence.

Their worldly goods were confined to what their camels could carry. These were the bare essentials: tents and blankets, knives and guns, and brass coffee pots. They were a philosophical people who lived in a simple and extreme world; a world that consisted of one line – the horizon: brown below, blue above. Baking by day, freezing by night. A people, oddly, with a poor understanding of the third dimension; a consequence of living in a flat world of two dimensions, a world with nothing to cast strong shadows. Hence, the desert Arab developed an unequalled appreciation of pattern and calligraphy at the expense of architecture and sculpture.

After the Bedu had established their camp outside came the construction of the two enormous water towers shaped like toadstools, one ten per cent smaller than the other. The larger was to receive the purified water, the smaller to collect the same water after it had been around the city, used by its ten thousand occupants and treated at the sewage works. This recycled water provided the irrigation that sustained a false green landscape that would die in a few days if the water ever stopped arriving from Al-Khobar.

This was Empty's task: to put in place the irrigation system in advance of the planting but following on immediately behind the villa and building construction. Thousands of miles of black plastic pipe and pop-up sprinklers. All of Empty's work was to be reviewed by Basil on behalf of the Saudi Arabian National Guard. Empty had to fulfil this task using 150 Rajasthanis, two Korean ship designers, a stammering Pakistani boxer, and a Jehovah's Witness from Buckinghamshire. Basil had to fulfil this task despite working for a huge American management consultancy.

In the Portakabin, Francis was smoothing out a site plan on the small table. Several red pencil lines had been added to the drawing. "We've hit another one," he informed Empty.

"Somewhere different?"

"No, in the easternmost sector … here."

Empty and his crew had been provided with drawings showing the location of every underground electricity cable, sewer pipe and telephone line, so that they could avoid them when digging their own trenches. They, like everyone else involved, had not been told where the secret communication cables had been laid. Officially, they did not exist. Empty had been told not to tell anyone, including the reviewers, when and where his men cut through one. He was to report it directly to a designated Saudi military coordinator. After the third time in as many days, Empty decided that Francis should keep a record of these routes in their little site office to help avoid future problems. They kept them at the back of the drawing cabinet.

Most of these secret cables appeared to run out of the site towards the satellite complex being built on the nearby low, craggy ridge. There was, however, a concentrated cluster over in the easternmost sector near to the sewage works.

* * *

If Sir Cecil had not cancelled surveillance of 'Gregory', Mannington would have known that he was on Iberia Flight IB372 to Madrid that Saturday morning, the first day of

May. Laurenti Malenkov, his real name, was in charge of accommodation provision for embassies of the USSR. This was the level of responsibility given to Georgians in the Soviet Diplomatic Service. He was booked into a three-star hotel near the residency block under construction around the corner from his embassy.

If Sir Cecil had not cancelled surveillance of 'Nabil', Mannington would have known that he was on Saudia Flight SV535 from Jeddah to Madrid that Saturday morning, the 1st May. Sheikh Abdullatif Al-Rahman, his real name, was sat in first class wearing a Lanvin suit and a Ferragamo tie, looking every bit the Mediterranean businessman. He was booked into the Hotel Palace, and a chauffeur-driven Mercedes was waiting to whisk him away from International Arrivals in the beautiful warm spring sunlight.

As it happened, nobody overheard the conversation between 'Nabil' and 'Gregory' as they sat on the large, comfortable sofas under the Belle Époque stained-glass dome which is the central feature of the Hotel Palace.

At 8.30pm Nabil found himself alone in a nearby recommended restaurant. He made a mental note not to invest in the Madrid area if this was the extent of free capital available. After boiling hot garlic soup with a raw egg poaching in the liquid, he picked at the *codornices al mojo*; two very small quail. This is a main course that results in a net loss in energy expended over calories consumed. He ordered a black coffee, was driven back to the Hotel Palace and watched Real Madrid on television. Between 10pm and 2am while Nabil was snoring, the *Madrileños* had come out to eat and the city was humming.

Before breakfast he telephoned his brother in Jeddah to

say that he had had a successful meeting with Gregory and was flying home.

* * *

Ross Smith walked into Jack's office. "Do you want the good news or the strangely interesting news?"

"Good news first … I might die before the other news."

"Nabil has had a face-to-face meeting in Madrid with Gregory. He has just telephoned his brother."

"That's bad news, isn't it? We should have been watching… and listening."

"We now know that he is really Sheikh Abdullatif Al-Rahman, the Saudi sponsor of the Honourable Basil le Strange Wynne."

"Really? That's his real name?"

"Definitely."

"What? Abdullatif Al-Rahman or Basil le Strange Whatsit?" Ross smiled back.

"Ross, old buddy, old pal, I think that we have a way to embarrass Sir Cecil of the Arthritic Knee."

"Is that his real name?"

* * *

Jack was elated. His mind was racing. He drove out of Mannington onto the Cirencester road and roared back towards Cheltenham. He had made a major breakthrough on Zugdidi, had a way to score points over Sir Cecil, and two weeks with Victoria in Cyprus to look forward to. He was a lucky man.

Unfortunately, his luck was in the balance. The Escort and the Rover followed him along the road. He turned down Birdlip Hill towards Great Witcombe. Victoria was a very happy bunny and he wanted to take full advantage of the resumption of normal servicing. He looked at the clock: 4.40. She would not be back for at least half an hour. He drove straight past the turning without a glance and on into Cheltenham to the travel agents, where he picked up her tickets. Tomorrow evening he would surprise her with them.

An hour later, the passenger of the blue Escort was speaking on his radio phone to Hamish.

CHAPTER ELEVEN

By Sunday 2nd May the Argentinians had twelve thousand troops on the Falkland Islands and the British had decided to make their landing via San Carlos Water and face the long march across the width of East Falkland to Port Stanley. The *Canberra* was still at Ascension Island, where everything was practised or rehearsed as much to relieve boredom and keep people fit as to prepare for the assault. Anything broken was repaired aboard the Stena *Seaspeed*, a North Sea oil-rig maintenance ship whose facilities had been supplemented by the addition of the contents of several naval workshops. If this wasn't enough to contend with, a *Primori*-class Russian surveillance ship watched even the most mundane of activities.

At dawn on that Sunday, a lone RAF Vulcan attempted to bomb Port Stanley airfield. It may have done more damage trying to land on the runway than by missing with all but one of its bombs. It had flown from Ascension Island accompanied by Victor air-refuelling tankers, which were themselves refuelled by other tanker planes en route. Perhaps they should have used all of the fuel to set fire to the airfield; they used enough of the stuff.

* * *

On that Sunday, Sir Cecil was about to tee off from the first tee at Staunton Grange golf course. He topped the ball fifty yards into the heather, failing to reach the fairway.

"Oh, bad luck," one of his three playing companions offered.

Sir Cecil straightened his arthritic leg and inferred by the odd grimace that this stiffness might account for the shot.

Robin Mills, playing with Lawrence Dodds of the Foreign Office, found the ball gripped by the springy tentacles of the innocent-looking heather. "It's sitting up," he called across to his limping boss.

"It looks like it's down to you, Miles." Sir Cecil peered at the lie of his ball.

"Don't be too greedy, Cecil. Just chip it onto the fairway," Robin encouraged, and two hacks later the ball reached mown grass and they all progressed down the hill.

Staunton Grange was a little-known and hidden gem of a golf course cut into the pines and heathland of Surrey. The sign on the road was six inches square and did its best to dissuade visitors. This was a truly private golf club that only had 120 members, of whom, it was rumoured, only sixty were living. Two of these were dukes, and of the lady members only three did not have titles. There was no annual membership fee. Whatever the year cost was divided by the number of members and that is what you paid. The course was always in perfect condition for the simple reason that hardly anyone played on it. You would have to get up pretty early to see any serious golf when the occasional Open champion used the empty course to play a practice round with his caddy. The club had certain traditions, one of which involved the automatic associate membership of certain members of the Foreign and Commonwealth Office, and other key civil servants.

In truth, it was rare for Sir Cecil, Sir Miles, Robin and Lawrence to play together, but today Sir Cecil had some important news.

"I don't want to spoil your golf," he said, approaching the first green, where his ball now sat just off the closely mown surface after five shots, "but I have some disturbing news."

"Really?" Lawrence asked.

"Jack Pennington is having an affair."

"He doesn't look the type."

"Not only that, but yesterday Hamish's men found out that he's off to Cyprus with her when he's supposed to be working at Akrotiri."

"No!"

"I'm afraid so."

"That won't do Mannington's reputation any good, will it?"

"What are you going to do?" Sir Miles asked.

"Oh, I don't know. It's come as a bit of a shock," Sir Cecil lied. "I'll decide before I see the Foreign Secretary in the morning."

He walked over to take his shot, carrying his putter only to find that his ball had ended up on the wrong side of the sprinkler head that irrigated the green. "Do I get relief from this?" he asked out of courtesy, knowing that he did.

"Of course."

"I know they have to water the greens, but what sort of idiot puts a sprinkler that close?"

At that moment, the idiot was three thousand miles away in the desert, trying to fix a broken print machine because its stammering Pakistani operator was, not surprisingly, nervous of playing with electrics.

* * *

"… and keep your fingers out of the sockets!" Empty shouted out of the pickup window as he drove off slowly to avoid creating a cloud of red dust.

Ashiq exposed his sweaty armpits to the heavens, standing in the Portakabin doorway and proclaiming his eternal gratitude to Empty. In his excitement, the stammering reached a new peak and 'eternal' proved to be a particularly treacherous word, seeming to take forever.

Empty followed his disjointed route back across the desert to Riyadh. The incongruously slick dual carriageways enhanced the dreamlike quality of his journey, sweeping him on elevated sections up over villas resembling scattered brown sugar cubes and down into the central metropolitan area. It was an urban facade; neo-Dallas, neo-Atlanta (or should that be mock Georgian?). Empty had made his way onto the flat roof of his Riyadh head office soon after his arrival in Saudi to gain a third-floor view of his new city. Leaving footprints in the lunar surface as he walked through drifts of ochre dust, he had paused behind the vast neon advertisement for Sumitomo tyres that projected upwards seven metres above the rooftops. From pavement level at night it was 'Japanese technology meets Hollywood'. Viewed from behind on the roof it owed more to 'Meccano meets the twelve-volt battery'.

That Sunday early evening he had kicked around his flat for half an hour; not kicking too much because it boosted the static to lightning proportions. Frosted glass in every window turned the flat into a prison. At least in most prisons you could see out through the bars to the sky. He missed green countryside, he missed wallpaper. He would break the rules and telephone Dawn. No, he wouldn't. The cream telephone with its black handset sat assuming disproportionate importance in the large room devoid of clutter and quarter-filled by big old furniture. Even Echo the Gecko, his friend, on his early evening gravity-defying saunter around the white walls, was staring at the telephone. Empty needed distraction. He walked around the flat again. He suffered another blast of static from the light switch. He would go downtown … again.

One of the joys to Empty of working in Saudi Arabia was that he worked six days a week excluding Friday, which kept him occupied. For him these were long days with much travelling to and from the site; when he did get back to the flat he basically wanted to eat and jump into bed. His sponsor, Sheikh Faisal, didn't get up until late morning, having performed his morning prayers next to his bed, and, having had lunch, did most of his formal business until the early evening. Thereafter he wanted to talk late into the night with people like Empty, in his palatial villa over a meal of lamb and rice. Eating late at night doesn't suit most Brits, and it is even harder to keep the greasy food down when you are subjected to two hours of *Starsky & Hutch* on video and endless debates about why the British put their grandparents in old people's homes.

Empty had been summoned to Sheikh Faisal's after nine o'clock. Two-and-a-half hours to kill as the build-up to *The Dukes of Hazzard* and roast lamb. He made a quick sandwich of cheese slices in white bread, grabbed a handful of cashew nuts and left the flat.

He was fast gaining the reputation for being the biggest nutter in Riyadh. This was not entirely surprising as he already had the reputation as the biggest nutter in High Wycombe. His use of the heavily subsidised and efficient bus service was often cited as odd by the other expats. When you are earning so much tax-free, why pay one riyal to sit with half of Asia on a bus? "Why not?" was his reply. It was worth it just to see things like all of the women, wrapped from head to foot in black, getting into their segregated section at the back via their own automatic door.

He jumped off, as he did most other evenings, into the bustle of the Arab souks. The orange glow of the fading sun was being replaced by the stark blue-white of bottled-gas lights and fluorescent tubes. A heaving mass of manhood, talking and selling and buying. The only women, completely hidden in black, sat cross-legged with hennaed hands on the roadside, selling nuts and spices.

There wasn't a great choice: the electrical souk, the clothes souk, the gold souk and, of course, the cassette shops. Social intercourse was limited (if you excluded the mosques and the vicarious pleasure of mixing the smell of your own sweat with that of others to a background of Marlboro cigarette smoke, sandalwood, Givenchy for Men, and sewage from any excavation below ground surface). Down a tight alleyway, already hot from the day's blistering temperature and perspiring bodies, he dodged the projecting air-conditioning units which expelled their fiery breath into his face. He walked into the cool of a music cassette shop … as he always did. The sweat under the armpits and down the back of his safari suit instantly went cold.

"*As-salaam alaykom*," the shop owner welcomed Empty.

"I prefer Adam and the Ants, myself. What's new?"

"Many things … take a look."

The walls were covered in row upon row of cassettes made in Singapore and on sale for sixty pence each. Cilla Black rubbed shoulders with David Bowie, Diana Ross with the Band of the Coldstream Guards; everything was randomly arranged. Logic would not help you to find your favourite music. To tennis elbow and housemaid's knee could be added 'cassette shop neck'.

The Saudi censors had been so enthusiastic with their black felt tips on the cellophane wrappers that it was hard to work out what was inside. Any cleavage or bare flesh above the knee was hidden by a felt-tip scrawl. Empty had soon realised why his Penguin Classic book cover had been ripped off at the airport. *Abraxas*, the studio album by Santana, was now essentially black, resembling an Ad Reinhardt abstract painting. Buying it was a leap of faith, which reminded Empty of when Dawn had bought a case of tins very cheaply from a grocery shop because their labels had come off; they were either pears in syrup or Irish stew. It made mealtimes interesting and saved money. Similarly, in Riyadh, Empty was torn between the desire to save every riyal to shorten his time away from his family, and the need to keep his head together for the couple of years he might be away. He really wanted to buy a cassette player with a radio to bring a bit of life to his flat; one of the new stacking mini systems in black. Maybe tomorrow.

After standing around outside the shops during prayer time, he eventually made it across Riyadh and at 9pm prompt was standing outside the grand gates to Sheikh Faisal's villa. He pressed the buzzer to gain entry and a security guard let him in, surprised that Empty had no car. He walked up the entrance drive with professional satisfaction that the palms and oleanders were thriving. It had been a little different on the first day, when the irrigation system was turned on and several thousand plastic emitters shot into the air because of a pressure fault; the myriad mini fountains among the plants had looked beautiful if unplanned.

Sheikh Faisal was on good form. "Greetings! *Marhaba!* Take a seat!"

There were hundreds of sofas and cushions.

"No. Don't take a seat. We will sit through here, it will be cosier," he corrected himself while negotiating a route through the furniture like a DFS salesman.

The twenty-year age difference had not even registered with Empty when they had first met; nor had the sheikh's obscene wealth. It was like meeting a panda or a Martian – just … different. The sheikh appeared to spend most of his life in a vast, linked space consisting of a bedroom, an anteroom and a lounge. The functions of each room were confused and duplicated. He often slept in the anteroom, ate in the lounge and worked from a desk in his bedroom. The women in his life lived in a totally separate part of the villa with their own front door.

"How's Nefud-al-aan?" he asked.

"Just dandy," Empty replied.

"What's 'dandy'?"

"Great. Fine. Super. Lovely."

"OK. That's a new one. Dandy. Will you make the deadline?"

"On the nail."

"I am assuming that 'on the nail' means 'yes'? Have some mango juice." Sheikh Faisal poured the most exquisite of fruit juices with crushed ice from a cut-glass jug. "I have more projects for you."

"Do you have any more hours? Only, I seem to be using the usual twenty-four each day already."

"Don't worry. Relax. I am so pleased with you, I have appointed an assistant for you. He is Canadian."

Empty let loose the startled innocent look.

"Don't worry. I regard it as promotion. I will increase your salary by five thousand pounds a year. What do you think?"

"That's mighty dandy."

"Mighty dandy … I like that."

They talked for an hour about two irrigation projects. The first was around a new library in Mecca, the Islamic holy city. The other scheme was for the sheikh's own new villa on the Red Sea Coast.

"What do you think? Dandy? Mighty dandy?"

Even Empty's innocence was rarely this startled. He was staring at a model of the two proposed villas; one for the men, one for the women. The men's villa was in the shape of a Spanish galleon; the ladies' was in the form of a Rolls-Royce. They were separated by a serpentine wall that meandered to the sea, where two gates gave onto a jetty which pointed across a coral sea to Sudan.

"What do you think? Here … look."

The photographs of the building site were surreal: a Spanish galleon and a car. Time travel in shuttered concrete.

"What's that out at sea? Another galleon?"

"No, don't be silly; that's the desalination tanker. It will be moored offshore. It's more convenient than running a pipe all the way from Jeddah."

"Of course." *Silly me*, thought Empty to himself.

Just before the meal arrived, they were debating how Empty could visit Mecca given that he was not a Muslim.

"No problem." There are no problems when you are a billionaire in your own country. The sheikh shot a strange look at Empty. "We will dress you as an Arab, anyhow. I will give you the clothes. No one will question you."

"Don't they look at your passport? You know, to check if you are a Muslim?" Empty was nothing if not practical.

"Ah, yes. No problem. I will give you somebody's … and my driver. No one will ask."

"Is it that important?"

"I want only you to supervise the irrigation contract. It is a very important library." The sheikh stepped into the bedroom and began lifting bundles of passports out of a drawer.

"Here. Yes. Here."

"Is my passport there?" Empty asked out of interest.

"Yes, I expect. All the passports are here unless Wafic takes them to the Ministry to get exit visas."

"How long does my visa last?"

They checked, only to discover that Empty had been given a short-duration, single-entry visa in London. This was a common occurrence due to the haste to get new employees out to Saudi Arabia.

"Is that a problem?"

"No, but you must fly back to London. It will only take a few hours."

"Dandy. Mighty dandy."

"Now, let's eat. Have you seen *Hawaii Five-O*?"

* * *

It was a regular Monday-morning meeting in London to apprise the Foreign Secretary of the latest events. Twelve men sat around the walnut table on high-backed chairs with green leather inlays. There was a somewhat formal air to the proceedings. The mood, however, became buoyant with the news that the Argentinian cruiser *Belgrano* had been sunk by the nuclear-powered submarine HMS *Conqueror*. The information which led to the decision to sink the ship had been collated by Mannington from several sources; the most useful signal had come from the Chilean naval command in Punta Arenas to the British Military Attaché in Santiago. It gave the location, course and speed of the *Belgrano*, showing it to be moving around the outside of the Total Exclusion Zone to the south of the Falkland Islands. Satellite photography, submarine reports and Nimrod reconnaissance data had already established that there were two Argentinian frigates inside of the zone.

"Well done, Marcus." The Foreign Secretary was clearly relieved. "It was a clever move by the Argies, and may well have come off. Of course, we'll take some flak in the press because we can't tell them about the frigates, but they'll know in fifty years when the Cabinet minutes become public."

Almost everyone laughed.

The meeting continued through coffee until lunchtime approached. 'Any other business' was always at the bottom of the agenda but was usually a short item. Not today.

"Right, gentlemen. Anything else, or can I close for today?"

"Just one matter, Foreign Secretary," Sir Cecil began, opening a dossier before him. "You may wish to deal with this outside of this meeting, but Hamish Dawes, our Head of Vetting, has made a serious discovery during routine surveillance."

Most of the men around the table were already picking their lunch from a mental picture of one of the nearby restaurant menus when they were brought back to the meeting with a jolt.

"As it concerns Mannington, perhaps we need not detain anyone other than Marcus?"

But they all knew now that it concerned Mannington. Sir Cecil would be impossibly discreet about the whole affair, knowing that the damage was done. When the others had left, he and Marcus joined the Foreign Secretary at the head of the table. There was an uncomfortable silence. Marcus was livid. It should have been discussed with him prior to the meeting, but he kept calm just in case it was a serious matter. This, however, was the final straw; it would be open warfare between Mannington and London.

"Have you discussed this with Marcus?" the Foreign Secretary asked.

"Ah, no, I'm afraid not. It literally came to my attention as I left to come here."

Marcus said nothing.

"It concerns Jack Pennington, who is, as you may know, Head of Middle East at Mannington."

Marcus was glad that he had said nothing. He had hoped that one of the security guards had been caught siphoning off petrol.

"He is having an affair."

Not with a Soviet agent, Marcus pleaded in his head. *Not with a male Soviet agent.*

"He is planning to go to Cyprus with her next week under the ruse of visiting Akrotiri."

"Is this an affair of the heart or is the female concerned working for the opposition?" the Foreign Secretary inquired.

"We are still investigating."

"What proof do we have?" Marcus asked.

"He was followed to a rendezvous, and to a travel agent where he picked up her tickets. Since then Hamish's team has been following them."

"So you knew some time ago?" Marcus glared at Sir Cecil.

"Ah … Hamish knew on Friday."

Marcus looked at the Foreign Secretary. The Foreign Secretary looked at Sir Cecil.

"These are photocopies of her tickets, if you would like to see them."

Marcus glanced at the A4-size sheet. "Victoria Moss?" he read. "She works at GCHQ, doesn't she?"

"Ah … yes." Sir Cecil was losing some ground.

"What level?"

"Second-level secretary."

"Not a prime threat to national security, then?" Marcus asked rhetorically.

"Any secret affair opens the parties up to blackmail. You know that." Sir Cecil fought back on reasonably firm ground.

"Have you confronted them yet?" the Foreign Secretary wanted to know.

"No, I wanted to discuss it with Marcus first."

"Then the two of you remain here and sort this matter out." The Foreign Secretary picked up his papers and said goodbye.

"That was shitty."

Sir Cecil didn't answer.

"Jack Pennington is exceptional and I don't want to lose him."

"He'll have to go … won't he?"

Marcus did not answer.

"If it's any consolation, I don't think this is anything more than a silly affair."

"So I can have him back when it's all been sorted out?"

"Possibly."

"In the meantime?"

"I take it that you do not want him suspended and sent home to his wife and kids?"

"No."

"How about if he goes to Geneva to cover OPEC instead of Peter Morgan while we investigate further? But you mustn't speak to him about the affair yet."

Marcus tried to find a catch but it sounded better than the alternative. A week or two listening to oil producers argue about the price of a barrel should keep Jack occupied. "OK. When would he have to go?"

"In the next couple of days."

CHAPTER TWELVE

Marcus was writing on a pad while speaking. "Jack, with the satellite now fully functioning over the Falklands, are we still heavily dependent on the Americans for stuff in the Middle East?"

He continued talking while swivelling the paper towards Jack. In a scrawled hand, he read:

> Keep talking as normal.
> Play along.
> Join me in the car.
> Leave your pager here.
> Do not say anything of consequence until
> we are out in the open.

They stepped out of the lift via Security.

"Tell Control that we are going to the West Sector. We do not need an escort. We are not leaving the site."

Marcus steered his old Jaguar out of the hangar and across the endless sea of tarmac. "They're suggesting that we allow gliders to use the runway. Apparently it would give greater credibility. Whatever next?"

The small talk continued. In the West Sector, Marcus stopped and they got out. A warm breeze teased the barley crop, which nodded coyly.

"Sir Cecil knows that you are having an affair, and he is investigating anything and everything."

"Oh … shit." Jack was taken off guard.

"Not brilliant timing?"

"No … sorry." Jack stood looking across the broad landscape to a chicken farm beyond the fence.

"Is it serious?" Marcus asked, meaning the affair.

"It is now." Jack was thinking of the wider implications for his life.

"Shall you leave Sarah?" It sounded archaic, biblical … moral.

"I don't know."

"Putting it off to the last moment?"

"Probably."

They were stood next to a pair of old Nissen huts inside the fence. Immediately outside were six further huts and several newer chicken sheds. Very close examination would reveal that one of the huts outside of the fence was not given over to the rearing of poultry. Instead, it was the outlet for the air-conditioning and heating system (together with a backup generator) for the six underground floors at Mannington. The farmer who rented the land outside of the fence had signed the Official Secrets Act and knew only about the one shed; he was content with the very low rent. From any Soviet satellite far above, the farming unit read as a logical whole. The heat generated from each shed was typical for a chicken farm, where the birds lived at a constant seventy degrees Fahrenheit and their droppings generated huge quantities of methane and hot air.

"I think that we are being followed and bugged," Marcus whispered, despite standing in the middle of nowhere.

"I'm really sorry."

"Don't worry about it. If it hadn't been you they would have found someone else and, failing that, they would have made it up."

"What can I do?"

"I have no doubt that you can come back eventually. Sir Cecil knows that you are good … but he needs to score points at the moment, so you are off to OPEC in Geneva … tough!" 'Tough' was said in as non-judgemental a way as possible; matter-of-fact.

"What happens to Mannington and Zugdidi?"

"Don't worry about Mannington. We'll survive and thrive. I do think that there is one useful thing that you can do to help."

The tips of the toytown evergreen trees picked up the southerly wind and passed it on to a row of poplars marching away to the right. If Jack's world was in turmoil he concealed it well, focusing on the far distance and ignoring the foreground. Marcus, meanwhile, seemed to be reflecting on his last statement.

"You could contact that chap we've been monitoring in Saudi. It would be interesting to know what is going on. Here's three thousand pounds in cash."

Jack turned to Marcus in disbelief as he was handed an envelope. "What? What for?"

"It's the Christmas party money."

"What … you really …?"

"I have given it a lot of thought, and don't worry. I thought that there is a certain irony in using the Christmas money, don't you think?"

"You are serious, aren't you?"

"I am afraid that Sir Cecil has gone too far this time. You may clock up some incidental expenses." Marcus was following a thought process that made sense to him. "It's the only uncheckable cash I have."

They were speaking in code; 'Christmas' was the low-level GCHQ desk officer who had been caught passing on secrets to the Russians. Together with some other minor indiscretions, it was not a great time for GCHQ. The money had been left in a dead-letter box for 'Christmas' to collect; some of the messages had been written on the actual banknotes and, together with the letters and photographs, had ended up at Mannington for decoding. After 'Christmas' had committed suicide, no one seemed to know what to do with it, and Marcus had kept it under lock and key for a rainy day. The irony came from the Soviet controller of 'Christmas', who happened to be a Georgian long expelled from the UK.

"Jack, if we crack this Zugdidi affair it will be the end of Sir Cecil, and Mannington will eventually get Collection and Control."

"I know that."

"This …" Marcus struggled to find the word, "… 'event' has given us an opportunity. At least now you know that you will be followed, but probably not too rigorously. They think that they have their prize."

"At OPEC, I should be able to sneak out for a few minutes between the snoring."

"Whatever happens, you must put Victoria and your family on the back burner for a few months."

They were partially downwind of the chicken farm, and a strange smell of warm methane reached their nostrils. A pair of crows swept by in a series of stalling loops; they had presumably mistaken the stench for rotting carrion.

"Can I speak to Victoria?"

"Do it once. Do it 'publicly' so that Hamish and his boys overhear, and you should say nothing contentious. Ross and I will help you, but remember we are being monitored as well."

Jack's face finally betrayed some emotion. If he had been worried about Marcus, what was he going to say to Ross?

* * *

In Saudi Arabia it was a religious holiday. Empty was on cloud nine (if that was possible under a desert sky of monotonous blue). A temporary bridge over his deepening trough of loneliness had been provided by the unscheduled trip home the day after tomorrow and a pay rise of five thousand pounds a year; the public holiday was a bonus. To cap it all, he was about to develop a social life. He had been invited to a picnic sixty miles out in the desert; apparently there was a rock outcrop with some prehistoric paintings nearby. Perhaps he had been premature, he thought to himself. Perhaps Saudi Arabia was not such a madhouse.

The invitation had come as a bit of a shock. Empty was counting the contents of three rusty sea-freight containers as they were being unloaded into the secure compound on site: twenty thousand emitters, two hundred solenoid valves, and the long-awaited control panel. He emerged from the mouth of one of the containers, which had been nicknamed 'Tandooris', for a drink. The tepid water failed to quench his thirst and instantly spurted from every pore like he was some crying circus clown, or so it seemed.

"Water. The key to everything, eh?" a voice said.

He turned around to see Basil looking at him from under a panama hat.

"It's kept me employed for a few years," Empty said defensively.

"Everything arrived intact?" Basil inquired.

"Yes. So long as it doesn't say 'Made in Israel' on it, we normally get it through OK."

It was very unusual for Basil to wander around or make light conversation. Theoretically he was the gamekeeper to Empty's poacher. He looked uncomfortable, and not just from the heat. "How are you enjoying Saudi?" he asked.

"Nice beaches but the sea's a long way out." Empty was beginning to wonder what Basil wanted.

"Your wife's not with you, is she?"

"No, she's digging the tunnel from the other end. I should be out of here by Christmas."

"I don't know if it's strictly according to the rules, but as we're Brits together, I wondered whether you would like to come on a picnic-cum-barbecue with Gaynor and the kids … and a few friends?"

What did Basil want? Empty couldn't think of one reason, beyond altruism (and he wasn't sure what that meant, anyway), why Basil would want to socialise with him. However, he would love a day out. He would love to see a woman's face, and to see kids running around.

"I'd love to, thank you." Empty paused. "At least it won't be too difficult to light the bastard out here."

"The what?"

"The barbecue."

* * *

The following day, when his bag of fruit juices and water had been placed in the boot of the Ministry Mercedes, Empty joined the young children on the back seat. Well, he thought that they were children; they could have been adults dressed in children's clothes.

"What's your name?" The boy stuck out his hand. Was that a Masonic greeting?

"Empty."

"Why?"

"Leave Mr Tanner alone, Simon." Gaynor turned around and reprimanded her son in a surprisingly deep voice.

"But he said his name was Empty."

"You'll call him Mr Tanner."

"'Empty' doesn't sound quite right," the nine-year-old persisted.

"Then call me Half Empty?" Empty offered.

Was he back in the madhouse? The children were adults and their mother was a man?

Basil started the car. "We're going in convoy," he said, "just in case we get lost or stuck in the sand. Klaus – do you know Klaus? From the Ministry of Housing? Well, he'll bring up the rear in his big … what is it he drives? I don't know … some Jeep thing. Anyway, it's a four-wheel drive."

"It's just like *Wacky Races*, isn't it?" Empty asked Simon as the six vehicles chased each other out of Riyadh into the desert.

"What's *Wacky Races*?"

Some miles later (a mile doesn't mean much in the desert), the convoy turned off the road, heading along a dusty track towards a ridge.

"That was a quick sixty miles," Empty said.

"No, no. We are going to look at the place where Abdul Aziz Ibn Saud, together with his Bedu army on camels, laid up before attacking Riyadh in 1902."

Until the last minute, there was little to see. Dipping bands of rock had created a large, deep cave, down into which they walked. The air was surprisingly cool and the children's voices echoed off the walls. At the bottom of the incline, an underground stream gave a tantalising glimpse before slipping back into its artesian strata. Empty stared in disbelief at a Volkswagen Beetle that had been rolled down and dumped in the water. This was one of the most important places in the history of Saudi Arabia. If it had been England there would be Beefeaters standing outside and an entrance fee of five pounds. There wasn't even a car park as such; after all, it wasn't treated as an attraction. Saudi Arabia doesn't attract tourists. There was, however, a sea of compressed aluminium drink cans which glinted in the sun. It made a change from tarmac.

"Wacky car park?" Empty asked Simon.

"What does 'wacky' mean?"

An hour of cruise control along an arrow-straight road with the family from hell drove Empty to desperate measures. "I spy with my little eye …" they had quickly exhausted 'desert', 'sky' and 'road', "… something beginning with 'M'." Empty swivelled his eyes so as not to give any clue.

The children were pensive, then restive, then aggressive.

"Mercedes!" Simon was ecstatic.

"No."

"Mummy!" one of Simon's friends offered.

"She's my mummy, not yours!" Simon was now moving from aggressive through possessive to depressive.

"I think that you had better tell them, Mr Tanner," Simon's mother suggested.

"Mirage!"

A little light relief was provided by a sentry box which appeared out of the shimmering haze. In it were some Bedouin in military uniform carrying rifles, and behind was a dark brown tent surrounded by barbed wire.

"Don't worry, Mark, it's there to catch Yemenis on their way to Riyadh without visas. They won't stop us … especially with the Ministry logo on the side of the car." Basil was at his most reassuring.

Everyone waved at the bemused Bedouin.

The final destination fifteen minutes later was even less impressive archaeologically or touristically than the first stop, if that was possible. The lowest of a string of stony hills revealed a few scratched animals on some of the larger rocks near the summit. The graphics reminded Empty of the children's game Hangman, so he suggested it for the way back.

"Apparently, this one here is a reindeer, which proves that the desert was obviously green when these wallahs painted them," some half-wit from another of the cars informed everyone.

"Or Father Christmas was on his way to Riyadh?" Empty suggested to Simon.

"We don't have a chimney in our villa," Simon began, and Empty immediately foresaw where this might lead: tears.

"That's not a reindeer … that's where his chisel slipped." Empty grinned.

"Food's ready!" came the cry from below, and everyone bounced down the slope in imitation of astronauts on the moon.

While scraps enough to feed the five thousand were being shovelled into rubbish bags, Basil wandered over to Empty, who was watching pipits through his binoculars.

"Mark, can I ask you something?"

"So, there's no such thing as a free lunch?"

"Quite. It's just that I'm a bit troubled."

"Don't worry, Basil. We may not be doing everything exactly to the drawings but it will all work out in the end."

"No, it's not that. It's more serious, I think."

"At Nefud?"

"Well … sort of. I wanted a chance to discuss it with you."

"Empty! *Kommst du mit?*" Klaus was calling. "Do you want to come in the Jeep with me?"

"Sure! One minute!" Empty replied, and turned back to Basil. "Can we continue talking in the morning? Only, I fly back later tomorrow."

"Yes, I rather think we should."

The convoy regrouped on the sand, with the Ministry of Housing Jeep bringing up the rear. However, there was no difficulty regaining the tarmac road and the five cars pulled away from Klaus, waving goodbye.

"That was pretty boring." Klaus rolled one word into the next in an American drawl.

"Not as boring as the journey here."

"Wanna drink?" Klaus pulled out a bottle from the door pocket. So it was alcohol, not an American education, that had given him his drawl.

No, Empty thought to himself, *the journey back will not be so boring*. He was back in the madhouse, sat with a drunk German whom he did not know in a land where alcohol was banned. How had this happened to him?

A few minutes later they were approaching the sentry box at about thirty miles an hour when two Bedouin walked into the road.

"Oh, shit! Let me do the talking, Klaus!"

The soldiers flicked back their headdresses, and another appeared out of the sentry box.

"I had better get out or they will smell the drink."

"OK, no problem."

"Passport?" the first soldier asked as Empty stepped down onto the melting black road surface.

He didn't have his passport. What should he say? "It … is … in … Riyadh."

No response.

"Ri … ya …dh."

"I will get it for you," Klaus shouted through the window, revving the engine and driving off into the distance.

The Bedouin did not seem to understand or care. Empty was standing slack-jawed, overtaken by the speed of events. He watched the Jeep become a dot and disappear over the horizon.

After five minutes, Empty was on his hands and knees, drawing in the sand. This cunning ploy was a last resort to stop his incarceration in the dreaded brown tent. How had Kamal taught him to write 'Riyadh' in Arabic?

"Riyadh," one of the soldiers mouthed.

"Riyadh." Empty stood up.

"Riyadh." Another pointed along the road.

"*Aiwa*, Riyadh," Empty confirmed. Now he was getting somewhere.

Then they started poking him with their rifles. "Riyadh," they mocked in chorus, pushing him along the road.

"Riyadh," Empty said, a little less enthusiastically.

They flicked their hands to encourage him to start walking. Empty started walking. He took stock. The good news was that he was not in a tent full of Yemeni illegal immigrants sixty miles from Riyadh. The bad news was that he was alone on a road sixty miles from Riyadh.

What had Klaus done? Buggered off? Thanked his lucky stars? He couldn't get Empty's passport even if he wanted to. He wouldn't come back drunk, would he? Oh dear. Empty could feel a nasty attack of the wallpapers coming on, and just when he had thought that he had it all cracked. He kept walking. There was no traffic. If he walked all night, how far would he get? Would anyone pick him up? Did he want to be picked up? What would he do in the heat of tomorrow? Tomorrow! He was flying in the afternoon.

It was at that moment that the explosion occurred. The desert air cracked and the hills echoed. A pall of black smoke mushroomed over the horizon ahead of him. *Not another two oil tankers with kamikaze drivers*, he thought to himself. Twenty-five minutes later he reached the first ridge to find that Klaus was flat on the ground watching the security post through Empty's binoculars.

"*Schnell!* Quick!"

They roared off in the direction of the explosion and Riyadh. There was little left of the burning Mercedes by the time they arrived on the scene. A few paper napkins blew around the feet of the sobbing picnic party. One branch of the Earls of Mallow and Blackwater had just been wiped out.

I spy … Empty thought to himself.

* * *

Jack followed Ross into the car park of The Merry Ploughman's Rest lodge and diner. Not so long ago it had been The Wagon & Horses, or was it The Drayman's Arms? With all equine associations lost (except on Gold Cup Day), it now sat incongruously off a roundabout on the edge of Cheltenham, orientated to the ring road rather than the Roman route to Cirencester. Inside it was reminiscent of Noah's ark, with two of everything: two businessmen chatting; two locals drinking pints; two women tearing pages out of a magazine; two bricklayers eating voraciously in silence; and, now, two members of the Intelligence Services. They chose without difficulty a noisy corner where the background music competed with the electronic toccatas, adagios and fugues of the games machine.

In the car on the way down, they had talked only of the Falklands and the need for a dual carriageway from the M4 to the M5.

"That would get rid of the rat run down Birdlip Hill," Ross had commented.

Jack had said nothing. It was the closest they came to talking about Victoria. The lull before the storm?

In a form of diversion therapy, Jack began to fold up his empty crisp packet and place it under the heavy ashtray.

"I've left a set of that chap Basil's plans in your drawer. You may need them when you talk to this 'new' man," Ross began.

Jack looked for an indication of Ross's feelings but he was speaking matter-of-factly.

"I've pulled together a file on our 'new' man, including contact information," Ross continued. "I hope you know what you are doing, Jack?" At last, a measure of censure – or was it concern?

"I don't have a lot of choice." Jack knew as he said it that he was laying himself wide open, but the lecture never came.

"He's coming back tomorrow to London for a visa before you fly to Geneva on Saturday."

"Oh, that's handy. How do you think I should meet him?"

"His visa's being handled by an agency, so that's out. You'll have to see him at his house."

"Oh, good! I'll be popular if he is only back for a few days." Jack stood up and walked to the bar to replenish their glasses, and prepared for Round Two. "I'm sorry if I've caused you and Margaret any embarrassment," he began on his return.

"No …"

"I'm in a bit of a mess at the moment and I had thought I would use my time away to sort my head out."

"Well …"

"I meant my trip to Cyprus, not Geneva, although that will do equally well." Jack was on a roll. "Sarah couldn't tell Cyprus from Geneva anyway." Although what this had to do with anything never materialised.

Ross kept quiet.

"If I say that I can conceive of life without Sarah but not without Mannington, you will probably be shocked."

"No."

"Really?" Jack was diverted from his flow of consciousness.

"And nor will Sarah."

It was Jack's turn to be quiet.

"She's known for some time. So has Margaret … so have I."

The earlier chat with Marcus had not been what Jack had expected, and neither was this.

"I probably put more effort into hiding it from Mannington than from my family. You may find that hard to understand."

Ross, of all people, did not.

* * *

Sir Cecil was in fine fettle; he must have been, for he was practically running up the stairs.

"Come into my office. Tell me all about it."

Black Sea Bob, as he was known, had never been so feted. He was the son of an Uzbekistani doctor who had fallen for a nurse while on a secondment to Leeds and, consequently, had grown up partly in England; they had all relocated to Tashkent after a few years. He provided a special service to the Soviet republics in the Caucasus by travelling to the West and 'stealing' their medical technology. Sometimes he physically sent the equipment back East and sometimes he made drawings for his paymasters to produce copies. It placed him in a unique position whereby he could fly freely to the West and move easily around places like Georgia, Chechnya and Armenia. His successes had brought him respect and special privileges such as a dacha near Sochi. All was not quite as it seemed, however. He was a British spy. The medical equipment was given to him. He travelled around the Caucasus in an ideal position to monitor troop build-ups and new missile sites, and to detail the complex political interrelationships. In London he was also respected and given special privileges. Rarely was anything that he did urgent, and, certainly, he had never met the Chief before.

"I'd offer you a vodka but I expect that you are sick of the stuff."

"Tea will do fine, thank you." Black Sea Bob was used to making small talk; he was a salesman. A big man with black hair and dark features, whose face was punctuated by a blue mark near his right eye where he had been stabbed by a pencil in his youth. His black suit was just a bit too shiny and his yellow tie a little too bright.

"Sugar?"

"No, fine, thank you."

Despite what he had said, they were not in Sir Cecil's office or his usual office building, and Robin sat on the other side of a soundproofed divide listening to everything being said. There was a limit to how much you trusted an agent such as Black Sea Bob. Knowing Sir Cecil's name would not be a startling revelation in Moscow; giving Bob access to Cecil's real office might be asking for problems.

"So what did you discover?"

"I could have sent the information to you." Bob was worried that he had done something wrong.

"No. No need. I wanted to hear from you directly." Sir Cecil definitely did not want a record of this conversation.

"The *Ikiz* is full of carpets and …" Bob took a shopping list from his pocket, "carved oak beams, brass balustrading, ship's chandlery …"

When he had finished itemising the cargo, Sir Cecil asked, "And you checked?"

"Yes, absolutely. There was no problem. I have shipped many items through the port myself. Plenty of acquaintances confirmed this information."

"And no big, unexplained boxes or … whatever?"

"I cannot say of small items, of course, but nothing big."

"Good. Very good … where is it going?"

"Istanbul and on to here … I do not know how to pronounce it." A name was written at the bottom of Bob's cargo list.

"Where is it?"

"On the Red Sea Coast of Saudi Arabia."

Ten minutes later, Sir Cecil and Robin were alone in the room.

"It must be Christmas," Cecil remarked. "First Jack Pennington, and now the *Ikiz* is full of harmless junk."

"What next?"

"Nothing. That's why I wanted to see him personally. I don't want Mannington to monitor any communications."

"You're not going to tell them?"

"Good heavens, no. Mannington's already caught on the hook, but we might as well let them swim into the landing net."

CHAPTER THIRTEEN

"But I wasn't being blackmailed." Jack's voice was calm and soft to emphasise the point. "She's not a security risk. I'm not a security risk. Together we are not a security risk."

The drab 1960s single-storey brick building added nothing to the proceedings. Overpainted window frames and grey plastic floor tiles turned the interview room into an interrogation room. He was at GCHQ for a 'debrief', 'reprimand', 'it's for your own good', 'are you sure it won't happen again?' session. Mannington was restricted for space, with only minimal and essential administration. GCHQ provided a spreading campus above and below ground, offering such luxuries as 'interview rooms' and 'counsellors'.

"But you *could* have been blackmailed." His counsellor sat across the table, flicking the top of his fountain pen like one would a cigarette lighter. "If you had told your wife, told us, left the family and joined … Victoria, we would not be having this chat now."

Jack adopted his 'politely unconcerned vicar' look.

"It's a serious matter." His tormentor was getting nowhere, slowly. "*Are* you going to tell your wife?" He was trying below the belt.

"Sir Cecil has kindly given me three weeks covering OPEC in which to decide."

"What does … Victoria think about this?" The counsellor was torn between calling her 'Victoria' and calling her 'Miss Moss'.

"I haven't spoken to her yet. I was hoping to see her after this … with your permission." Jack adopted his 'politely concerned vicar' look.

"Well, I—"

"That's very kind of you." Jack helped him decide. The rubbing of the pen top was reaching frenetic levels, such that spontaneous combustion could not be ruled out.

Jack was allowed ten minutes with Victoria, after she was given her version of the counselling session, at which it was suggested that she use the three weeks while Jack was away to consider the delicacy of the situation.

"So?" Victoria opened when left alone with the seated Jack.

"I'm terribly sorry. What can I do?" He turned his palms heavenwards in entreaty. The words 'bugged' and 'make small talk' were written on one palm; 'nurse – the screens' and 'ASAP' on the other. The amateur dramatics that followed would not have discredited a daytime soap opera on ITV.

Forty minutes later, Victoria, suitably chastised, walked through the campus to the medical centre block. Next to the toilets was a row of rooms down a side corridor available for medical examinations; these were really only used by visiting doctors or during the mass inoculations which happened infrequently. The display outside Room 3 was illuminated to warn that a medical examination was in progress; it came on automatically when the door was locked. There was no sign of activity in the short corridor, so she knocked and waited.

The light went off, the door opened and she stepped inside. They fell into each other's arms as they had done in this room a dozen or so times before when they had worked together.

"They're going to be watching us when I get back," Jack said.

"What are you going to do?"

"I'll tell Sarah when I get back, I promise." But whether this was certain to happen or just procrastination was hard to tell.

"I can't wait."

"I'm sorry about Cyprus. You enjoy the holiday. At least this has brought it all to a head."

"Oh, Jack, I cannot wait."

"Just count off the days and I'll see you when I get back."

* * *

In the South Atlantic, the commanders were getting very nervous about the vulnerability to air attack of the big ships. Without any AWACS, the American airborne early warning and control system planes, or enough of their own Nimrods, London was receiving inadequate early warning of missile launches. In an attempt to protect the aircraft carrier *Hermes*, a group of frigates and destroyers was deployed around her. The *Sheffield* was one of the Type 42 destroyers in this protective shield. Unbelievably, her radar was switched off while she used the newly positioned satellite to transmit directly to C-in-C Fleet Northwood. The Exocet fired from a Super Étendard aircraft went undetected and the destroyer was turned into a blazing inferno of melting and exploding aluminium.

This one event quelled in the British public any notion that this war was going to be a simple, painless operation. People started to ask questions; so did the Foreign Secretary.

"Why didn't the satellite warn us of the Exocets?" he asked Sir Cecil over a secure telephone line.

"Wrong sort of satellite, sir. This one is for photography and communication."

"So far, the only benefit from this satellite has been that I get to see instant photographs of a burning ship instead of having to wait to hear about it thirty seconds later via Ascension."

Sir Cecil did not correct the Foreign Secretary, who was patently not having a good day.

"And another thing – if aluminium burns, why are we building bloody ships out of the stuff? Not learnt much since the *Mary* bloody *Rose*, have we? I'm going to have a closer look when this is all over." He was talking to himself; it was nothing to do with Sir Cecil. "What's the quickest way to find out, Cecil?"

I've always found buying a first-class rail ticket from Chippenham to Paddington works. Sit at a table next to any three men who are wearing ties with a seahorse motif. They will have boarded at Bath, where they work for the Admiralty. Pay no obvious attention to them, and before the 125 pulls out of Reading, you'll know all there is to know about laser-guided rockets and beam-to-weight ratios, is what went through Sir Cecil's mind. He actually decided on, "It's not really my area."

There was silence at the end of the line.

"I should speak to Bath rather than London, or you'll get the sanitised version. Or you could just ask the Defence Secretary?"

The Foreign Secretary put down the phone and made a

mental note that, come the revolution, Sir Cecil would be first against the wall. He loathed the man.

* * *

If the *Sheffield* had showed that technology can work for and against you, it was also being demonstrated at that moment in Saudi Arabia. Two men were about to make a telephone call. Sheikh Abdullatif Al-Rahman was behind a mahogany desk with inlaid gold; large enough for the entire United Nations to sit around its perimeter. The desk was in an office with a larger floor space than some United Nations member countries. There was no desktop clutter: no filing trays; no blotter pads; no Newton's cradle. There was just one item in pride of place: his father's dagger in its dull beaten-silver sheath was set in a block of gold. Abdullatif never wanted to forget where he came from. On a low hexagonal table to his right sat a telephone console; it was state-of-the-art, with conferencing facilities and a hands-free unit that allowed him to sit in his plush chair and control his empire under the watchful gaze of the three framed photographs of Ibn Saud, the King and the Crown Prince.

He had just dialled a very good friend of his in Riyadh. The telephone rang in the office of Sheikh Faisal Al-Shaqra. He, too, had this state-of-the-art system. He, too, was sat in a large chair, master of all he surveyed.

At the forefront of technology it may be, but the telephone system was not designed for two big egos and the background noise from buzzing air-conditioning vents. Each telephone was programmed to override the other on picking up sounds on its own microphone. The result was chaos. Never was a microchip so tested. Chopped into staccato clips, the conversation became meaningless. When they eventually gave up trying to talk, a new battle ensued as the noise from the air-conditioning units at either end caused the system to swap back and forth. The two men were worth a billion dollars between them but were unable to conduct a simple telephone conversation with each other. During a particularly bad break-up, neither heard the other say that he would pick up the handset because there was something wrong with the other one's phone.

"Hello, Abdullatif, that's better."

"Hello, Faisal, that's much better."

"Is this new telephone company one of mine or one of yours?"

It was a standing joke. They owned so many franchises between them that they lost track.

"Whoever it is should sell it."

Almost immediately they forgot who had telephoned whom, asked after each other's families and discussed each other's current medical problems. Only then did Abdullatif update his friend on their latest joint business venture.

"Are the villas at Khaburah ready to receive everything?"

"Very, very soon. The desalination plant is moored offshore and the jetty is built. The villas are a few weeks from completion, Insha'Allah."

"The *Ikiz* is entering the Mediterranean tomorrow. She is fully loaded with all that we ordered."

"By the time she reaches Khaburah, we will be waiting, Insha'Allah."

"How is Nefud-al-aan?" Abdullatif changed the subject.

"Insha'Allah, we are on schedule," Faisal replied.

Although it appeared that British and French companies were building the military city with an American company reviewing their work, the underlying reality was different.

Faisal was sponsor to all of the construction companies and Abdullatif was sponsor to all of the reviewers.

"Sadly, an English reviewer of mine was killed in a car accident yesterday. We will look for a replacement. I hope that there has been no inconvenience?"

"None," Faisal replied.

They reminisced about a recent hunting trip with some new saker falcons, wished each other a thousand years of happiness, and thanked Allah for their good fortune.

* * *

Empty was on automatic pilot; it was the only way he was going to cope. Outwardly he still grinned inanely and joked at every opportunity. Inside his head the events of yesterday went round and round, and he needed to concentrate on his impending trip home tomorrow in order to break the swirling thoughts. He wasn't mad. It was Saudi Arabia that was mad. Or did you have to be mad to be there? Gas bottles don't just blow up. Mercedes don't just incinerate in seconds. Why Basil? Why Basil's kids?

He felt guilty. The assembled expats at the scene of the explosion had decided quickly who needed to disappear and who was squeaky clean and could stay and talk to the police. Klaus was top of the list of those who needed to leave immediately, and had driven back to Riyadh so carefully, apologising to Empty every few minutes.

Empty felt relieved. *His* family had survived *his* fire. He had not been shut up with all of those Yemenis. He had not been caught with a drunken German. He had not been caught without a photocopy of his passport or the open letter from Sheikh Faisal.

He snapped out of it yet again. How would he get on the plane to come back out here in a few days' time after seeing Dawn and the kids?

That evening, Empty picked up his passport from Sheikh Faisal's rooms, where it had been placed on a coffee table with a short note. He looked around the acres of white walls. If ever a place needed wallpaper, it was here.

Empty needed some light relief, so he kept the appointment for his third calligraphy lesson at the flat of Kamal; officially his Syrian secretary at the head office in Riyadh. The arrangement was a perfect trade: Empty learnt how to read and write phonetically, and in return Kamal had his 'woulds' and 'shoulds' corrected and began picking up idiomatic English.

"How many?!" Empty screamed across the kitchen table. "Over a hundred? We've only got twenty-six letters in our alphabet."

"No, you have fifty-two. You have capitals also."

Kamal was sat in his chair, twisting his tight, curly black hair. He pushed back with his feet and began brushing biscuit crumbs off his blue shirt. To begin with, Empty had thought that his young secretary only had one shirt, but it transpired that his mother had bought him five, all the same colour, before he had left Damascus. Empty and Kamal had hit it off from the second they had met; they shared a silly sense of humour, were both gentle souls, and had decided to make the most of their time in Saudi.

"Yes, OK. But reading and writing backwards is a bit much."

"No, *you* read and write backwards." The fluorescent tube above Kamal's head made his shirt luminescent.

"Touché."

"What is 'touché'?"

"It's a French word." Empty wrote it down. "It means that you have made a good point."

"And what is this over the letter 'E'?"

"It's an acute accent."

"I have not known that European languages have accents."

"You mean you *didn't know* that European languages have accents."

"Touché."

"English doesn't."

"We have many in Arabic."

"Not hundreds?"

* * *

RSA Typing and Shorthand at the local technical college had not prepared Victoria for the world of the Secret Services. This fact did not prove to be a problem for her as she was clearly naturally gifted at out-thinking the system. She was certain that her cottage, car, office, telephones and mail were being monitored, so when she decided to go to Cirencester, she devised a circuitous route. After driving to Cheltenham she parked in Royal Parade and proceeded to zigzag through the town on foot; she went in the front door of Cavendish House, visited all of the floors in the department store and went out the back door. She eventually ended up at the bus station just in time to sneak onto the 11.15 to Cirencester. Slumped in the back seat, she checked every car that followed the bus for more than a few minutes.

In Cirencester she had lunch in a small café tucked down an alley before criss-crossing Market Place and sneaking past the imposing parish church into Dollar Street. There was absolutely no one in view. Victoria stepped into a tiny, old-fashioned shop, announced by the tinkling of a bell. There were no other customers.

An old man dressed in a tweed suit, waistcoat and wool tie that managed to contain the full colour spectrum of the autumnal forest floor from moss green to russet brown looked up above his glasses. "Good morning, or, should I say, afternoon." The red veins on his cheeks indicated that he had either walked to Cirencester from Tetbury for a couple of hours that morning, or had just spent a couple of hours drinking brandy in a local hostelry.

It was not the most inviting of travel agents Victoria could imagine. The brochures were unhelpfully piled in heaps on shelves and the very few posters on the walls promoted the British Overseas Airways Corporation, the precursor to British Airways which hadn't flown for years. The posters had at various stages been current, out of date, trendy and, now, tired and faded.

"Where did you have in mind?" the old man asked.

"Geneva."

"Skiing? Business? Or sanatorium?"

"To see a friend. I just need a flight and a hotel."

"When would you like to go?"

"The day after tomorrow."

"I'm sure that's no problem. Heathrow or Gatwick?"

"Nicosia."

He tried to focus on a poster bleached by the sun, but failed. "Nicosia?"

"I'm flying to Cyprus tomorrow and I want to fly as soon as possible on – or is that back? – to Geneva and then home."

He thumbed through a flight timetable book of impossibly

large dimensions. How big would a book have to be before it collapsed like an accordion on maximum air intake? He read out a choice of three services. Victoria chose an Air Mediterranean flight which meant that she need not leave Nicosia airport and waste money on a hotel.

"How would you like to pay?" He looked up from the book but this action seemed to disorientate him. Staring out of the window at the buildings opposite helped him to reset his focus. Eventually he came back to Victoria's face, gradually feeling his way along the walls with his eyes. A pilot with a drink problem now running a travel agents, Victoria concluded.

"Cash."

"And where would you like to pick the tickets up from?"

"At the Air Mediterranean desk at Nicosia airport. Could you telex them and request that?"

"Of course."

She gave her name but used her mother's address. Twenty minutes later she was on the bus back to Cheltenham.

CHAPTER FOURTEEN

"This is James Melrose from the Foreign Office." The Undersecretary of State for Trade introduced Jack Pennington to the other four men present using a pseudonym. "While Adrian here is our official interpreter, James will play dumb and act as our unofficial eyes and ears. It's an old trick but it always turns something up. I understand, James, that you had a quick introduction to the world of petroleum yesterday from Tony. So long as you've read *The Ladybird Book of Oil*, you're more than prepared."

"It's all becoming clearer," Jack said.

"That's oil processing for you." The Undersecretary seemed in flippant mood. "We're here today to agree our objectives and the timetable for attendance in Geneva and, afterwards, in Riyadh. Sorry about the circular trip but we need to attend both and the Saudis hold all of the cards." The Undersecretary sat bursting out of his shiny suit; the product of too many lunches and trips around the world. "Any questions, James?

Only the rest of the team here went last year and are pretty au fait."

"What is my official title?"

"Chairman, Consultative Committee on Energy," one of the senior civil servants chipped in.

"How long are we in Geneva?"

"You'll be there about three weeks. I want you to be an observer at a lot of fringe sessions which happen afterwards. We will all convene in Riyadh on the 29th May for the follow-up conference. Here are the hotel details for your loved ones."

Jack picked up the sheet and thought about his loved ones.

"And here are the flight details. We fly out Friday, late afternoon, from Heathrow."

This gave Jack only Friday morning to see Mark Tanner, who was flying in at that moment.

After his meeting, Jack wandered around London, killing time before catching his train from Paddington. The swirling wind buffeted him, sweeping dust and fumes into his eyes. He found himself reading the humorous cards on display in a gift shop window, and stepped inside as much to avoid the gale as to actually buy anything. Scanning the cards brought back memories of all of the key events in his life from birthdays to getting married. He had already made up his mind what he was going to do. The next three weeks or so away from everyone gave him a stay of execution; it wouldn't change anything.

He picked out a 'MISSING YOU' card from the wire carousel. This was not the act of an old romantic at heart. He was deep in thought about the impossibility of sending it to Victoria. Not being able to post it to her cottage or workplace. Not even being able to send it to her via her mother. Until his return, communication with Victoria was going to be impossible. The thought of her sunbathing on a Cypriot beach for two weeks stirred up a cocktail of emotions. He closed the card, noticing that it was particularly expensive. On the back it offered the opportunity for the purchaser to ring a telephone number and, included in the price of the card, record a personal message. There was a unique code number on each card. The recipient could telephone, quote the code number and hear the recorded message, which would remain accessible for one month, after which it would be erased. Jack's mind was racing. He bought some cards without registering the total cost or checking his change. Outside, the wind was so strong that it tried to blow his coat between his legs as he headed along the pavement towards Paddington.

While waiting for his connection at Bristol Temple Meads station, he dialled the number on the back of one of the cards from a call box. When prompted, he began reciting *The Rime of the Ancient Mariner*. Forty minutes later, he was on Cheltenham station, where he found a call box and telephoned again, giving his personal code number and listening. Trying to ignore the idiosyncrasies of his accent being played back to him in his dull monotone, he counted the seconds on his watch. He reached thirty just as '*The Mariner hath his will.*' The message had a maximum length of thirty seconds. Perfect.

He took a taxi home.

* * *

Marcus was leaning over Ross's shoulder to watch the satellite sequence playing on the larger of his monitor screens. The Sea of Marmara to the south of Istanbul filled the screen with a murky greyness. Ross rolled the mouse along the rubber mat to select 'zoom in', and in a couple of computer blinks they were staring at a small ship ploughing westward towards the Dardanelles.

"The good ship *Ikiz*," Ross explained.

"At last she is within satellite coverage." Marcus stepped around the chair in front of him to peer more closely.

"Good." Ross did not sound overenthusiastic.

"Well, what did you expect? Crates lashed to the deck marked 'RADIOACTIVE'?"

"No, I was thinking how harmless she looks."

"We'll track her now through the Aegean, across the Mediterranean, through the Suez Canal and down the Red Sea to … where is it? Khaburah."

"Here's the actual transcript." Ross put the conversation between Sheikh Faisal and Sheikh Abdullatif on one of his smaller screens.

"A desalination ship moored offshore is a bit over the top for two villas, isn't it?" Marcus asked. "And what about the jetty? How big is it?"

"I can show you, hold on."

Marcus went on reading the text while Ross brought still aerial photographs of Khaburah onto the central screens.

"The *Ikiz* is a day late entering the Mediterranean. Did she stop in Istanbul?" Marcus went on musing as he read each word of the translation. "… all that *we* ordered … why *we*?"

"There's the jetty. It's not big. He probably has a motor yacht in Puerto Banús bigger than most people's houses."

Marcus was still transfixed by the text on the screen to his left. "Basil Wynne's death … why did he ask if it had been inconvenient?"

"This must make Nefud-al-aan the most likely site, surely?" Ross was busy typing in more commands.

"When's Jack seeing our new friend?" Marcus leant forward and spoke more quietly.

"Friday lunchtime, I should think, before Jack flies to Geneva."

"This chap must know this site backwards. He should be able to give us some pointers."

They talked around the subject, discovering little new but reconfirming each other's views that this was becoming a very serious matter. After a while they returned to Basil Wynne.

"I know that we are trained to look for coincidence, but it's frankly amazing that Sir Cecil's lot ask this chap Basil a couple of questions and a few days later his car blows up," Marcus said.

"I think that Jack had better be extra careful with this new man," Ross remarked.

"Is Jack contactable?"

"Only over the telephone. Do you think that I should pop round tonight to update him?"

"Yes, but do it out of earshot."

In the word 'earshot', Marcus could never convey the size and sophistication of the 'ear' that concerned them.

* * *

Other sections of Mannington had been working overtime to establish the exact number of Exocet missiles held by the Argentinians. The current estimate was five. They had already used three firing at the *Sheffield* and the *Yarmouth*. Five struck most people as a ridiculously low number, and no one would stake their life on this total despite there being no information to the contrary. Off the Falklands, the bad weather was causing its own problems and two Harriers disappeared into low cloud and crashed, leaving the task force with twenty-two split between the two carriers. Several of these were being repainted hastily, having been seconded – or, rather, commandeered – directly from the British Aerospace factory, where they had been decked out in the colours of the Indian Air Force.

If Mannington was under pressure, so was Sir Cecil, who had to answer three questions on an almost hourly basis: *How many Argentinians are there on the Falklands? Where do they think we are going to land? When do they think we are going to land?*

Despite diplomatic efforts to avert a ground war, the general consensus was that the landing would take place in a fortnight's time.

* * *

In High Wycombe, the Tanner family was at fever pitch. One child remained on lookout at all times, while Dawn found pointless jobs for everyone else to undertake so that another few minutes passed by. She was as bad as the children. It may have only been a few weeks since Mark left for Saudi but, after the trauma of the recent past, it felt like a year. She knew in her heart that they wouldn't last a month living in a small flat with Mark there permanently. A couple of days would be fine, although he was guaranteed to go back to Saudi Arabia with a pair of bruises on his hips from bumping into the central table. It was a good job no one checked the children or they would think that they were being beaten up.

Every car driven down the road caused much screaming, jumping, and several more bruises.

"He'll be another half an hour yet!" Dawn tried to calm them down, without success.

"I can't wait half an hour!"

Their prayers were answered almost immediately when the doorbell rang.

"Daddy! Daddy!"

The door opened and the children rushed out, grabbing Empty around each hip. It was a good job he had no bruises.

"We didn't see any car arrive."

"I flew from Heathrow on this." He had a huge inflatable Boeing 747 under his arm.

"You look red," Dawn said, rather unromantically.

"So would you if you'd just walked from the bus station, pulling a suitcase and trying to blow this up."

Inside the flat they played 'chase me around the table'. This was not a game. It was the only method of reaching either the lounge, the bathroom or the two small bedrooms. The children wanted to launch the inflatable plane off the balcony; no training, no flight simulation, just a maiden flight. Empty stared down the six storeys and sympathised with the idea. He carried his suitcase into the bedroom while the children turned the kitchen table into a runway. The increasing violence of the landings would have had the designers at Boeing reaching for their professional indemnity insurance policies.

"Is that a new jumper?" Empty asked Dawn inside the bedroom.

"No, I'm knitting them to order. It makes a few quid."

"Are those marks on the wall where you have been trying to swing a cat?" he asked awkwardly.

"No, you silly sod. They're from Christmas cracker boxes."

Empty looked nonplussed. His arms hung down by his

sides, from carrying the suitcase and because he didn't know what to do with them; he was lost in his home; his own temporary home.

"Before the jumpers, I applied to make Christmas crackers. They give you all of the bits and you roll and fill them." Dawn waved her arms. "Unfortunately, the cardboard boxes filled the flat and I had to sleep with the kids for a week."

They laughed, hugged, and he knew that he couldn't stay in Saudi Arabia for another month, let alone a year.

"You do look red," she observed.

"We've been through that. It's probably sunburn."

"Is it awful?"

"Not if you put cream on it." He smiled. "Do you mean Saudi Arabia, the job or life in general?"

"Any of it."

He pulled out his wallet with a flourish. "This is what keeps me going."

The large cheque bore no resemblance to anything Dawn had seen before. It was closer to the scribble pad at the Parker pen counter in WHSmith. "Are those signatures?"

"I hope so."

She looked at the amount and her eyes opened wide. "Gosh. We are going to get there," she said, putting on a brave face.

"No problem," he replied, putting on a brave, sunburnt face.

"Perhaps we are beginning a wonderful new phase of our lives … with no problems?"

"Dad!"

Empty and Dawn emerged from the bedroom to see a Boeing 747 steamrollered flat on the kitchen table.

"Depressurisation problem, I think." Empty picked it up and began blowing it up again.

"You're very red, Dad."

"It's a long story," he said between puffs. "There. Problem solved." He winked at Dawn.

"No problem."

The telephone rang. It was a James Melrose from the Foreign Office.

* * *

There was only one word to describe Geneva – 'grey'. Victoria was not impressed. She was meant to be sunning herself on a beach in Cyprus. She had expected Geneva to be crisp and clean and … Swiss. Of course, it might be if she could only see through the mist … although there seemed to be a surfeit of grey concrete everywhere. Not to worry; she would be together with Jack soon for a whole fortnight.

If it was hard to tell where Geneva stopped and the mist started, so it was hard to tell where Victoria's hopes stopped and reality began. She would see him for lunch if he had evening sessions, or in the morning if he had to work all through the night; either way, every day and most nights.

She had read enough issues of *Woman's Journal* to know that men did not leave their wives and children for their lovers voluntarily. If allowed, they would have a whole chain of cake shops and eat them at the same time, or whatever the expression was. Men at Jack's stage of life never jumped; they always needed to be pushed. With such an array of proven excuses, such as kids, illness and finances, it was ultimatum time. She did not want to hit him in the pockets, just very close to them.

Ironically, it was the debriefing at GCHQ that had truly galvanised her into determined action. She was loyal, hard-working and good at her job. She put up with enough restrictions on her life from working at GCHQ that she was not prepared to be told not to see Jack. National security was hardly being placed in jeopardy. He wasn't just any lover; he was Head of Middle East at Mannington, after all.

She was not going to let GCHQ or Geneva on a grey day get to her. However, after a bitter cup of tea in her hotel room she did begin to ponder the mechanics of actually contacting Jack.

CHAPTER FIFTEEN

Jack Pennington was sat in the reception of the Golden Hind Hotel near Heathrow. It was Friday morning and his flight to Geneva left that evening. He was also awaiting the arrival of Mark Tanner, who had agreed to meet him under the flimsiest of pretexts.

The hotel was an anachronism tucked awkwardly between runways, dual carriageways and chain-link fences; cars and planes criss-crossed on merging tarmac. It had two types of client: African businessmen meeting customers by day, and African businessmen meeting escort girls by night. There was a darkness and a dinginess about it, caused in equal measure by the overgrown garden and by a complete lack of building maintenance. It had seen better days. If you scraped off the yellowing paint you would reveal a yellowing patterned wallpaper of the '60s.

When Jack telephoned to book a meeting room, he had been offered a bedroom at a discounted day rate as long as he was out by 4.30pm. Thinking that this would give the wrong impression to Mark Tanner, he reserved the Drake Room for twenty pounds including tea, coffee and flipchart. On arrival, he was horrified to find that the Drake Room was of sufficient importance in the hotel to warrant prime position on the black pinboard welcoming guests. Showing great innovation and delicacy, the white letters forming the word 'ROOM' had been removed, doubtless to provide the backbone of the word 'MELROSE', which sat proudly beneath the word 'DRAKE'.

The telephone conversation with Mark Tanner had been odd. By way of recognition, he had offered to wear a dandelion in his lapel, and to dye his *Daily Mail* pink as he was not prepared to buy the *Financial Times*. Jack had not needed to invent much of a story because Mark wittered on and on, inventing his own windmills at which to tilt; mention of the words 'passport', 'visa' and 'Foreign Office' appeared to be enough.

A DC-10 on reverse thrust tested the double glazing to its limits. Jack shifted on his seat, realising that in telephoning Mark, he had crossed a significant line. So many of the important developments in his life had happened quietly, almost without notice and often through subtle external forces. He had gone to Oxford through the influence of a friend of a friend, he had joined GCHQ through meeting someone in Egypt, and had married, had children and even met Victoria without any planning or great forethought. The Secret Squirrel world had provided patronage, protection and a structure to his life; he hadn't needed to think, just translate from Arabic.

Even the discovery of his relationship with Victoria need not be a big deal. He could avoid her and rejoin Mannington in a few months. It was easier for the Secret Services to keep him (and his knowledge) in-house than to have him expelled, where they would need to watch him for years to come. In telephoning Mark and in booking the hotel room using the cash from Marcus (and he could still not believe the money), Jack had crossed a line. Very small steps they may be, but he had jeopardised his career and probably his marriage as well. Was he tempting fate? Did he know deep down that, unless he was sacked, he would never end up with Victoria? Was he subconsciously engineering it? Did any of this really have anything to do with Mannington's battle with London? Jack gradually became aware of how much of his own as well as Mannington's future rested on Mark Tanner. The man sounded desperately ordinary from the collated biography given to Jack by Mannington – apart from the house fire, and that could happen to anyone.

Empty's black hair and tanned face came through the automatic doors fractionally later than his flared trousers, owing to his rather 'laid-back' style of walking.

Jack approached him, recognising him instantly from his photographs. "I'm James Melrose. You must be Mark Tanner?"

"Hello, Mr Melrose. Nice place you've got here."

Jack's overwhelming urge to walk straight past Mark, jump into a taxi and catch a plane soon evaporated; first impressions weren't everything, he kept telling himself.

It was a delicate mix of amateur dramatics and job interview that took place without an audience in the Drake Room. In the years to come, Jack could only remember two things about the meeting. The first was Mark Tanner's addiction to the mint imperials on a saucer in the centre of the table, and the second was the psychedelic green light show caused by a strong ray of sunlight striking the lime cordial bottle.

"Mr Tanner, I haven't been entirely truthful with you …" was the way it all began. Six mints later they had reached, "That sounds like espionage to me." By the time that our budding spy had poured, sipped and abandoned a glass of lime cordial, they had reached, "So, what's in it for me?"

Jack made a series of financial promises based on a successful outcome which he hoped Mannington or someone would find some way to honour.

"I could get my soft parts chopped off for this, you know?" Mark was beginning to get cold feet.

"We are not asking you to do anything you are not supposed to do except look out for the oddities I've just described. I'll explain how you can contact me if you see anything. Do you realise how much the British Government is relying on you?"

Mark puffed up his chest and grabbed another mint to take away the taste of the lime cordial.

"Your mother in Worcester would be very proud of you."

"What mother in Worcester?"

Jack hesitated. "*Your* mother."

"You know where my mother is?"

"Yes."

"She left me at birth with my aunt."

"Would you like the address?" Jack was using his trump card. "Will you look at a plan of Nefud-al-aan and tell me where there could be any secret installations?"

He rolled out a copy of the plans originally given to Julian by Basil. The discussion was more to orientate Jack than to find a location for the missiles, but he was in for a shock.

"Where did you get these from?"

"I'm sorry, I can't tell you that."

"They're a bit out of date."

"Are they? By how much?"

"Well, the extra tanks for the sewage treatment works for a start. Here." Empty, as he had now insisted on being called, pointed near the Bedu camp at the edge of the military city.

"Do you think that this is significant?"

"Well, I've been wondering for some time why they need a sewage works twice as big as is required by the city."

"Anything else?"

"Well, it's conveniently near the Bedu … and all of the secret cables go in that direction."

"What secret cables?" Jack could scarcely control his voice.

So Empty explained everything that he had noticed.

"You couldn't mark up these plans … you know, to the best of your memory?"

"Why?"

"Because it would be helpful."

"No, why mark up *this* plan? Get someone to call round and collect the plans."

"That may prove difficult in Riyadh."

"No, High Wycombe."

"The plans are in High Wycombe?"

"Yes, I sent them back DHL to Mr Richards so that he can calculate all the pipe flows and stuff."

Jack sat dumbfounded. Marcus or Ross could probably arrange for someone to pick up a set.

"You're looking for a missile site, are you?"

"What?" Jack was way out of his depth. James Bond always had to fight so hard to collect any information. Here, he was confronted with all the information he needed by someone who had already worked out that they were probably looking for a missile site. "It could be. It's probably best if you don't know too much."

"I bet that Abdullatif Al-Rahman is involved. I never took to him."

Jack stared at the lime cordial bottle, wondering why we bothered to have embassies, GCHQ and the rest. "What is it about this man?"

"Oh, I can't put my finger on it. I'm going to my sponsor's new villas on the Red Sea next week and Abdullatif Al-Rahman is supplying all of the interior furnishings."

Jack poured himself a lime cordial.

* * *

Eighty miles to the west, Marcus and Ross were in The Selwyn Arms. This was not one of their usual haunts; in fact, they didn't have usual haunts of any kind. From the outside it was an ivy-covered pub with an old arched gateway. Inside, it was one of those disorientating pubs where the small courtyard has been covered over and incorporated into a bar. Dusty leaded windows from the upper rooms looked down not onto draymen's horses delivering wooden kegs of beer, but onto half a dozen tables with a token candle as decoration. They had selected a quiet corner under an old balcony and were enjoying a home-made steak and kidney pie and chips.

"We must press London to board that ship," Marcus suggested before attempting the near-impossible task of breaking into the puff pastry monstrosity that sat on top of the meat and gravy.

"Don't we need an excuse? And where should we do it?"

Marcus waved his fork to indicate that he would answer

when he had swallowed his piping hot mouthful. "Doesn't matter. Where are they now? Calling into some Turkish port?" Between every few words, he blew out air in an attempt to cool the food. "Anywhere between Turkey and Suez? Or *in* Suez? We can always spin some yarn about drug smuggling, you know?"

"If I had …" Ross paused to choose his words, "… *that* … on board, I wouldn't stop too often. What are they doing in a Turkish port anyway?"

"No idea, but they're pretty safe. I'm sure that they will have somebody important in their pockets so that they don't encounter any problems."

"Will you go to Sir Cecil or direct to the Foreign Secretary?"

"I'll do both at the same time by secure telex. I want to keep our workplace's involvement recorded in writing."

They continued eating without talking, acknowledging the commitment needed to eat the food, with Ross finally revelling in his free access to the gravy once his pie's pastry top had been removed intact.

"Do you think they reuse these pastry lids?"

"What? To tile the toilet walls?" Marcus jested.

Ross put down his knife and fork. "I wonder how things are at Heathrow?"

"Only twenty minutes to find out. I'm not expecting miracles but you never know what lines of inquiry might be opened up."

The cheesecake proved to be a reverse of the main course. Having savoured with ease the soft kiwi-flavoured topping, they would have impressed Uri Geller with their spoon-bending antics on the biscuit base.

"I think I've discovered how they reuse those pastry lids," Ross suggested.

"Cross this place off the list."

"I already have."

Marcus walked to the payphone in its small booth and dialled the number from the back of one of Jack's greetings cards. He listened. In the thirty-second recorded message, Jack managed to convey the key facts about his meeting with Mark Tanner.

Marcus walked back to the table. "You're never going to believe this."

* * *

Jack was staring down from the aircraft window at rivers which resembled slug trails across the earth. He marvelled at how the sun always managed to find a surface off which to dazzle you. He turned away from the window. It had been a long time since he had been in Geneva. In fact, the last time was also at an OPEC meeting when he was a lowly interpreter, never dreaming that he would progress through GCHQ to Mannington. Would Geneva have changed much? Actually, he couldn't remember much about it.

His mind turned to Mark Tanner. He hoped that he wouldn't poke his nose in too far at the Red Sea Villas or anywhere else for that matter. One minute he appeared to be a complete idiot of the most irritating kind, and the next minute he was asking penetrating questions. Whatever happened, Mark Tanner had probably already provided Mannington with the answer it needed; Nefud-al-aan looked increasingly like the final destination. The more Jack thought about it, the more it made sense. He hoped that Marcus or Ross had heard his message. He would leave it a day or two and then telephone using another code number to hear any reply from Marcus or Mark Tanner. It was a little cumbersome and restrictive, but relatively foolproof if you didn't use any keywords which might just trigger interest from GCHQ or elsewhere. He had bought every recorded-message card in the shop in London, much to the delight of the owner. Perhaps he could buy some more in Geneva?

When he had exhausted the worlds of missiles and messages, he looked at his watch. Victoria would have spent the day sprawled beside the hotel pool in Cyprus, drinking orange juice on ice and soaking up the sun's rays. He really must sort out his affairs … literally.

Victoria, for her part, it is true, had been swimming in a hotel pool, but of the indoor, heated type. There was no orange juice on ice and no sunshine. However, on the question of her affair, she was completely sorted out.

* * *

Sir Cecil was not listening to the Foreign Secretary. Instead, he was striking the delicate balance between drinking his white wine and leaving enough in the glass for the inevitable toasts. There were over a hundred people in the room, around tables of eight and also barely listening to the speech. Those not wearing dinner jackets and black tie were in dress uniform; everyone was waiting for the next course, which was slow in coming. In fact, it was the serving staff who were trying to catch the Foreign Secretary's words as they were temporarily banished from the room. He was joking about transparency in the modern Secret Services, making reference to the sparkling chandelier hanging in the centre of the room. Sir Cecil looked up lazily. He didn't see a multifaceted, transparent entity cleverly concealing its internal workings. What he saw was a collection of sharp, heavy glass shards held up by five rusting screws and some antiquated wiring ready to drop.

Sir Cecil smiled. He must be getting cynical in his old age. After all, he had had a very good day.

Earlier, Marcus Billingham had – what was it? – 'set out his stall' in front of the Foreign Secretary. 'Put his neck on the line' would have been a better expression. Mannington was pressing as hard as it could for more information on the *Ikiz* and its cargo. Marcus had urged Sir Cecil to agree to the idea of having the ship boarded as soon as it sailed across the Mediterranean, or into Suez with the agreement of Egypt if necessary. Sir Cecil had put up as much resistance as was necessary to force Marcus into showing his entire hand and asking outright. Sir Cecil's acquiescence had been the performance of his life, making it crystal clear (in a chandelier sort of way) that Mannington must take full responsibility if the ship turned out to be carrying carpets or Turkish delight. After some discussion, it was agreed to ask the Egyptians to allow a search for drugs near Suez. Marcus had left the meeting quietly confident that this would underpin his argument that Mannington should have a wider role. Sir Cecil had left the meeting even more confident that, between Jack Pennington's misdemeanours and the *Ikiz* being full of carpets, Mannington would be back under his complete control. He would wait until after the boarding of the *Ikiz* to play his final card in the game with Mannington.

* * *

It had taken Victoria only three telephone calls to establish in which hotel Jack had a reservation. She had a light early dinner, packed a few night-time essentials into her largest handbag and walked the few blocks to his hotel. The lounge offered comfortable armchairs that gave clear views through to reception. She ordered a gin and tonic with extra ice; this was a drink that she could sip for hours by using the remaining tonic in the bottle on the melting ice cubes. The price of anything alcoholic in Switzerland was at the limits of Victoria's budget. Reading a magazine brought for the purpose, she avoided the gaze of every conference attendee wandering into the lounge waiting for friends or looking for company.

She thought that it was highly unlikely that Jack's room telephone would be monitored but she couldn't take a chance. It was equally unlikely that his colleagues on this OPEC mission would know about her but she had a story prepared for Jack in readiness; she would be an interpreter. With his real past it would be quite credible that he would know many interpreters in many countries; she would be an old friend visiting Geneva for work.

Jack had one thought on his mind as he wheeled his suitcase into the hotel: he fancied a brandy and lemonade. Perhaps it had been the free glass of sparkling wine on the Swissair flight that had set him on this path. On landing in Switzerland, he had felt that his problems were far away and to be forgotten about for a few weeks. Things had rather crept up on him in the UK; what he needed was a holiday, even if it was a busman's holiday.

Victoria recognised his back immediately. He appeared to be alone. This was great news as she had expected him to fly in with the rest of the delegation. Even better. She watched him fill in his registration form and hand over his passport. The receptionist gave him his key and handed him Victoria's note. She imagined him reading her words:

Miss G. Witcombe, the interpreter from the Cypriot delegation, is waiting for you in the lounge bar.

It took a long time for the penny to drop. Twenty years of Arabic, cryptography and lateral thinking did not seem to help him decipher the words. *Miss … Great … Witcombe … Cypriot.* He turned instinctively towards the lounge and back to the receptionist. With his luggage taken care of, he walked through the double doors into the lounge.

Victoria was down to her last warm mouthful of diluted tonic water. In the simple act of sitting down opposite her, he took another major step in his life. When he told her about Mark Tanner, he unwittingly took a major step for his country.

CHAPTER SIXTEEN

It may have looked bizarre but it was effective. Marcus and Ross were travelling down to the third floor at Mannington in a lift, accompanied by a large traffic cone. As the doors opened they were confronted by more cones up and down the connecting corridors. They were neither a pedestrian-control measure nor an indicator that their usual lift had broken down two days before. They were to show that an 'outsider' was in that area of the complex; in this case repairing the lift. He was accompanied by a security guard at all times, even when he went to the toilets, but the cones were the simplest device to warn approaching staff that they should adjust their conversation and not discuss anything secret; in fact, the repairman must have thought that he was in a monastery because most people found it easier to remain silent than to suddenly make small talk.

At his workstation, Ross selected the satellite view over the Eastern Mediterranean. A colleague had been following the *Ikiz* as she left the Dardanelles and entered the open sea. He had also been following HMS *Erebus* since she left Gibraltar, steaming eastwards past Malta on her way towards Crete. It now looked as though, after a week of political deliberations, Friday 14th May was to be the day of action; the day of boarding. Ross was able to listen to all radio calls from the *Ikiz* and HMS *Erebus* by way of the listening station at Ayios Nikolaos on Cyprus; a place he knew well, having spent many months at the base. Ironically, Jack would have been there had he not wound up listening to Oil Ministers in Geneva.

"How far apart are they?" Marcus asked.

Ross tapped in some commands. "Twenty nautical miles."

HMS *Erebus* had on board a group from the Special Boat Service and six military police from the Sovereign Base Areas on Cyprus. Interpol had agreed to allow the British police, acting in an international capacity, to board the *Ikiz* looking for a major drugs haul. The SBS were there in case it turned nasty or in case the *Ikiz* needed to be sent to the bottom of the Mediterranean.

After a while of watching real-time images of the two craft in the sea between Crete and Cyprus, Marcus suggested that they have a break for coffee. They walked to an empty restroom at the corner of the section. To keep support staff at Mannington down to a minimum, most catering, office supplies, maintenance etc. came from GCHQ. If possible, material was handed over at the security control to a few trusted individuals who distributed it throughout the underground floors. So it was with the coffee. There was no lady with a trolley at eleven o'clock. The coffee machines were filled each morning and no one minded having to walk to the rooms to collect their own drinks; it provided a welcome break from monitors and earphones.

"You should remember the next few hours, Ross. They will be the making of Mannington."

"Are you not worried that London gave in too easily?"

"You don't know the people involved, their arrogance or their apathy."

Marcus had finished his first cup before Ross had begun his own. While pouring a second, Marcus listed the facts as he saw them.

"We have the Georgian, we have Nabil, the activity at Zugdidi, the *Ikiz* and the Madrid meeting. We have the Red Sea Villas and Nabil's relationship with Abdullatif. There is their joint involvement with Nefud-al-aan, the murder of Basil Wynne, and our Mr Tanner's description of the extended sewage works. It is very difficult to put another interpretation on those events."

"True, but I would have thought that London could see all of that as well?"

"London is too busy enjoying its successes in the Falklands from tapping up old chums in Uruguay and Chile who happen to be ex-Eton or ex-Sandhurst. Anything else, and especially routine intelligence from the rest of the world, is of little concern to them."

"Perhaps Jack won't be needed in his new role and will be able to return as soon as possible?"

"Jack is the victim of Sir Cecil's personal vendetta with Mannington. In a couple of hours' time, Sir Cecil will have lost the ascendancy and I will be able to ask the Foreign Secretary for whatever I want."

"I wonder how Jack is enjoying OPEC in Geneva? It's a long time since he has done anything like that."

* * *

Ross was correct; it had been a long time since Jack had done anything like this, and he had never done it in a woodman's hut halfway up a Swiss mountain. It was a rest day at OPEC and, on the pretext of seeing an old interpreter friend, he had picked up Victoria in a hire car for a day in the mountains. The weather forecast was good, with the gloom settling on Geneva soon to lift. The talk in the car was of blue skies, wild-flower meadows high in the foothills, and clanking cowbells. They talked of transhumance, romance, anything ending in '-ance', and laughed uncontrollably at their shared jokes as only the besotted can. When the clouds became denser instead of thinner, they laughed even more loudly. Finally they stopped in a forest car park that advertised a circular walk nearby. They sat in the car and speculated as to when (or if) the low cloud would clear. They played with the radio. They played childhood games. Before they knew it, the cloud had lifted and they could see a hundred yards. They set off to find their alpine meadow.

Inauspiciously, the walk took them through a pig farm where the mud stuck to their shoes. Then they discovered that it wasn't mud, and the smell followed them both for days later. Walking through the pine forest, they confided in each other. Jack spoke of Mark Tanner, of the greetings-card messages and of the *Ikiz*; Victoria spoke of cottages, eating in public together, and children. She hoped that this was a turning point. He knew by telling her everything that it was. When they were back in Gloucestershire, either he would move in with her or he would never see her again. He knew that as long as he kept Mannington informed there would be no problem. Even if he wanted to, Sarah, Victoria and Mannington would not allow him to enjoy the best of both worlds. And, like all cowards who find themselves in the lead, he claimed full credit.

The damp pine needles on the forest floor absorbed all sound and there was a pervasive feeling of peace. The path meandered along the contours to a clearing. They stood spellbound as a giant steel door slid back to allow an Army truck to drive into the mountain.

"Busman's holiday," Jack said, and they ran on through the trees, laughing at the thought of a post-nuclear world inhabited by scorpions and the Swiss.

In a woodcutter's – or was it cowman's? – shed, he told her more vehemently than before that he loved her.

* * *

"What are you doing in the office today?" Empty asked Amira. He was back in Riyadh and this was the first time that he had gone into the main office on a Friday; supposedly his day off each week.

"It causes less problems," she said.

The silence which followed was entirely due to Amira bending over her drawing board in tight black velvet trousers. Even the ever-talkative Empty was lost for words. He was in a country where women cannot work or drive and must be covered up apart from their eyes and hands at all times when outside of their home. This made the sight of a girl's face or arm something surprising … and yet here was a young, black-haired girl in tight trousers and blouse working away at a drawing with her Rotring pens. But, then, Amira was unusual. She was the daughter of one of the heads of the Ministry of Finance who had given her the chance to study interior design in Washington in a very progressive relaxation of what was normal. Of course, she had been chaperoned day and night, but had revelled in her three years in the USA, gradually becoming more and more Westernised. She loved Saudi Arabia too, but was faced on her return with the dilemma that she could not work. That was, until Sheikh Faisal, a close family friend, had offered her the chance to work in his architect's office providing that she obeyed all the religious and social laws when not in it.

She was probably the only young Saudi woman working in Riyadh; she was a novelty. She was also stunningly beautiful. The expat men in the office may have snapped their pencils in frustration and found every excuse to have plans amended by her, but they also treated her with kid gloves, knowing who her father was. Empty, oblivious and socially inept as always, treated her like everyone else, and they soon established an easy relationship.

"What are you working on?" Empty asked.

"The garden walls at Nefud-al-aan. All the new layouts have been sent through. Have you seen them yet?"

"No. I shall need to see them so that I can adjust the pipe runs."

"They're next door. Shall we have a look?"

There was a soft American lilt to her English that made her all the more attractive. Of course, she could have spoken with a guttural Serbo-Croatian drawl and still been attractive.

'Next door' did not mean the room adjoining. As with so many businesses in Riyadh, they had quickly filled their office space over a row of shops, which had necessitated the renting of more offices next door and along the street. Without connecting doors, one had to descend in the tiny lift, walk into the street and enter the neighbouring property.

"My father would like you to do a private garden for him. I will do the main design," Amira said as the lift sank the two floors to the marble entrance hall. She was putting on her dark glasses and beginning to wrap herself in a fine black abaya.

Their footsteps echoed across the hall as they walked towards the glare of the outside world.

"It's a large garden around a new villa with …" She stopped talking as the door opened and they stepped onto the pavement where she dropped back a few paces behind Empty. Only her hands and face were bare to the world. They entered a door thirty yards along the street and she began unwrapping the black cloth and removed her sunglasses. "… a series of swimming pools which cascade into the main pool."

"Does that, you know, bother you?" he asked, going up in the next lift.

"No, it might cause a few evaporation problems." She smiled teasingly.

"You know what I mean."

* * *

In the Eastern Mediterranean, the moment of boarding had arrived. Two Sea King helicopters lifted from the deck of HMS *Erebus*, while three inflatable craft skimmed across the swell towards the dwarfed Turkish trawler. Radio conversations between the two captains had been muted and altogether low-key; this added to the expectancy on deck, within the boarding parties and at half a dozen other places around the world.

The sunbathers on the Lady's Mile Beach at Akrotiri were unaware of the role that the five tall pylon aerials were playing in the event. They passively collected the radio transmissions to be sent on to Cleeve Hill on the edge of Cheltenham where, in temporary buildings which were gaining a sense of permanency after twenty years, computers modulated the transmissions. In parallel, the real-time satellite pictures were beamed down to the Mount Olympus radar station in the Troodos Mountains and directed on to dishes in the GCHQ complex. The conversations and pictures were conveyed eastwards from Cheltenham by secure landline to London. The new fibre-optic line was tamper-proof. The thin glass rod in its protective coating was spun in coils of twenty-five miles. No one could 'plug into it' and any breakage was instantly obvious. Only at the joins was there any weakness, so, to counter this, the landline took a zigzag route in roughly twenty-five-mile stages between secure military sites in central Southern England: Cheltenham to Mannington, Mannington to RAF Lyneham, RAF Lyneham to RAF Welford, and so on along the M4 valley.

Marcus, Ross and the team were packed into the Floor C computer room, watching and listening intently. In the furthest corners of the room, operators collating translations of the latest verbose rantings of a mid-ranking ayatollah with statements made in the Iranian press could not help but cock one ear to the group in the centre of the room.

The two Sea Kings hovered in a stationary position over either side of the *Ikiz*, flattening the surface of the water and causing her flags to flap in all directions. Meanwhile, the SBS, in black balaclavas with sub-machine guns strapped to their backs, climbed up at several points, followed by the police in slightly less threatening attire. There was an all-too-casual air to the three scruffy crew members who stood amidships, awaiting the boarding parties.

Andrew Clayton had been at Century House a long time. He could remember when GCHQ sent almost everything up to London. In those pre-Mannington days, he would sit at his station collecting the telexes and ciphers and distributing them round the building. Then came Mannington. Now everything came in distilled versions direct to workstations or occasionally by computer reels; the whole atmosphere had changed. So it was an unusual day for him to find the Head, Deputy Head and a whole bunch of senior officers sat behind his hastily rearranged desk and monitors to experience at first hand events off Cyprus. Even Sir Cecil seemed in relaxed mood, perching on a desk corner in preference to the available chairs.

The pictures came up on the screens and the conversation turned to the operation.

"Oh, I see – we're doing it in force. A frigate, two Sea Kings and three inflatables?" someone commented.

"You can never be too careful. Turkish carpets can be deadly. It's so easy to trip, or stub a toe."

And so the banter continued.

"We should be careful. They might be flying carpets!"

"… and there's Ali Baba!"

The captain of the *Ikiz* was now on deck, talking to the senior British police officer. Some wag behind Sir Cecil was saying, in a deep 'PC Plod' voice, "I 'ave it on the very best hauthority that you 'ave been smuggling hillegal carpets hinto Saudi Harabia."

Andrew Clayton kept his head down. Something very strange was going on. It was as if his superiors wanted the exercise to be unsuccessful.

"Do you think all of the crew or just the captain know about the cargo?" Ross asked.

"I expect the captain and first mate know all about it and the rest of the crew know that it is a special, valuable consignment with a hefty bonus if it arrives safely," Marcus replied.

"They've gained access to the two holds," someone monitoring the radio traffic interpreted.

"Excellent. The Geiger counters will soon locate the goodies."

The next few minutes dragged. Some more rolled carpets were transferred onto the deck to provide better access. The captain became more vociferous, wanting to know where he would get compensation if the carpets or furniture for his Saudi customer were in any way damaged.

"Clean as a whistle." The radio report back to HMS *Erebus* was heard simultaneously in Mannington and London. "She's only half loaded. We had pretty good access. There's nothing radioactive on board. There's nowhere to hide anything very big," the voice added. "We'll go on looking but there's only so much you can do at sea; we can't dismantle her."

On Floor C, previously unregistered sounds were heard or imagined in the sudden silence. Clocks ticked. Air conditioning hummed. Nothing was said. Ross and Marcus walked out of the room and into the lift.

"I think that we've been set up," Marcus whispered.

"We'd better let Jack know. There's no point in going any deeper." Ross stared at the button marked 'Help'.

CHAPTER SEVENTEEN

"What were you doing, Mother?"

"It wasn't me, it was your father."

"Well, what was *he* doing?"

"Dusting."

"Dusting?!" Marcus asked incredulously.

"Dusting."

"At five o'clock in the morning?"

"As good a time as any."

Marcus watched his aged parents dither around the bed-sitting room. Visiting them was like going to the insect house at the zoo; you didn't sit down and you were always aware of the door to the corridor. "Matron fitted a panic button in each room for *emergencies.*"

"It was an accident. Your father was dusting."

"Matron told me that you asked for some soap?"

"That was the time before."

"Please only use the panic button for real emergencies."

Marcus hated coming here. He didn't recognise the two people in their nineties before him. They, for the most part, didn't recognise him. Today he hoped that the pain of this visit would help to mask the other pain inside him after his failure at Mannington. It had never dawned on him that he had never really failed before. His successes at GCHQ and in establishing Mannington had come in an almost continuous sequence. But now he had gone a bridge too far, having been lulled into a false sense of security. There is no hatred as deep as self-hate, and Marcus was currently at a pretty low ebb. He now worried that the painful experience of seeing his parents would in fact *not* be a diversion from this pain, but rather combine with it and make matters worse. It was a risk.

Every time he approached the residential home where his parents now lived he vowed to stay calm, but in that nightmare lack of synchronicity only achievable within families, he lost his temper when they were at their most vulnerable and they were at their most cantankerous when he was feeling the most guilt. The rare moments of lucidity served only to emphasise their senility. Conversations were a long sequence of non sequiturs that still managed to resemble sensible discourse; events and people from their lives separated by seventy or eighty years were mixed up and paired at random.

"You been caught with that girl again?" his father asked.

"Which girl?"

"They can soon prove adultery, my boy."

"Which girl?"

"You know."

"Do you mean Sally?" Marcus made a wild guess.

"Yes, you know."

"No."

Sally had been a childhood sweetheart who had sent Marcus Valentine cards when he was ten or eleven. Her father owned an egg-packing factory.

"Don't you have any honour?" This from a man who had joined the fire service in a quiet rural area at the outbreak of war to avoid the call-up, and afterwards bought widows' houses to sell on to soldiers made homeless after active duty.

"Only that which I inherited from you." Marcus was getting irritated.

"Or have you had your fingers in the till again?"

Marcus could feel the blood pumping through his veins. "What *are* you talking about, Father?"

"At the bank."

For the past thirty years Marcus had told them that he worked in the City at a financial institution.

"We want you to know that there is always a place here for you … you know, if things go wrong." His mother was fumbling with a packet of custard creams. "We can always get Matron to make up a spare bed."

"No! Don't touch that button!"

"I was just getting a side plate for you, Marcus. You are silly." She beamed, perhaps benignly, perhaps maliciously. It depended on what you wanted to see. "Your father's not entering anything in the flower show this year," seemed to follow on quite logically from her lips.

Bloody good job, since he hasn't had a garden or an allotment for twenty years, Marcus thought to himself uncharitably.

"There's no point in running." His father was somewhere else.

"Running where, Father?"

"You can't hide from them."

"From whom?"

"The two men I spoke to yesterday."

"Were they from the flower show? What did they want?" Marcus gazed abstractedly across the garden.

"I ..." His father lost his train of thought.

"Not to worry, they probably went away happy."

His mother started to shuffle towards him with the biscuits. "I don't think so, Marcus, because they're sat out there in that blue car."

Marcus could just make out a blue Escort through the shrubbery. There are times when we all need a panic button.

* * *

Empty woke with a start. He had never seen this bedroom in daylight and he needed to get his bearings. He had driven to the palm nursery located in a wadi way out in the desert on his way to Sheikh Faisal's Red Sea Villas; the wadi provided some natural shade, some sweet soil and a little water at depth, although it only flowed through the valley when there was a rainstorm every decade or so. He'd needed to break his long journey somewhere and the nursery was as good a place as any. Francis had recommended it, having visited a few weeks before. Arriving in the dark, Empty had found the so-called accommodation block and a note telling him in which room and which bed to sleep. It said that there were other people in the room, so he hadn't turned on the light but had undressed by the light from the corridor.

In the morning the curtains were still closed but he could make out that there was no one in either of the other beds. Somewhat to his surprise, two men were kneeling on the floor, searching for something under the beds.

"What's this? Room service?" Empty asked.

The two men jumped, the taller man banging his head.

"We were trying not to disturb you, you daft bastard," he said, rubbing his closely shaved head.

"You found us all right?" the other asked.

"Your directions were excellent. Drive across the desert; turn left."

"Welcome to the Empty Quarter … Empty."

"What are you stupid idiots looking for on the floor?"

"Sid."

"Sid who?"

"Sid the Scorpion."

Empty lay very still. "And he's in here, is he?"

"He's escaped from his box."

"I crept in here quietly last night as you were asleep in the other beds and got undressed in the dark … and there was a scorpion running around on the floor?"

"He is only a small one."

"They are the most poisonous!"

The two nurserymen, who were a very long way from their greenhouses in England where they had begun their careers, continued their search.

Over his breakfast cereal, Empty stared uncertainly at Sid, who was back in his crudely constructed polystyrene-and-Perspex box alongside his cousins. Looking around the room with its bare concrete walls, Empty decided that Sid probably had the better accommodation.

"We're in a wadi in the middle of nowhere. What did you expect? Tablecloths and fish knives?"

"It's very kind of you to let me kip overnight. I shall love you and leave."

Empty stayed long enough to watch the lads pack Sid and his relatives into Jiffy bags ready for posting back to the UK.

"They're worth a lot of money back home."

Empty was not sympathetic.

"You'd be surprised how much those big charcoal-grey ones are worth."

"Not half as surprised as the postman who tries to deliver that package."

"They can survive nuclear explosions."

"Not the last postman I spoke to."

Having checked his Datsun pickup thoroughly for unwanted hitch-hikers, Empty set off for the Red Sea Coast. So much for his Friday off.

The sea, when he finally saw it, was indistinguishable from the shimmering mirage which had been hovering just above the sand and tarmac all day. The coastal area had a few more palm trees than inland but not enough to give continuous shade. Close up, the Red Sea was the richest turquoise, and it lapped white coral beaches that were backed by low, hardened cliffs of limestone. Empty got out of his pickup and took in the panorama. It was the most beautiful thing he had ever seen … he was stunned. There was not a person or building in sight. He jumped back in and continued along the coastal track northwards until he was even more stunned by the Disney-esque silhouettes of a Spanish galleon and a car which appeared over the horizon. The villas were all but complete but they sat in a hot, dusty building site. Some way offshore lay the desalination ship at permanent anchor. Its three fake wooden masts attempted to fool the eye into believing that this was another galleon carrying ships and spices back from Zanzibar. Moored to the jetty was a ship, the *Ikiz*, which on account of its age and wooden construction did not look out of place between the *Santa Maria* and *Pinto*, or whatever the desalination ship and the villa were meant to be. Half a dozen workers in grey or brown dishdashas ferried rolled carpets, wooden caskets and brass artefacts up to the two villas.

A few minutes later, the helicopter bringing Sheikh Faisal from Jeddah landed, creating a dust storm which turned the sky temporarily grey. The workers wrapped their headcloths around their faces and dived for any cover. The pennants on the *Ikiz* and on the villas fluttered in all directions.

The sheikh waited a couple of minutes before stepping out to survey the site and the progress. "I would like the rose garden here."

Empty stood staring at the most barren, arid patch of land. *And people thought that they had trouble keeping their roses alive in South-East England during the hot, dry summer of 1976*, he thought to himself.

"How many palm trees have you ordered for the avenue, Empty?"

"Twelve."

"And they are big?"

"The biggest money can buy."

"They must look – how shall I say it? – impressive."

"Oh, they'll look impressive."

"When do they come?"

"They are being wrapped with hessian this week in Hawaii. The chartered cargo Boeing 747 flies into Jeddah next week. The irrigation system will be in place by then."

"Empty, you are my top man."

Inside the men's villa, they were stood together on the 'bridge'. Did galleons have bridges? Where there would have been the controls on a modern ship, there was a stereo system with rows of knobs and sliders.

"Empty, actually, I have two more jobs for you."

"If I work any more hours I will make mistakes ... or break."

"Do not worry. I am arranging for you to have an additional person. His name is Randy Coleman. He is Canadian."

"Oh, good." Empty did not make it sound as if everything was ... dandy.

"I want you to go to Mecca next week to the Mumtaz Building which I am constructing with my friend Abdullatif. It is a very special building and I only want my good friends to work on it."

Empty was just wondering again how he, a non-Muslim, was meant to go to Mecca.

"I also want you to go to London for me."

Empty was just about to complain that he had only just been to London when he bit his tongue. Paid trips to London he could handle. "What do you want in London? A rose garden in London will be no problem."

"They are called apostilles, and I want someone English that I trust to get them."

Empty did not even bother to ask what an apostille was. He didn't even get an attack of the wallpapers. He was living in such a complete madhouse that such lunatic requests were almost to be expected. "When do I fly?"

"Monday. Coming back, actually, Tuesday."

When alone on the galleon's bridge, Empty stared out across the Red Sea. He remembered the days when all he had to worry about was a couple of sprinklers on a Surrey golf course. It seemed like yesterday. What was he thinking? It practically *was* yesterday. He thought of Jack Melrose. Did that meeting really take place? Was the bridge on which he was standing in the villa a triple bluff; a stereo system disguised as a ship's bridge when it was secretly a missile control pad? Of course not. He realised that he was losing the plot – a plot more suited to *Thunderbirds*. Mind you, there was so much crazy clutter in every room that you could stand a couple of missiles up in the corner and no one would bat an eyelid.

He broke his long journey back to Riyadh in a small hotel in preference to another night with the scorpion catchers at the nursery. Despite an overwhelming weariness, he telephoned one of the numbers that James Melrose had given him. In his message he dismissed the Red Sea Villas, asked what the Mumtaz Building in Mecca was, and said that he was coming back for a day to London to get an apostille. In his own bed, he fell into a deep sleep free of nightmares that couldn't possibly begin to compete with reality.

* * *

Jack was daydreaming. Without the pressure of being the official interpreter he found it hard to concentrate as some Nigerian Oil Minister argued for or against limiting oil production. Having discovered through his recorded-message system that the *Ikiz* was missile-free, his mind wandered from the consequences this had for Mannington to consequences for his own future. This line of thought inevitably brought his fortnight with Victoria to the fore, reminding him that she flew back in only a couple of days. Their time together had worked almost better than if she had gone on holiday to Cyprus, where he would have had to work long hours at the base there. The occasions they met each day in Geneva were governed by the OPEC meeting, and this gave them an unpredictability and spontaneity. The fact that they were apart for some of the day made the evenings and nights more special. Geneva, too, had cheered up once the sun had dried out the wet greyness to a more colourful palette.

A change of slide projected behind the speaker's head brought Jack's attention back to the meeting, but only for a few seconds. In the semi-darkness of the interpreter's booth, he began reviewing the sequence of events which had led to Mannington advocating the boarding of the *Ikiz*. It was all very well London crowing and Mannington apologising, but their internecine battle was in danger of dismissing the whole Zugdidi affair because of one, albeit large, mistake. What were the possible scenarios? Which pieces belonged to the jigsaw that had the *Ikiz* delivering carpets to a rich Saudi sheikh, and which pieces belonged to a different jigsaw that somehow included the transfer of nuclear materials out of Georgia? He examined each piece of intelligence in turn, metaphorically fitting it into either of the two jigsaws or, where necessary, throwing it away.

Jack started with what he believed to be true. The Georgian, Laurenti Malenkov, had specifically mentioned Zugdidi in his first monitored communication. There was an outside chance that this had nothing to do with the missile site or the nuclear material itself, but surely this was unlikely. He had spoken to 'Nabil', who was undoubtedly Abdullatif Al-Rahman. They may have been referring to Georgian ethnic antiques, but with Abdullatif's involvement in the construction of military cities they were more likely to be interested in military hardware. Jack was convinced that they were dealing in some sort of nuclear material or equipment. However, he was less certain about the satellite images of logistical movements at Zugdidi or of the *Ikiz*; they could have been misinterpreted. Times and locations may have been close to those mentioned in the communications between 'Nabil' and 'Gregory', but had they also been misinterpreted by Mannington? Was it seeing what it wanted to see? He also pondered the *Ikiz*. Did they have the wrong ship? Could it have been a coincidence that the one identified just happened to be on its way to Saudi Arabia? Or was transportation to be by some other method, over a different timescale and, worst of all, to a different destination?

He tried hard to remember the actual text of the interceptions between Gregory and Nabil. The original ideas that Syria, Lebanon or Iran might be the final destination came back into his mind. Had they been too quick in dismissing them? What if the two jigsaws were interconnected? What if Gregory was supplying by ship old artefacts and trinkets to Nabil for his (or his friend's) new villa? What if the warheads were separately en route overland, having been completely missed by London and Mannington, obsessed with their game of one-upmanship?

Another change of slide by the Nigerian Oil Minister brought a flash of white lightning to the conference room. Jack wasn't translating because he was speaking in English.

"For that much of an oil price increase, we would not leave our beds in the morning."

What would Sheikh Abdullatif get out of bed for in the morning? Jack thought to himself. *Would he fly to Madrid for a few carpets and some brass balustrading?*

* * *

Something almost undetectable on the surface had changed with Marcus Billingham. The white hair was still neatly in place and his emotions were equally kept to a narrow band. Yet today there seemed to be some added purpose. He was sat in Room 409 chairing a meeting under the relevant protocol on the situation in the Falklands since yesterday's landing. One of the biggest concerns was the freak loss of eighteen SAS men in a helicopter crash. Many of these would have fed intelligence back to GCHQ and Mannington in the coming days. The other matter of import was being described by George Kemp, Mannington's expert on Argentina. He was a big man with girlish eyes and a soft blond quiff, and was wearing a green blazer.

"It nearly worked like a dream. A stripped-out Sea King with additional fuel tanks flew in the SAS to the Chilean coast. We knew it couldn't make it back, so we ditched it." He took a sip of coffee. "Of course, the helicopter will give the Argentinians something to think about now that it's been discovered. Sadly for them, the SAS couldn't make it too close to the two airbases. They have left our standard listening devices which will tell us when the Super Étendards take off. This will give us, the task force, twenty minutes' warning."

"That's still useful."

"It's even better because the Argentinians are looking for the SAS all over the South, telling everyone that we have failed to sabotage anything. Our boys are already back on *Hermes*, having rendezvoused with the patrol submarine HMS *Onyx* off the Argentinian coast."

There were smiling faces around the table.

"And it was our idea to set up the listening devices. *Muchos kudos.*"

Marcus smiled more than most. He may have lost a battle over the *Ikiz* but he hadn't lost the war with Sir Cecil. He now knew what he was up against, and that the gloves were off. By having him followed to his parents', Marcus felt that Sir Cecil had made it a personal vendetta. Marcus had underestimated his enemy once but he had lived to tell the tale; he would not fail again.

CHAPTER EIGHTEEN

In life you need the odd lucky break. Right up until the last minute, Jack thought that he was going to be tied up at the conference. After such a wonderful fortnight, he wanted to accompany Victoria to the airport and say goodbye. However, no one else could have predicted the call for a recess while calculations were being verified by several delegations. Jack walked slowly out of the building, ran around the side and jumped into a taxi. He arrived at Victoria's hotel twenty minutes before her own taxi was due to arrive.

It was a slightly dishevelled couple who emerged from her room sometime later; they were still laughing at something crass he had said about Lady Luck being a long time coming.

At Geneva airport she checked in her luggage at the Saudia desk; it was only an hour-and-a-half flight back to London. They went for a coffee, leaving her passage through passport control to the departure gate until the very last minute.

"I want to buy myself some chocolate. They sell imitation

gold bars in the duty-free shop," Victoria said. "I've bought all of this for the girls back in Cheltenham." She pulled out a Larnaca airport plastic bag from her hand luggage.

"What's in that?"

"I bought a load of Cyprus delight at the airport in Larnaca while I was waiting for the connection. I even sent some postcards to people."

"God, you think of everything. Mind you, it's not a patch on Turkish delight."

"I don't bloody care so long as they all think I've been in bloody Cyprus for a fortnight."

"You've rehearsed your story, have you?"

"I shall pretend that I've met a nice bloke and I can be as secretive as I like."

"And to explain why you're white as a sheet from spending so much time in the bedroom?"

"Fortunately, Jack, you can buy a tan out of a bottle."

"You really are cut out for the Secret Squirrel stuff, aren't you?"

She sipped her cappuccino and moved on to things of a more personal nature. "And when we both get back to Gloucestershire?"

"Vicky, I don't know what's going on back at base or its relationship with London. I gather it's not good."

"They'll let you back in, won't they?"

"I would think so. Perhaps I'll be demoted and sent back to your place?"

She smiled at him. "That would be good, wouldn't it?"

His face displayed equal amounts of 'yes' and 'no'; yes to being with Victoria, no to being away from Mannington. "I still have a slight problem with Mr Tanner. I can't make contact with him until I get to Riyadh to stop him wasting his time looking for … you know what."

"He won't do anything stupid, will he?" She plainly had not met Empty.

"I just wish there was a quicker way of contacting him. I gave him two card numbers so he could leave me a message, not the other way round."

"Is there anything I can do?" she asked.

"No, we daren't risk it." He paused. "I must listen to see if he's left a message when I get back later. I wonder what the silly idiot is up to?"

At that moment, the silly idiot was sat five hundred yards away at Gate 2, waiting to reboard the Saudia 747 flight from Riyadh to London via Geneva.

Victoria's flight was called over the loudspeaker system. Everyone was asked to proceed to Gate 2.

"I'll get a note to you as soon as I get back from Riyadh," Jack promised.

"We must fail to go to Cyprus more often," she suggested.

"Perhaps we could fail to go to Barbados next time. Why be cheapskates?"

They kissed, and she turned and waved from the other side of passport control. In a few minutes she was through and approaching her gate.

"Whatever you do," Empty was saying to some bemused Swiss businessman, "don't drink that cardamom tea they give you. It makes you fart."

Victoria walked forward, praying that she would not be sat next to someone as uncouth as that all the way to London. Lady Luck probably did not know what to do for the best. In the end, she sat them a fair distance apart.

"The first time I flew out, I was sat next to a peregrine falcon," Empty was saying to the old lady with small eyes and a hooked nose who was sat next to him. "Oh, sorry, no offence."

* * *

"Ross, we're doing fine but we need a whole string of successes to put the *Ikiz* way out of people's minds," Marcus was saying. "The Falklands episode is going well – in fact, we're doing well everywhere – but we need to score some points in the Middle East."

"I've got a few additional pieces of work under way in Saudi Arabia. Firstly, I've asked GCHQ to check on the Exocets held by the Saudis at Ta'if, their new military city over near Mecca that they are building. It's not finished yet but they have all of their planes there already."

"How many of these cities are they building currently?"

"Five. Nefud, Ta'if, Jeddah, Dammam and Hofuf. One in each corner and a big one in the middle, if you see what I mean."

"Unbelievable."

"Secondly," Ross picked up his thread, "following our friend's message, I've asked that calls from Sheikhs Faisal and Abdullatif are monitored for the word 'mumtaz'."

"Obviously we can't search for the word generally because it's too damn common."

"What do you think 'mumtaz' means in this context?"

They were both in ponderous mood. In Arabic it means 'excellent' but it is an adjective – you have an excellent something, but what?

"Perhaps our friend got it wrong? Perhaps he was just

saying that the building in Mecca was excellent?" Marcus suggested.

"Well, if we listen to the sheikhs and if our friend visits the building, we should find out."

"If you wanted to store even small amounts of nuclear material, you wouldn't choose Mecca and you wouldn't invite our friend to wander about, would you?"

"Who knows? The outskirts of Mecca may be very clever; it has very restricted access. As to our friend, they seem to like and trust him. Nobody suspects a fool."

George Kemp knocked and entered the room.

"Got some good news for us, George?"

"Ugh, no. *Ardent* and *Coventry* have gone and … the *Atlantic Conveyor*."

"Oh, no," Marcus and Ross said in unison. The ensuing silence hid the question on their lips.

"All the Harriers got off but we lost all but one of the Chinooks … and four thousand tents … and quite a bit more."

"Shit."

"They've fired Exocets at *Invincible*."

"No!"

"How many have they got left?"

"They should be down to three or four."

"It's a shame that the SAS couldn't take out some planes when they paid their visit; just bad luck."

"I haven't given you the bad news yet." George stunned them. He handed them a single sheet of paper. "They seem to have succeeded in buying four Sparrowhawk missiles."

"Where from?" Marcus asked.

"From some middleman working out of Mexico City."

"Have they got them yet?"

"No, they are currently in transit to Mexico City."

They all knew that Sparrowhawks were ship-launched missiles which could be fired from outside of the Total Exclusion Zone, threatening our aircraft carriers.

"Any bright ideas how to stop this?"

* * *

The Foreign Secretary was staring at the portrait of Jeremiah Wesleyan Judd. Why were the subjects of eighteenth-century oil paintings always sitting in that dark chocolate near-blackness? Sir Charles Finch had made a marvellous job of the picture; it said so much. Judd's eyes were lifeless, his hands weak and loose over the arms of the chair. The dog at his feet, however, was captured to perfection. It was the dog's eyes that followed you around the room.

"It's a bit like losing a couple of wickets five overs before lunch, isn't it?" Sir Cecil was asking. It was not the best analogy for the loss of Her Majesty's ships.

"Yes," most of the room agreed sycophantically, but without any great conviction.

"We think that they are down to their last three or so Exocets, and we now have good warning of their planes taking off from the Argentinian mainland."

"But what about Mannington's discovery that they're about to get Sparrowhawks?" the Foreign Secretary asked, moving his gaze from the sharp eyes of the dog in the painting to those of Sir Cecil.

"Something to be monitored," Sir Cecil replied.

The Foreign Secretary moved his head so that the light was reflected from the painting. The bumps on the surface appeared to bear no relationship to the brush strokes. In fact, the brush strokes bore no resemblance to the shapes of the subject matter. "We need to do a little more than just monitor the situation, don't you think?"

"Quite right, Foreign Secretary, but I have every faith, and I do mean every faith, in Mannington's ability to collect quickly all there is to know."

The Foreign Secretary waited for a subtle jibe at Mannington but nothing came … if you excluded Sir Cecil's emphasised 'every faith'.

"I'd like to talk to you about Mannington." Sir Cecil became oddly humble.

Here it comes, the Foreign Secretary thought to himself. There had to be some point to this meeting other than to confirm the loss of ships that he already knew about.

"In fact, my concern today is even wider than Mannington." Sir Cecil was losing his short-lived humility. Finch would have had real trouble painting Sir Cecil. His eyes didn't follow you around the room; they were already there ahead of you. Any dog at his feet would, of course, have had a look of terror; that's if you could get a dog to sit near him for that long. "The computer is revolutionising the Secret Services …"

The Foreign Secretary's jaw dropped.

"… we know more, and we can analyse more. The future lies in winning the technological war."

There was something wrong about hearing this from the lips of someone who probably searched for the Third Programme on his valve radio.

"Mannington …"

Here it comes, the Foreign Secretary thought to himself, yet again.

"… has been enormously successful. But, if I may be critical in a constructive way for just a few moments, I do not think that they have appreciated their success."

Was that it? Finch would have snapped his brushes or limited himself to three oranges in a fruit bowl.

"You see, Foreign Secretary, they are like the successful spin bowler who thinks that he can be an opening batsman as well. Instead of trying to become an even better bowler, he becomes a mediocre batsman and then his bowling goes off as well. Mannington has been far more successful than anyone predicted, but instead of looking to even more success at collation, they are looking towards peripheral areas better handled by others."

The Foreign Secretary was fascinated.

"I would like to suggest three major changes to prepare the Secret Services for the twenty-first century."

It may have been a trick of the light, but did Jeremiah Wesleyan Judd's eyes flick down towards Sir Cecil?

"Firstly, I would like to suggest concentrating the various offices in London and the Home Counties into a new, purpose-built building in Central London. We have more personnel than years ago, our old buildings are inappropriate for their modern tasks, and unnecessary duplication can be removed. Secondly, I would like to propose increasing Mannington's budget so that it can build on its collation success. If necessary, we should consider physically expanding the site at Mannington."

The Foreign Secretary was now sipping tea in stunned silence, listening to Sir Cecil. Far from clipping Mannington's wings, he was proposing an extension of their budget and site.

"Finally, in recognition of the importance of electronic communication and collation, I feel that we cannot have all of our eggs in one basket at Mannington. If we were to lose their function because of accident, terrorism or war, we would be in some difficulty. I suggest that we locate a safety-net duplicate system in the basement of the new building in London to cover any eventuality. I know all of this is a lot to take in while we're fighting a war, but I wanted to sow the seeds now to be backed up by a series of reports which are being prepared for you."

"Well, that's all very interesting … and encouraging, Cecil," the Foreign Secretary said, to general nodding and agreement around the table. "I'll wait to receive the reports but, providing that there are no budgetary implications that we cannot absorb, I'm in general support."

"Oh, that's very helpful. Thank you, sir."

"Have you mentioned this to Marcus Billingham?"

"Not yet. I thought that, with your agreement, I would bring the matter up when we all meet on Wednesday."

"I'm sure that he will be thrilled."

Nobody said a word. Only Judd's dog tried to warn the Foreign Secretary, smelling a rat.

* * *

"Is that it, then?" Empty asked the woman behind the counter.

"No. Please take a seat. We will give you back your papers with the apostilles attached in a couple of minutes."

"This is a cushy number." Empty was not always aware that he was not helping his case.

He sat down on one of the dozen chairs, weighing up his fellow apostille hunters. *Not one of these people is English*, he thought to himself, but fortunately he did not say anything.

The only light came from some high leaded windows, and the room was made dimmer by the wooden dado panels that had been scratched by people leaning back on the uncomfortable chairs. He leant back on two of his chair's legs and took stock. *Relax*, he told himself. *Enjoy yourself. If some nutter wants to pay you to fly back to London to have a postage stamp stuck on a couple of sheets of paper, who cares?* He had managed to see Dawn and the kids the previous night, and this had really helped. When he had flown out to Saudi Arabia he had thought that he would not see them again for six months. Instead he had been back twice in a few weeks. Crazy.

"Mr Tanner?" The woman slid back the glass.

Empty stood up and walked to the counter.

She pulled both sheets out of their envelopes to show him that the apostilles had been attached.

"And that's it?"

"Yes."

"What does it mean, then?"

"It means that the Foreign and Commonwealth Office on behalf of the British Government has verified that the Notary Public signatures on these pages are correct."

"What's a Notary Public?"

"Someone who witnesses other people's signatures."

"So I've just flown back God knows how many miles for you to confirm the signature of someone who confirmed the signature of someone else on these papers?"

"Yes."

"So, if I can't have your job, how do I become a Notary Public? Sounds like a very cushy number."

"You have to be a solicitor."

"There's always a bloody catch, isn't there?"

"That looks like a volcano. Why am I looking into a volcano?"

"You shouldn't be. Hold on while I move the sequence forward."

Marcus Billingham pulled back from the monitors, picking up a printed transcript.

The operator tapped his keyboard to bring up on display the satellite images of the area a few miles to the west of the volcano in Mexico. "There we are," he said.

Marcus put down his papers. "Is that where he lives or where the Sparrowhawks are at the moment?"

"Where he lives, and where they will be in three days' time according to those transcripts."

"When are they being collected and how are they getting to Argentina?"

"By C-130 transport with air refuelling."

"When?"

"The day after delivery from the USA to Mexico."

"Four days' time?"

"Yes."

"Thank you. Can you give me the printouts?"

Forty minutes later, Marcus walked into a room in which four men were sitting. Two were Sir Cecil's colleagues who had convened the meeting at the safe house in the suburbs of Cheltenham. One of the others, Mitchell de Jong, was in the Navy, where he specialised in armament testing. Mitch had been born specialising in armaments; conceived on Guy Fawkes Night. He was a technician obsessed with the details and the mathematics. Joe, just plain Joe, made up the convened group and was based in Hereford, where he too specialised in armaments. Usually he carried them to obscure places in the world where he holed up for a few days before firing them at somebody or something important.

Marcus was introduced under his pseudonym. To Mitch he gave the telex messages, freight list and schedules. To Joe he gave the aerial photographs and two maps. To them all, he explained in broad terms the various sources.

"I have two questions," one of Sir Cecil's men began. He could have come out of the same mould as Sir Cecil, with the emphasis on 'mould'. "One question follows the other."

They normally do, Marcus thought to himself.

"Firstly, Mitchell, is it possible to sabotage the Sparrowhawk missiles so that they either are permanently harmless or, even better, they blow up the user?"

"The answer is yes, with a few provisos."

"If you need provisos, we'll get you provisos," Sir Cecil's man joked in a mouldy sort of way. "Joe, those photographs are of a hacienda in the countryside outside of Mexico City. What's the area called? Oh … Cocoyoc. The owner is not a big drug baron or anything. How quickly could you or your friends visit him and perform any adjustments Mitchell might suggest?"

"We can be in his area in twenty-four hours. It's not the time or the security that bothers me, it's the technical work."

"Excuse my ignorance," Marcus lied, "but surely you would have to take someone like Mitch with you?"

Mitch looked at Joe. Their worlds were the range of an intercontinental missile apart.

"No offence, Mitch, but we prefer to do this sort of work in-house," Joe said. "Our teams have taken quite a few years to get used to each other … and things."

Mitch did not look too happy about the '… and things'; he normally sat at a desk in Portsmouth.

"Mitchell, I think you do need to be there," one of the two London suits suggested.

"I would need about twenty minutes and a bit of kit." Mitch was torn between the excitement of going and being scared shitless.

"How much kit?" Joe asked.

"Do you mean what type?"

"No, what weight?"

"Thirty or forty pounds, I suppose."

"Is that all? No problem."

"How many people would you need, Joe?" The other London suit asked.

"Eight. Four to get us to the hacienda and four to look after Mitch. Just joking, Mitch."

One hour later, Marcus was back at Mannington talking to Ross.

"What do you think Sir Cecil is up to, Ross? Why invite us to that meeting?"

"Do you think that he's trying to show us how Mannington might fit into operational work?"

"And I'm the Queen of Sheba."

"There's no better time for Sir Cecil to concede something small to keep us happy than when he's in a position of strength. Instead of waiting for us to regroup, he's decided to devise a system acceptable to him."

"Hmmmm."

"Being at that meeting is an important step for us."

"I still don't trust him."

"Once you are on the pitch, you can show off your skills. You cannot do that on the substitutes' bench."

"That's very profound for five o'clock in the afternoon."

"I think Sir Cecil's putting bromide or Valium or something in the tea."

"Chance would be a fine thing."

The telephone rang. Marcus answered it. "Billingham. Hello, Brian. No, I don't. No, never." He put his hand over the receiver out of instinct. "Have you ever heard of a 'Project Canute', Ross?"

"No. Never."

"No, Brian. Let me know if you find out." Marcus replaced the receiver. "Canute. Now there's a man I have certain sympathies with." He let his mind wander.

It was Ross who broke the silence. "If this is to be the new relationship between London and Mannington, we have done pretty well. I don't think that we should do anything to upset things for a few weeks."

"Then let's hope Jack has manged to call off our friend in the desert."

CHAPTER NINETEEN

It was Wednesday 26th May and the searing sun of Riyadh was defying the sky to produce even a wisp of cloud. 'A good drying day', as Empty's stepmother would have said while hanging out the washing. Her stepson, at that moment, was delivering some papers with apostilles attached to Sheikh Faisal. He had promised to be ready to receive Empty at eleven o'clock, having made a special effort to rise early after another heady night of grilled mutton and *The A-Team* on video. It did not come as a total surprise to Empty that the sheikh was not up; no doubt he had spent a troubled night fretting over why Mr T, if he had so much gold around his neck, would need to spend his time chasing psychopathic bank robbers.

Empty walked into the huge living room that resembled an MFI showroom. *Now, which settee shall I sit on today?* Navigating through the furniture, his daydream was shattered by a softly spoken 'hi' which emanated from the folds of a white leather sofa.

"Hi. I'm Randy." The middle-aged man with the gap between his teeth finally struggled free from the marshmallow cushions.

"Hi. I'm Empty."

"Well, this seems as good a place as any to fill up."

"No. My name's Empty."

"Why?"

"Because they are my initials: M. T. My name is Mark Tanner."

"My name is Randy Coleman. 'I'm R. C.' doesn't sound right, does it?"

"It depends how offensive you want to be. Are you a Catholic?"

"No … just arsey?" Randy's American, perhaps Canadian, accent was wavering.

In the hour it took for Sheikh Faisal to make an appearance, Empty discovered that Randy was to be his irrigation 'help'. Unfortunately, it did not sound too hopeful as far as Empty's projects were concerned as Randy was to live and work in the new Sabaramco oil compound on the east coast; Empty had never heard of it. Randy was also neither American nor Canadian but from Boston, Lincolnshire (although he sounded more from Massachusetts). True, he had a Canadian passport, but not his own. At some collision point in his chequered past he had borrowed it from a flatmate, renewed it with his own photograph and done a bunk. He was in Saudi on a British passport but he was not specific about whether it was his own. Randy told Empty that he kept his money in launderettes; not literally, he owned them. "Notes are traceable," he said; "nobody gives a hoot about coins … and you always have clean clothing." Nothing about Randy Coleman seemed remotely plausible.

Empty felt that he had lived a rather mundane existence by comparison: a wife, two kids and a house in High Wycombe. Of course, there was the fire … and the lunatic asylum of Saudi Arabia … and spying for MI5, or was it MI6? Perhaps he wasn't doing too badly himself.

By the time Sheikh Faisal walked into the lounge area, Randy and Empty knew more about each other than most neighbours and workmates in England would know in a lifetime.

"Don't mention the passport to His Royal What's-His-Ness, will you?" Almost all traces of an accent west of Cambridge were temporarily gone.

"Empty! You are back, by the grace of Allah."

"And Saudia."

"And you are Randy Coleman?" The sheikh broke his name down into four clear syllables.

"I have that privilege, sir, and I am at your disposal." The American drawl had reappeared. Elstree Studios had obviously missed out on a B-movie actor of staggeringly low standard. Boston, Lincolnshire had also lost a promising plumber when Randy Coleman chose desert irrigation over blocked sinks.

"You have the papers, Empty?"

Empty handed over the brown envelope together with his passport. The sheikh threw the passport onto a coffee table with such casual abandon that Empty felt like pointing out how easily it could fall into a wastepaper bin or be picked up with a magazine.

"A multiple-entry visa would be much better." Empty tried to keep the passport in the sheikh's mind. "This one's only valid for three months."

The sheikh was busy reading. "Good. I will give these papers to my lawyers. I am buying an island."

He said it as casually as he had thrown down the passport. Randy stood, smiling in an experienced, disinterested way, waiting for the sheikh to get round to him again. He had to wait a little longer.

"I was stuck in Geneva for two hours." Empty was still thinking about his passport.

"No problem, Empty. Next time that happens, you can use my BMW 745i. It has white kid-leather seats with blue piping. Bentley made them for me; BMW don't have that option. Tell the porter at the Royal Continental Hotel; he will give you the keys. It is a very special blue."

"Why do you keep a BMW in Geneva?" Empty asked all of the questions anyone else would leave echoing around their head unsaid.

"Because I go to bank there."

Of course you do. Probably when you need to pay for an island.

* * *

Fringe gatherings were happening within the main meeting at a natural break. The Foreign Secretary had made a point of singling out Marcus Billingham, who was sat as far away as possible from the Century House mob.

"How are shares in Collation faring?" the Foreign Secretary asked.

"I wouldn't put your life savings into it," Marcus replied.

"Sold all of your Turkish interests, have you?"

"The market in carpets and warheads seems to have fallen through the floor."

"I hear from Sir Cecil that you are doing good things on the Sparrowhawk front?"

"He credited us?" Marcus sounded surprised.

"And more. He said that you were the best thing since sliced bread. He is advocating increasing your budget and even your premises."

The Foreign Secretary's eyebrows fought to stay inexpressive. Marcus fought not to spill his coffee.

"Really?" was all he could say.

"It seems that Sir Cecil's wife has bought a microwave oven and now he is a total convert to the world of technology. You are so vital," the Foreign Secretary began to whisper, "that you are to have a duplicate system under a new Central London building being proposed." He nodded to encourage agreement from Marcus.

"Wonderful," was all Marcus needed to say. He deserved an Equity card for hiding all of the pent-up aggression and fear it so graciously concealed.

The meeting was almost ready to resume. Marcus was up next with a short presentation on Mannington's analysis of the situation in the Falklands, which concentrated on the additional Argentinian troops mostly at Goose Green. There was just time for the Foreign Secretary to say to Marcus that he hoped that the result of the official report into the *Ikiz* in two days' time would soon be consigned to the fourth tray, as he liked to call his waste basket.

* * *

The inevitable had happened on the evening before. A man whose doctor had advised him that the tablets and a quiet life would keep his epilepsy under control should not have gone to Saudi Arabia. It was not just the physical and mental exhaustion. It was not just the disruptions to his sleeping patterns. It was the living nightmare from which bad dreams would have been a welcome relief. He just wanted to work hard, earn the money tax-free and pay off the debts resultant from the fire. He wanted to be back with his family.

But that was the evening before. Unlike normal nightmares, this one did not end when he woke up. His colleagues in the Mercedes that morning were unaware of his state. The Syrian electrical engineer and the Iraqi telecommunications expert may have presumed that Empty always travelled bolt upright, sporting dark glasses and restricting conversation to 'yes' and 'no'. Externally on automatic pilot, internally he was switching from Plan A to Plan C to Plan B, all involving rapid and final departure from the Middle East. By the time that the chauffeur delivered them to the building site in the holy city, he was well up to Plan Z.

The offer from Yiannis, the Greek architect, to come for dinner with his family had appeared harmless enough. Perhaps Empty should have remembered that the last time he was invited to a family event in Saudi Arabia, they had been blown up in their car by a faulty gas cylinder. Offers to socialise were few and far between, so Yiannis's was accepted readily. They were the only non-Arabs in Empty's small block of flats, living diagonally across the hall on the first floor. Starting work early, coming home late and spending disproportionate amounts of time in planes, cars and pickups meant that it was some time before Empty realised that the New York-trained architect and his American wife Annie lived so near. He had still not actually met her or their two young children. Not knowing their ages, and with alcohol out of the question, Empty settled on a box of chocolates as an appropriate gift.

With ridiculous punctuality, he closed his flat door at eight o'clock and took the five paces across the marble floor, clutching his Belgian mint chocolates. The box was already moist in his hands and he realised that he was sweating in his ironed white short-sleeved shirt. After dithering in front of the mirror, he had finally taken off his tie before he left his flat.

"Hi! How you doing? C'mon in. Right on time!" Yiannis was a ball of curly black hair stuffed into a beige pyjama suit. Only the large whites of his eyes seemed safe from the encroaching hair.

Empty walked into the flat, which was in exactly the same configuration as his. He thrust the chocolates towards the vision of Lily Munster that floated towards him.

"Hi! I'm Annie. Good to see you. This is Ari and …"

Empty never caught the name of the other child. He was struck by Annie's hair, which was long and straight, extending all the way to her backside; it was an odd mixture of white and black, resembling salt and pepper. Her eyes were pale grey with minute black pupils.

"Take a seat. Have you come far?" She burst out laughing and floated across the lounge to the kitchen.

The white walls of the flat were punctuated by crudely painted hippy images of female genitalia, bright flowers and orange sunsets. Within seconds Empty forgot he was in the desert and, temporarily, which decade he was in.

"I hope you like lasagne … it's vegetarian."

"Fine.

"Ari, I would rather you didn't do that."

Empty couldn't see what the child was doing around the corner from the lounge. He looked at the orange-brown nylon carpet and sofas which seemed to fit so much more easily into this flat. Why did it feel so different? Was it that there were scattered toys and clutter everywhere?

Annie handed him a glass of home-made wine and he was invited to take a seat at the dining table. "Do you work with Yiannis? He just loves the freedom out here." Had she noticed that she was in Saudi Arabia? "Ari, please don't do that, and come and sit at the table."

"We work for the same company but our paths haven't really crossed."

"Is your wife coming out here?"

"No – ooh!" Empty leapt up as Ari stuck his fork through the cane panel of the Habitat dining chair into his back.

"Ari, please don't do that. It will hurt Empty."

Ari wandered off barefoot clutching his fork as Yiannis walked back into the room.

"You working at Nefud-al-aan?" Annie continued her questions.

"Yes." Empty was gingerly beginning to eat a flatbread with taramasalata which had been placed in front of him before Ari returned for a second prod.

"Crazy architecture, huh?" Yiannis beamed.

Empty had not really paid much attention to the architectural styles; to him they were large concrete boxes. "They're certainly building them fa ... asst!" He was skewered from behind again.

"Ari, please don't do that."

This time Yiannis rose from the table and escorted an unrepentant Ari to the sofa. "Please do not stick your fork into our friend like that, Ari. You know that's not a good thing to do." He was speaking in a soft voice. Smacking the little bastard around the back of the head did not look like it was a possibility, Empty was thinking, but he kept it to himself.

By the time that the key lime cheesecake arrived, Empty was reeling from Annie's red wine. "We shouldn't be drinking this," he said, without much conviction.

"Ari, please don't do that!"

Empty instantly sat bolt upright as a Pavlovian response, but there was no fork in his back. He turned to see Ari trying to force the fork into an electricity socket on the wall. *Here comes the big smack*, Empty was thinking, but instead Annie flounced across the room in a confusion of black and white tie-dyed fabric to pull the budding electrician away.

"We like our children to learn by experimentation rather than by punishments," she offered as an explanation.

"Don't you get through a lot of children that way?" Empty asked.

"It's the most natural way to learn."

Given the choice of 220 volts up the arm or a slap on the back of the neck, Empty would have gone for the slap every time.

"Don't you think that restricting children is awful?"

"Shocking." Empty regretted using the word immediately.

Within an hour, the children had disappeared into some bedroom to sleep or electrocute themselves or see how long they could breathe with their head in a plastic bag. It did not seem to concern Yiannis or Annie.

"I've got something to show you," Yiannis said, draining his cup of coffee.

If you had asked Empty he would have said that he had not been feeling one hundred per cent all evening. He also did not like drinking alcohol in Saudi Arabia, especially crap-tasting wine made from supermarket grape juice fermented in a dirty glass jars. He stood up and followed Yiannis into the smallest bedroom. Immediately, he felt as if the wallpaper was peeling from the wall, rolling up and disappearing. The room had none of the furniture one would conventionally find, such as beds or wardrobes. Thick curtains covered the window and a thermometer hung from a wall. Six bright strip lights were suspended crudely on long wires from the ceiling, beneath which was a sea of dark green leaves. The cannabis was growing from wall to wall in plastic buckets up to waist height.

"What do you think? Brilliant, eh?"

Empty recognised the metallic taste in his mouth, the cold sweat on his skin, and his eyes receding into his head. He wouldn't remember hitting the floor or being carried back to his flat.

* * *

The morning afterwards, his skull felt hollow and echoed strangely within. Walls and surfaces moved unpredictably, viewed through a fish-eye lens. Somehow Empty managed to put on sunglasses, pick up his briefcase and walk down to the Mercedes. There were several grunted greetings and he slumped back in the comfortable seat. The long journey was a silent film set in the desert, viewed through tinted windows. He lost track of time, and by the time the car approached the outskirts of the city, he had none of the recent events organised in his head. With complete certainty he knew that living ten yards from a room full of cannabis was not a terribly bright idea in Saudi

Arabia. On the same scale, but much lower down, was entering a religious city if you were not a Muslim.

The chauffeur pulled up at a checkpoint that projected out into the road. Empty waited for the 'No good' he had heard frequently since his first day in Saudi Arabia, but it never came. The sheikh was right, he could pass for an Arab; maybe it was his swarthy skin from a lifetime of working outside? Whatever the reason, he was waved through even though he had no idea on whose passport he was travelling.

The Mumtaz Fateen Building, as it appeared to be called, proved to be nothing spectacular by Saudi standards. It was big and inverted; that is to say that its upper storeys projected more than the lower ones to maximise shade and reduce glare. Empty walked off with his notepad to look for the input valve near the gate where his irrigation work usually began. Although the building work was advanced enough for there to be glass in the windows, the immediate surroundings remained a dusty patch of desert peppered with empty cement bags and plastic water bottles. He wandered around the construction site with his plans, making notes and pacing out dimensions. Down one of the sides, he found himself against a half-complete block wall which offered some shade. Stepping across some foundations, he was faced with a long, deep, shutter-lined excavation which disappeared beneath him. Three floors of the building below ground could be seen, as well as two tall, central, circular towers; the whole complex really was deceptively large.

The consequences of the serious fit, or grand mal, that he had suffered the evening before had now disappeared and he saw everything with a fresh, crisp focus. It is true that his pinprick-size pupils, which made him look as if he had smoked a few leaves from Yiannis's indoor nursery, had yet to return to

203

normal. The bright sunlight was not helping, and he raised his hand to shade his eyes. This movement turned into a forehead slap as he saw with a frightening clarity the real purpose of the building. The meeting with James Melrose made complete sense. He clambered back up to ground level and stood on a hardened heap of waste concrete. Despite this being yet another nightmare scenario, there was no fear of another fit. He was numb and subdued, but clear-thinking. A succulent *Calotropis* bush, poisonous to goats and therefore left to grow as a weed, provided a shady place for him to gather his thoughts. He looked at his plans. They stopped at the half-completed wall which divided the future external space inside the substantial outer complex walls into two distinct areas. Sheikh Faisal clearly liked and trusted Empty, but surely not enough to let him loose around such a sensitive site? And what of the Syrian and Iraqi engineers? Did they know any more?

He had decided to ask his fellow travellers on the way back what they knew about the building, but the most they volunteered was that it would be a library. They were not forthcoming with any further details. Perhaps he had been too persistent with his questioning. Whatever the reason, the journey back to Riyadh was a quiet affair, with Empty watching the film in reverse out of the Mercedes' window; forwards or backwards, he still didn't get the plot.

* * *

Victoria had over-prepared her alibi for her return to work. No one was really interested in where a glorified secretary had gone on holiday beyond a cursory question about the weather or the hotel. She could have come back lard-white with stories of coach trips to Buenos Aires from Larnaca and no one would have said anything. They chewed a piece of Cyprus delight, thanked her for her postcard and told her the on-site gossip. The day after her return she slipped back into the regime and Geneva was no more than a remembered novel or film from years back.

There would be no contact with Jack for a few weeks while he covered the OPEC sessions in Riyadh. She did ring the telephone numbers he had given her, to listen for messages and just to hear his voice. It was from a red public telephone box outside a newsagents in Hatherley Road that she heard Empty's message about the Red Sea Villas and the Mumtaz Fateen Foundation. This meant nothing to her until three days later when she was collecting groups of messages for onward transmission to Mannington. She tapped the words 'Mumtaz' and 'Fateen' into her system during an idle moment as she was perfectly entitled to do; part of her job was to put messages and translations into coordinated blocks by subject heading to ease Mannington's workload. The two words occurred frequently but only once in the form that interested her.

As she scrolled the English translation down the screen, she realised that she needed to inform Jack as soon as possible. The Mumtaz Fateen Foundation, she read, was akin to the Church of Jesus Christ of Latter-Day Saints. Just as the Mormons, as they are known, keep a complete record of all living and departed souls in a vast complex beneath Salt Lake City, so Muslims were going to keep a database or library of all known believers in a facility to be built in one of their holy cities. Unlike the Mormons', the Mumtaz Fateen Foundation's system was to be secret and not available to the outside world. Jack would be able to cross that building off the list.

CHAPTER TWENTY

From their rooftop vantage point, they could almost see the tread on the tyres of the Lockheed TriStar immediately above them as it came in to land at the airport right in the middle of Riyadh. Empty and Randy Coleman were deafened by the roar as the plane yawed serenely over villas and palms. The swirling heat from the three engines mixed with the desert haze to form a dizzying mirage, and the red lights of the runway danced like sparks from a bonfire.

"I still don't know how they get off the ground." Empty was leaning against the parapet wall which surrounded the top of his block of flats.

"They don't look very aerodynamic, do they? Cor! Something smells good." Randy's eyes were overridden by his nose, which had just caught a waft of cooking onions. He walked across and leant over the wall around the shaft which penetrated the centre of the building. All he could see was the dull light from small, opaque kitchen windows, and a rat negotiating the treelike pipework that served all of the eight flats. He took a swig of lemonade from a plastic bottle to erase the memory of aviation fuel which was mixing with the onions. "I bet you'll be glad when the new airport opens in a couple of weeks' time?" he sympathised. "The noise of the air conditioning must be bad enough without aircraft a few inches above your head."

"When I'm working, I find this place totally absorbing," Empty began rather profoundly, "but five minutes after I stop work, boredom sets in, and five minutes after that, homesickness takes over."

"Keep working, then," was the unhelpful response.

"I don't think I can stand much more."

It was Friday, the day off, and Empty needed a heart-to-heart. Randy Coleman was the best of a poor bunch of potential confidants.

"But how else will you pay off your mortgage?" he asked, while ensuring that the rusty steel door was not about to slam shut, stranding them on the roof.

"I think it's called 'the horns of a dilemma'?"

"And we are talking rhino horn here rather than dik-dik, I think?"

"I think I know what you mean … either way, substantial."

Randy walked over to join Empty, who was looking down at the street two floors below. "Why don't you just steal the money?"

"There is the small question of morals."

"The insurance company stole the money from you."

"No, they didn't."

"Yes, they did … whatever name you want to give it."

"It doesn't change the moral question."

"The only reason people don't steal is fear of getting caught and punished."

"Rubbish."

"If you could, with absolutely one hundred per cent certainty of not being caught, walk off with that plastic sack of riyals in the back of that pickup down there, you would."

This was not the conversation that Empty needed at this moment in his life. A reassuring 'It'll soon pass' or 'Give it another three months' might have helped more.

"It is *his* money, not mine." Empty indicated the old sheikh carrying a sack into the Exchange House.

"The insurance company didn't say that, and they've messed up your life completely. I bet if you took that sack from that pickup it would have virtually no impact on that chap's life."

"You see the world in very clear black and white, don't you, Randy?"

"No, I see the world as grey, where anything goes."

"But aren't you worried about being caught?"

"Not really because I'm not stupid or greedy. Paying no tax and having a few passports is no big deal and I just keep a low profile."

A sombre grey Boeing 707 US Air Force tanker plane thundered over their heads. It was returning from refuelling the AWACS which were monitoring developments near the Iranian border with Iraq.

"Will they still be based here when this airport closes and the new one opens?" Randy asked.

"I don't think so. They are trying to move all of the big planes away from here, I think. This airport has too many buildings around it now and it will only get worse."

"I'm flying to the Sabaramco compound in Dammam tomorrow."

"You're not being driven?"

"No. Sheikh Faisal offered a flight so I took it."

"Why not?"

"Come and visit me if you need a break."

Now that was more what Empty wanted to hear.

* * *

'Never tempt fate,' her father had always said. Perhaps that was why her car had broken down a few miles from Great Witcombe on her way to work. All she had thought was that nothing should spoil such a gloriously sunny Friday morning with the promise of a hot weekend ahead. Victoria had set off from her cottage full of the joys of spring, having decided to call Jack at his hotel over the weekend before he left for Riyadh. She reasoned that no one had followed her on her holiday so they could not be too bothered about her. After all, Jack was in Geneva en route to Saudi Arabia and she was in Gloucestershire. They were probably monitoring her phone at home and work, but not much more. She had fretted most of Thursday and through the night about the Mumtaz Fateen Foundation. Mannington should know about it but there was no one for her to tell other than Jack; she was not meant to know about it. She could hardly say that she had been in Geneva for two weeks and that Jack had confided in her about the telephone messaging system. She did not want Empty and Jack pursuing a red herring. The foundation might be secretive but it was not seemingly a military outfit.

There was no alternative; she had to communicate with Jack directly, and the only method was the telephone. As

Cirencester had provided her with a safe place to buy an air ticket, she settled on a return visit during which she would find a public telephone and call him.

Fate having been tempted to intervene, it did not stop at loosening a fan belt or any other belt. Victoria's rusting Mini had come to a halt outside the home of someone she vaguely knew near the village of Brockworth. After futile attempts to restart the car with its flat battery, she walked through the gateway and under a stone arch towards the imposing Georgian residence of Monica. Her surname escaped Victoria. Monica was a lady of advancing years whose degenerating physical form belied her incredible sharp mind and limitless energy. She was a key fundraiser on behalf of most local charities; a redoubtable knocker on doors and supporter of good causes.

"Hello. You may recognise me. My car has broken down," Victoria spluttered at the stooping white-haired lady who opened the door.

"You live in Great Witcombe, don't you? Where is your car? You had better come in."

So Victoria found herself, at 8.30 that Friday morning, not crawling into Cheltenham listening to the radio, but walking through a large hall which had a real leopard skin on the floor and a grandfather clock with a beautiful etched face. She explained her predicament.

"Use the phone in there. I'm halfway through washing the kitchen floor, if you'll excuse me."

"Spring cleaning?"

"No. It's Friday."

Victoria felt a certain inadequacy sweep through her not-so-old body.

A fading photograph of a young Monica and a moustachioed

man, both on horseback in some African landscape, told Victoria almost all she needed to know. The framed copy of the *Rhodesian Times* announcing the posthumous awarding of the George Cross told her almost too much. She rang her office to say that she was going to be delayed, and then the local garage to arrange for a man to look at her car. All of the dark wood, which should have made the room sombre, was softened by the sunlight streaming in from two tall windows. She thought of Jack. She thought of telephoning him. No one could have known that she would be in that room. She hadn't known it herself.

"Hello?" She sought out Monica with her mop and bucket, busy on the red-tiled kitchen floor.

"Everything sorted?"

"Yes, thank you, but could I ask one more favour? If I get the operator to give me a cost, could I make a short call to Switzerland?"

"Of course … this is to your boyfriend?"

"How did you know that?"

"Well, it wouldn't be work, would it? You're not wearing a wedding ring and, judging by the car you drive, I doubt that you are ringing your Swiss bankers."

Victoria smiled even more, and especially as she thought about the man in the photograph who had been lucky enough to know Monica in her prime.

It was not long before the sing-song voice of the operator was on the line. Victoria knew that it was a fifty-fifty chance that Jack would be there, and she also knew that she couldn't leave a message.

"Room 217, please."

The ringing tone began.

Jack was at the hotel but not in his room. He was in a flower shop ordering a bouquet for Victoria to be delivered Saturday morning when he knew that she would be at home; thank goodness for Interflora. He had no other way of contacting her without using up one of his precious card numbers, which he wanted to keep for communications with Mannington. He was off to Riyadh with the OPEC circus on Saturday.

Victoria was annoyed with Jack for not being there even though it was not his fault. Fate had given her a window of opportunity that was unlikely to be repeated.

* * *

Empty did not receive many calls at his flat, so it was a pleasant surprise to have his tedious Friday evening disturbed by the telephone. More often than not it was Francis ringing in preparation for the next week's work on the Nefud-al-aan site.

"Lunatic asylum, chief nutter speaking. Oh … hello, Sheikh Faisal." Empty grimaced at the wall.

"You are enjoying your deserved day of rest, Insha'Allah?"

"Yes, thank you."

Echo the Gecko did a sideways shuffle back behind the heavy curtain. He had not long emerged to begin his nightly prowl.

"You are enjoying your stay in Saudi Arabia?"

What did Sheikh Faisal want? Someone to watch videos with? Another trip back to the 'Yookay' for an apostille?

"I am enjoying it very much," Empty said cautiously.

"You enjoyed your trip to see the new library?"

"Ye … esss."

Why couldn't he get straight to the point?

"The Mumtaz Fateen Building was … confusing?"

Empty froze in a panic of realisation. It had never dawned on him properly that, if James Melrose was right, Sheikh Faisal was implicated. If the Mumtaz Fateen Building was the secret location for something military, Empty had been asking a few too many questions.

"No. The plans you gave me didn't cover the whole area … so I couldn't make sense of the irrigation requirements." *Good*, Empty thought to himself.

"You know that there is some … secrets? No, what is the word? Secrecy with this building?"

"Ah … no. I thought that it was a library."

"You are right. It is a library. It is a special library. It is a Muslim library, and this is why it is in a holy city."

"Fine." Empty was trying to work out the reason for the call.

"I do not want the library to be … discussed." In the way he said 'discussed', Sheikh Faisal was leaving no room for misinterpretation.

"No problem. I didn't want to irrigate half the site because I didn't have all of the plans."

"You are right. I am wrong. You will have all of the plans but will say nothing of the building."

"I am not interested in the building," Empty lied.

"Enjoy your Friday evening, Empty."

"I will. Thank you for calling."

Empty walked along the hall into the bathroom, where the strangely located washing machine was trying to remove the dust from his clothes. He rotated a dial and clicked on the drying programme. In a fit of frustration, he tried to crush a cockroach that did not share Echo's understanding of the sensitivity of the situation.

* * *

The Friday-afternoon joint intelligence meeting was overrunning. The news was coming in thick and fast; most of it not good.

"What's the bloody use of us having the intelligence if the soldiers on the ground don't use it?" someone was asking. "We told them over a week ago that there were upward of 1,500 Argentinians in the Goose Green area. Why are they still relying on the original SAS estimate of five hundred?"

"It's the Navy's fault. Everything's got to go via the bloody ships and they're not up to it. What have they done in the last thirty years apart from chase a few Icelandic fishermen?"

"You are a heretic, Miles."

"These cock-ups are all down to the fact that we do not have a land-based Tactical HQ. Apart from Diego Garcia in the Indian Ocean, do we have a square foot of land more difficult to defend than the bloody Falklands? We need a land-based HQ on Chilean soil." Miles paused and then further expounded his heresy. "Then the Army could organise itself and leave the Navy to ferry stuff about and fire big shells at big targets on the Falklands that they might manage to hit."

"Underneath your crazy scenario, there is a seed of truth about the line of communication." The Foreign Secretary tried to calm nerves.

Another telex from Northwood was brought into the meeting, putting a temporary end to the discussion. Sir Cecil read it and handed it to the Foreign Secretary.

"Colonel 'H' Jones is dead."

Nobody was keen to speak.

"One battalion is not enough." Miles voiced what they all knew to be true.

"The telex goes on to say that progress is being made …
thankfully," the Foreign Secretary had finished reading, "but,
clearly, lessons must be learned."

"I agree."

An hour later, the news was much better and the mood in
the meeting had lifted. They broke for ten minutes, allowing
Sir Cecil to pin down Marcus Bellingham in front of the
Foreign Secretary.

"We shall be seeing you at the inquiry into the *Ikiz* incident
on Monday, shan't we, Marcus?"

"Yes, I'll be there."

"Don't worry, Justice Templeton is not a hanging judge."

"We advised on the best available information. I don't fear
the inquiry."

"Are you staying up in town?" Cecil asked Marcus.

"No, I'm going to see my parents in Oxford … but you
already know that, Cecil, don't you?"

CHAPTER TWENTY-ONE

She could have dozed under the warm duvet that Saturday morning, or taken her breakfast back to bed, or read the newspaper – such are the freedoms of the singleton. Instead, she woke early, grew bored with her thoughts and found the emptiness of the bedroom overpowering. Wearing her dressing gown, she stood in her tiny sitting room, ironing in front of the man on the television with his kipper tie, shoulder-length hair, and jumper which looked as though the arms had been cut off with scissors. He was explaining wave theory using a skipping rope. This was the Open University, which was the only option open to her apart from cartoons. Victoria wanted distraction. She had been thinking about her circumstances all evening and all morning since waking at six o'clock. The fact that she had blown all of her savings on the Geneva trip featured prominently. Re-examination did not change things, but she could not stop herself going back in time: her planned Cypriot holiday, their debriefing at GCHQ, Jack being followed, the feud between London and Mannington, and the *Ikiz* business. Victoria did not know half of the details about some of these matters but she was bright enough to guess. What she knew of the *Ikiz* affair did not make sense. If so much intelligence from so many sources indicated that there should be something on board, why wasn't it there?

The man on the television rocked a tank of water back and forth to simulate wave motion. Ping-pong balls rose and fell on the swell.

She knew that she only had a couple of weeks to wait. Jack would be back from Riyadh and, presumably, back at Mannington. He would discuss everything with his superiors, leave his wife and move in with her. Resting her iron on its base, she stared for some time out of the window, not really focusing on the countryside at its verdant best. When the spell was broken, she returned her attention to the wave expert. To her surprise, he was gone. Replacing him was S316, a module in the course on astronomy. To relieve the boredom, she went into the kitchen and put on the kettle. Carrying a cup of coffee back into the sitting room, she stared at an older man with a beard, tight sports jacket and bow tie. He was holding a black ball and a white ball – one in each hand.

"All evidence suggested that a black hole must exist, but we just couldn't find one," he was saying. "It was only when we looked into space beyond the twin stars of Castor and Pollux that we found what we were looking for."

Victoria never did finish her cup of coffee, but did remember to turn off the iron. She ran upstairs to dress with her mind racing all over the place. Unfortunately, it was still too early for her to check anything and it would be a long time before the public library in Cheltenham opened. Her impatience prevented her from waiting that long. Where else? WHSmith! She would look it up in a book in WHSmith.

Rushing into Cheltenham would gain her nothing, for she knew that she would have to wait until the shops opened. This did not stop her. She found herself parked and standing outside the shop, waiting for it to open. When the bemused staff unlocked the doors, they watched Victoria walk purposefully past the newspapers and the records and cassettes to the main bookshop area. She stopped at the language section and fumbled through the Langenscheidts, Oxfords and Harraps, looking for what she wanted.

It took only thirty seconds to open the dictionary, check her word and confirm what she had guessed at seven o'clock that morning. She must ring Jack, whatever the consequences.

* * *

There was a half-term feel at the conference in Geneva. Some, like the Undersecretary of State, had already flown back to Heathrow. Others, like Jack Pennington, were about to leave for Riyadh. The bright blue sky on the day of their departure rather mocked them after their arrival in that grey murkiness. Jack's bags were packed and positioned to hold open the hotel-room door. He was doing that unnecessary final inspection where you open drawers you have not used and lift up the bed linen to search for lost socks.

The telephone rang on the bedside cabinet. He expected this to be some last-minute changes to the pickup arrangements, but he was in for a shock.

"Hello, Jack?"

"Hello … Sarah?"

"Don't sound quite so surprised."

"I'm sorry. I was about to leave the hotel for the airport."

"This is probably not a good time to catch you?" She sounded unnerved.

"No … it's OK for a few minutes."

"I mean," she hesitated, "I had something … there was something I wanted to … discuss with you."

"Fire away."

There was silence down the end of the line.

"I know about your affair with Victoria, your secretary."

It was time for Jack to fall into silence.

"Jack, I'm not ringing to have a row … that would be hypocritical in the circumstances."

"You choose your moments, Sarah."

"I'm sorry. There will never be a right moment. You see … what do you think I've been doing all of those evenings you have been … occupied … at work?"

"I didn't think."

"No. I know that. I think we both looked for someone to fill the gaps."

"I—"

"Let's talk when you get back, but I felt there was no point deceiving each other any longer."

"No," he said rather meekly.

"The rest of the family are fine, by the way."

"Yes, thanks. I would have asked … normally."

"Have a good trip to Saudi."

"Yes. Right. I will."

The porter tapped the open door to collect the luggage.

"Thanks. I'll see you in reception," Jack said in French.

Random questions floated in his mind. Why hadn't he

guessed? Who was the other man – or men? Why had he spent so long concealing Victoria? Why had he bothered to go home? Would he now live with Victoria? And, finally, how could Sarah? He replaced the receiver, picked up his briefcase and stepped into the hotel corridor in a daze, leaving his raincoat hanging on the back of the door (fortunately for him, he wouldn't need it in Riyadh). The emotional extremes of sadness and elation, anger and relief managed to cancel one another out. He disappeared downstairs in the lift.

* * *

Victoria was deeply frustrated. She had dialled the hotel number from a call box outside the main post office in Cheltenham only to find that Jack's room phone was engaged. How long before she should ring back? Her dwindling column of fifty-pence coins on the black shelf would not last long. She waited five minutes and repeated the exercise. No reply. He must have gone out. Running out of money, she rang off in disgust. Why did she have anything to do with …?

She remained irritated all of the way back to her cottage. It would be Monday evening before she could leave a message at his Riyadh hotel; perhaps she could pop out after work to a telex bureau in Cheltenham and arrange for them to send a message to the Hotel Mövenpick – something along the lines of 'Please call – urgent!' She thought that they probably charged by the word so she was going to be as concise as possible.

She drove the Mini unnecessarily fast into Great Witcombe, preparing to swing onto the compacted earth which served as her driveway. A large white van was parked outside, blocking the entrance.

"Now what?" she muttered to herself.

A woman in green overalls opened the rear door and pulled out a magnificent bouquet of flowers. Victoria stepped out of the car, ready to help her find the correct house.

"Victoria Moss?"

"Yes."

"These are for you."

Victoria cradled the flowers unnaturally in her arms like a newborn baby. The message read:

All my love, Jack.

* * *

In Riyadh it was over forty degrees centigrade. The sun was defying the animal kingdom to survive. Those with brains hid under rocks or expired. Those with larger brains turned up the air conditioning, drank iced water and were oblivious to the challenge outside. Sheikh Faisal had abandoned the conferencing facility on his telephone and was holding the handset to his ear. The introductory asking after Sheikh Abdullatif's family and the offering of well wishes had almost been completed.

"Many thanks for all of the Turkish and Georgian goods. They look wonderful in the Red Sea Villas."

"I am thrilled that you are happy with them," Abdullatif replied. "You have chosen a most beautiful location on the most beautiful coast in Saudi Arabia."

"You must visit me when all of the decorations are complete."

"It will be an honour." There was a pause not orchestrated

by the electronic overload of the telephone system. "How is our ... friend?"

"He is fine."

"Have you spoken to him?"

"Yes, and I am reasonably happy with his answers."

"Do you trust him?"

"I think so."

"With the greatest respect, I ask if that is enough?"

"I do not know."

"My man on site tells me that he asks too many questions."

"Fools always do; so do the innocent."

"So do those with evil intent."

"You are right."

"Can we take any risks?"

"No."

"Is he indispensable?"

"No, but good irrigation engineers are hard to find."

"You will remember that I lost mine."

They both listened to the noise of the air conditioners, which was being amplified by the telephone system.

"What shall I do, Abdullatif?"

"I think it's time for an exit visa."

* * *

Empty was sat in the passenger seat of a brown Chevrolet station wagon. The front of the vehicle was in a different time zone to the tailgate, it was so long. In design terms it was also in a different time zone – about 1962; the year of the chrome trim. It was being driven by Amira's father, Mohammed, sporting a short-sleeved shirt and sunglasses. He owned fifty-one per cent of a cement-making company, among other ventures. The works outside Riyadh had some of the lowest environmental standards, but who is going to complain about dust emissions in the desert? Together with his separate transport companies, the cement franchise had made Mohammed a multimillionaire. He now, nominally, played an important role in the Civil Service. His time undertaking an engineering degree at Penn State University had made him more accepting of American freedoms and, later, more tolerant than most as a father of four daughters. Tolerance is relative and only Amira had made it to America, and even she had only the pretence of a job back in Saudi Arabia.

It was Speech Day at the girls' school. Mohammed's wife, Fatima, was present to see their younger daughters collect academic prizes. The Chevrolet was on its way to pick them all up after Mohammed had taken Empty to see a large farm that he had just bought. Empty had been stunned; this was irrigation taken to its limits. It was one of those ideas that sounds good on the drawing board. You take a patch of flat desert (any patch of desert) and bring in a desalinated water supply. You build a flat concrete platform, to which you anchor a very long pipe that is supported by up to a dozen tractor units at hundred-metre centres which circumnavigate the central platform with the monotony of a donkey on a treadmill. The two-kilometre or so diameter circular 'fields' support an arable crop or produce fodder for the dairy cows in their factory sheds. From the air, these arable farms resemble green records removed from their sleeves and thrown randomly onto a beige carpet.

But that had been this afternoon; a period when Empty had relaxed a little away from Riyadh and in the company of a gentle, educated man. Mohammed had been pleased with Empty's advice, especially his suggestion of installing an injection unit on the platforms which could provide additional nutrients. Now Empty was on his way back to his flat via a girls' school; so ridiculously normal in his own country that he had not thought through the implications.

The Chevrolet wallowed on its springs as it dipped and bucked across the unfinished roads of Riyadh; the tarmac may have been missing but the kerbs were always in place. They turned down a side road framed by the obligatory three-metre-high walls. Empty was transfixed. In front of him on the pavement there appeared to be a hundred Guinness bottles; women and girls completely wrapped in black, waiting for their cars. Mohammed pulled up among some of the most bashed up as well as some of the most expensive cars in the world.

"Excuse me asking," Empty began, "but how do you know which is your family?"

"I don't."

They both laughed.

"But they know my car."

Five black apparitions descended on the Chevrolet, opening the rear doors.

"Would your wife like to sit here?" Empty asked, having no idea what the rules were.

"No, of course not … but thank you."

Hot air swept into the car accompanied by the sound of swishing fabric. The air conditioning went into overdrive and the engine noise increased. The doors slammed and a strange sort of equilibrium returned to the vehicle.

"This is Mark Tanner. He works for Sheikh Faisal."

A chorus of female voices said hello.

"Amira, I am very impressed with Mr Tanner. You can learn a lot from him, I think." Mohammed turned to the three black shapes on the first bench seat behind him.

"I'm back here, Father," Amira answered from somewhere near the tailgate. "Don't you know your own daughter?" she teased.

They all giggled.

The normally loquacious Empty was thrown by the situation. He turned around to be confronted by five pairs of heavily made-up eyes peering at him from five slits in black fabric.

The gentle ribbing continued all the way across Riyadh. The car swept up the drive past a gatehouse, the tyres purring across the clay paviours. Outside the garages, which resembled the stable block at South Fork, they all got out. In the privacy of their high-walled garden, five females began unwrapping themselves, their conversation not missing a beat. The five Russian dolls became five beautiful clones of each other; their Western clothes immaculate, their Eastern eye make-up stunning. Empty was not allowed to decline an invitation to take tea. Mohammed slumped into a gigantic sofa while his four daughters perched precariously on the arms and back, telling him of their day with obvious family pride. The youngest daughter collected the tray from the Filipina maid and Amira poured tea for Empty. The contrast with the family of Yiannis the Greek would not leave his mind.

Back at his own flat, Empty found the lack of laughter and love overpowering. He missed his own daughters such that his stomach ached. He wanted to telephone them but he suppressed the impulse, knowing in his heart that he had decided to get out of the madhouse and fly home for good as soon as he possibly could. Instead he decided to ring one of James Melrose's numbers and leave a cryptic message about Mumtaz; no harm would be done. He would speak to Sheikh Faisal tomorrow about going home.

Empty dialled the operator.

"Hello. May I help you?" an effeminate male Arab voice inquired.

"An international call to London, please."

"What number?"

Empty read the number slowly from the card given to him by James Melrose.

"You are ringing your boyfriend?" the operator asked.

"No."

"A girlfriend?"

"No. My wife," Empty lied quickly.

There was a pause. "You don't like boys?"

Empty had a very strong urge to tell the irritating bastard on the other end of the line to just dial the number and put him through. This, however, would risk upsetting the young man who had the power to block his telephone line or, even worse, add hundreds of pounds to his bill. "I like everyone."

"So you don't like boys?"

"I like boys and girls, but I need to phone my wife, who is ill."

"Hold on. I am dialling."

Empty recorded his short message and spent the evening in a one-sided discussion with Echo the Gecko on why absolutely nothing in Saudi Arabia was straightforward.

CHAPTER TWENTY-TWO

The horse chestnut trees were still dripping from the heavy overnight rain. Cheltenham was at its drabbest. There was more to come as the clouds gave up the task of hoisting their load up over the Cotswolds. The oolitic limestone hills soaked up the water, filtered it and let it seep slowly, over tens of thousands of years, under Cheltenham – the source of the spa water. Sadly, the Georgian villas were made of cheap bricks and the rainwater collected on their flat roofs, creeping into cracks in the stuccoed walls to emerge not as pure mineral water but as mildewed dampness in the basements.

Ross Smith peered out of the bedroom window. He had heard the electrical whine of the milk float ten minutes earlier splashing along the road. Now there was no sign of human activity. He finished dressing by putting on the tie he had worn yesterday, having no choice if you excluded Jack's ties behind the wardrobe mirror, into which he was looking.

Sarah was sat up in bed with the sheets around her waist.

The smile on her face was a valiant attempt to make it easier for him to leave; showing half her body was a subconscious attempt to get him to stay a bit longer.

"We've reached Base Camp 1," Ross had said over dinner the night before, but Sarah did not know if they were numbered up or down the mountain and how many more there were. Telling the self-obsessed and unfaithful Jack was a quick walk in the foothills compared with telling Margaret, all of the kids and Mannington. Perversely, it was the calm ease with which Sarah dealt with the pressures of having a husband at Mannington that had attracted him in the first place. It contrasted vividly with the naturally rebellious Margaret, who could never miss an opportunity to bang her head against a brick wall; and there was no more solid, immovable brick wall than that metaphorically enclosing Mannington.

Ross and Sarah had speculated ever since Sir Cecil's men had discovered Jack's affair with Victoria as to which of them had been unfaithful first. This was not an academic exercise but an important opportunity to offload some of the guilt.

With the children at Margaret's for a night, Sarah had killed two birds with one stone – her home was empty and Margaret was tied up. The unequalled pleasure of a night in a comfortable bed with no worries about Jack, Margaret or the children was overwhelming.

Ross was contemplating the next step. It wasn't telling Margaret but the timing which was bothering him. Should he do it before Jack came back from his trip, while he was still out of favour, and possibly out of Mannington? Obviously, they couldn't work together again, so one of them would have to go. Working back at GCHQ would be difficult for both of them, even if it was allowed to happen. Ross knew that the post of Operational Head at Cyprus was coming up, and this might put sufficient distance between everyone. The very latest possibility he had only discovered from Marcus in the last few days; namely that there may be a duplicate Collation Unit established in London.

Ross's immediate problem concerned Sir Cecil's watchers. Had they finished their searching or were they still active? Having blown their cover, Ross felt that it was unlikely that they were still around, but he was not going to take any chances. Should he park his car in Jack's drive and brazen it out? It was often seen there. Or should he park next to the church around the corner, come and go by the garden gate at the rear, and walk along the edge of the sports field, risking prying eyes?

He had settled on a slight variation. He made the plausible suggestion that Margaret should use his car to ferry all of the children, while he used hers. He had parked in Jack's driveway so that any watchers driving by would not see his own car and he would not need to risk the walk along the sports field in the morning. Nevertheless, he waited for the milkman to go by and checked the street from the bedroom window just in case. Similarly, he was as quiet as possible opening and closing house and car doors so that he could make a quick exit before anyone was up at a window. After a morning at work he would return for the afternoon while the children were at school, provided that Margaret had not decided to stay at Sarah's drinking coffee.

* * *

It never felt like a Monday morning at Mannington; every day, every night was the same. The world never slept. Somebody somewhere needed to be recorded or watched. At his desk, Ross was presented with a list of priority intelligence that had come in over the last few days and had been collated. Near the top was a transcript of the telephone conversation between Sheikh Faisal and Sheikh Abdullatif about Mark Tanner. Ross read the text in its original Arabic to appreciate fully all of the nuances. Were they talking cryptically? Factually? Theoretically? After some discussion with his night staff, he decided to speak to Marcus as soon as he came in.

There are places where a white-haired man in a charcoal-grey three-piece suit looks right. Four floors below an airfield in the middle of Gloucestershire on a wet Monday morning was not one of them. Marcus had to go to London later for the inquiry into the *Ikiz* fiasco, so had dressed appropriately, but in the meantime had taken off his jacket to hide any incongruity. He still managed to look like a veteran snooker player. What earthly reason could there be for Mannington staff to wear a collar and tie when there was absolutely zero chance of anyone visiting them?

By the time Marcus was standing next to Ross, the somewhat cryptic telephone call from Empty recording his telephone call to Jack had been added to the pile for analysis and evaluation. How the world had moved on in just a few weeks. Marcus deeply regretted Jack's recruitment, if that was the word for it, of Mark Tanner. Now that the *Ikiz* affair was a dead duck, Tanner represented an accident waiting to happen. Marcus hoped that Jack could call him off via a quick personal visit in Riyadh before any accident occurred.

"What's this Mumtaz Building meant to be?" Marcus asked.

"I've no idea. It hasn't cropped up in anything else."

"Do we have an aerial of the building site?"

"Only a general high-level shot. It will be three hours

before we can get a detailed sequence. I am assuming it will not take us long to spot the building site he is describing?"

"We'd better check, but I expect our Mr Tanner is seeing potential missile tubes in every lift shaft and nuclear bunkers in every basement."

"Do you think the sheikhs have simply had enough of our nosy parker, or is there something more sinister?"

"We must be careful ourselves that we don't see 'murder' every time 'exit visa' crops up, and 'warhead' every time 'Turkish carpet' appears."

"They're up to something, I know it."

"Undoubtedly, but I wonder if any of it is really of British national interest?"

"Shall I find out what this Mumtaz Building is supposed to be?"

"Yes, and get the new aerials. Get our lot to see if everything's kosher, if you can have that in an Islamic holy city. I'll ring Jack to make sure that he calls Tanner off. We'll go on monitoring the sheikhs for old times' sake, but nothing more."

* * *

"Hello, Jack, it's Harry," Marcus began.

"Hello there. What a surprise." Jack was about to go down to lunch in his hotel; it was a day off before the meetings resumed.

"Jack, I'm speaking to our supporters later today about the future. I'll let you know where you'll be based on your return, hopefully."

"Excellent. Thanks."

"How was Geneva?"

"Refreshing."

"I hope that you are not going to bring me back a Turkish carpet. I've got enough Turkish carpets to last me a lifetime. In fact, don't waste time looking for one."

"Not much fear of that in Riyadh, but I was going down the souk tonight."

"Well, if you see a Turkish carpet seller, tell him the market's flooded."

"I'll call as soon as I can. When I get back to the UK, maybe we could have a beer?"

"Good idea."

Jack and Marcus had agreed a few code words before Jack had left Mannington, but not to cover every eventuality. 'The market's flooded', however, meant that Mark Tanner should be called off. Jack would get driven around to Empty's flat tonight about seven o'clock.

Before he had finished thinking through all of the implications of what Marcus had said, the telephone rang again.

"James Melrose speaking."

"Jack … it's Victoria." There was no point disguising her voice or changing her name. If they were monitoring the call they would trace it to her whatever she said or did.

"Ugh … hello." Jack was thrown off balance.

"I tried to call you in Geneva."

"Why? Is something wrong?"

"No. Not really. I wanted you to know that the … foundation is not what you're looking for—"

Jack could only think of Sir Cecil's men listening to this conversation. Why was she calling him like this? "Victoria, I'll speak to you when I get back."

"—but that's not why I am phoning. Well, not phoning now, if you see what I mean." Her prepared script had gone out of the window the moment she had heard his voice.

"Victoria, this is not a great idea."

"Jack! Jack! Look up the name of the boat in a dictionary." She was trying hard not to use the word '*Ikiz*'.

"Why?" Jack could see no point in stopping now; he was probably doomed.

"It means 'twin'! There are two of them!"

* * *

Despite being underground in Gloucestershire, Marcus could not escape the feeling that he was in the Middle East. He was staring at a dull brass coffee pot full of pencils and pens that sat on his desk – a present from some former colleague who was based in Oman – and listening to the air-conditioning system. In three hours' time he was off to London to present the reasons why so much of HM Government's time, money and effort had gone into boarding a small ship carrying Turkish house furnishings; hence the three-piece suit, and hence his preoccupation. To make matters worse, there was no coffee … yet. The excuse given was that it had rained solidly last night, although how this had prevented a large van from bringing the supplies to Mannington, Marcus was not party to.

The direct telephone on his desk rang. No doubt it would be London calling to wind him up before this afternoon.

"Billingham," he answered, achieving that Civil Service balance between authority in case the caller was of lesser status, and deference in case they were higher.

"It's Jack."

It was Marcus's turn to be thrown. "Hello, Jack." Deference, authority and everything else went out of the window … metaphorically speaking, of course.

"I've just looked up '*Ikiz*' in my handy pocket-sized dictionary," Jack lied, "and it means 'twin'. I think that there are two boats. We followed the wrong one, as we were probably meant to do."

There was silence.

"While you are at it," Jack continued, "I wouldn't waste too much time on the Mumtaz Building. I am inclined to think that it may be clean."

"Very interesting," Marcus said, with his mind in several places at once.

"I will try to see my new friend tonight."

"Yes, definitely. Tell him to go on holiday quickly."

Everyone relevant to the Middle East or the Eastern Mediterranean was summoned to the meeting room from their stations. Marcus was not going to breathe a word of this to London until he was one hundred per cent sure of his facts. He could not risk another fiasco. There was only one real question – where was the *Ikiz 2*? Marcus was hoping that it could be found by the time he walked into his in camera inquiry that afternoon.

With everyone gathered together, the meeting took less than five minutes and Marcus spent the next quarter of an hour ringing all of those people in the sections covering Arabia, the Black Sea or the Mediterranean who were at home. He grew weary of saying, "Hello, it's Harry. Aunt Mary is not too good, I'm afraid. She's in hospital … bring some clothes. You can always stay here if you need to stop over … I don't think she's going to make it."

With ironic timing, the tranche of information partly grouped together by Victoria at GCHQ reached the attention of Ross and his colleagues. Marcus was soon back in front of the monitors to hear the secret – but not threatening – raison d'être of the Mumtaz Fateen Foundation. The next few hours saw a frantic level of activity at the expense of all but critical other work. Satellite sequences were scrutinised again. Northern Turkish port records were retrieved and revisited. The details of the *Ikiz 1* and its crew were studied for anything relevant to its sister ship. Telephone calls between 'Nabil' and 'Gregory' were replayed for missed clues.

Marcus waited in the wings, rehearsing his lines, which was made all the more difficult as he did not know the play's ending. He practised the bullish 'I'm pleased to announce to this inquiry ...' and the apologetic 'I am sorry that the misconstruction of an unusual combination of intelligence ...' Between these two extremes, he was not too sure what approach to take. For certain, he would not be risking his neck further.

By the time that he left Mannington in the chauffeur-driven car, nothing had been found. Perhaps the first *Ikiz* had been lost very soon after construction? Perhaps they had named her replacement *Ikiz*? Perhaps the owner was a twin himself?

* * *

The inquiry was an informal affair held in a small committee room. It was predictable, without point-scoring from either side. Sir Cecil was so happy with his work that he was beyond rubbing Mannington's nose in the dirt. The general drift of the investigation centred on the inappropriateness of the boarding. The apparent weight of the evidence in favour of the *Ikiz* carrying nuclear material or equipment was not disputed. The inquiry decided that the ship should have been followed through Suez and the Red Sea. The SAS or SBS should have been geared up to deal with any matters arising once the proof of the cargo had been revealed by the unloading at the Red Sea Villas. The relative isolation of the villas on the flat, deserted coast would have made the task as straightforward as such ventures can ever be.

Sir Cecil was content that no harm had been done and that lessons had been learnt. He would report the outcome to the Foreign Secretary. As he wore a permanent expression of self-satisfaction, no one could guess how happy Sir Cecil actually was.

"Cecil, could I have a few seconds of your time?" Marcus asked afterwards when they were separated from the other departing participants.

"Of course. How can I help?"

"Jack's back from Riyadh in a couple of weeks. I would like him to take up his old job at Mannington."

"I can see no problem, so long as you monitor his domestic situation and he keeps his personnel officer informed of what's happening."

"Thank you. I'll let Jack know."

* * *

Jack had been staying in an American-owned hotel in Switzerland, and now he was staying in a Swiss-owned hotel in Saudi Arabia. The British Embassy was in Jeddah on the Red Sea Coast and there was not enough official accommodation in Riyadh for the British contingent at the OPEC follow-up meetings – so a hotel it had to be. This was about to change since the King had ordained that a new Diplomatic Quarter be created on the edge of Riyadh; a move about which the multinational diplomats were not entirely enthusiastic. Jeddah was cosmopolitan (if there is such a thing in Saudi Arabia); Riyadh was ultra-conservative and religiously correct. Jack read with a smile that, to avoid accusations of favouritism or intrigue, the proposed location of each embassy had been pulled out of a hat. Unfortunately, as with so many attempts at fairness, certain combinations were thrown up that should have been prevented by that master of intrigue, serendipity. Iran came up next to Iraq and the UK found itself next to Argentina. There were, of course, no Israeli or Soviet Embassies, but you would not have got long odds on them being next to the Palestine Liberation Organisation or the American plots.

Jack walked out of the air-conditioned shade of the foyer into the glare of the city. He had changed his mind and ordered one of the ubiquitous limousine taxis, a General Motors extravaganza with white-walled tyres, that was waiting for him at the kerbside. A small Filipino jockey (or so he seemed) in a uniform and cap stood ready to open the door. Two Lebanese businessmen in shiny light grey suits, also waiting for a taxi, exchanged insults about Jack in Arabic. Their heavy jowls, with permanent dark six o'clock shadow, barely moved as they cursed Jack, cursed 'Americans', cursed Jack's parentage and his sexual preference for goats and camels.

When one works in secret establishments or organisations, whether GCHQ or the SAS, the desire to brag about one's escapades or knowledge soon disappears. The rest of us would want to tell everyone we meet about our life, especially after a few drinks down the local pub. The one time when Jack had to bite his lip was when Arabs talked about him in his presence. They would never dream that his mastery of their language, culture, innuendo and insults was at such a high level. The things people said when they thought that you couldn't understand.

Jack encouraged Sammy the chauffeur to slow down a little. It was hard to tell whether he was using the large steering wheel to manoeuvre the car or as something to hang on to while he bounced up and down in his seat. When he had his two feet firmly fixed on the pavement of Sitteen Street, Jack smoothed back his hair and took a couple of calming breaths. He had looked on a map and knew where Empty lived. He chose a meandering route in and out of a modern shopping arcade where French fashion, German porcelain and Dutch flowers sat forlornly, like puppies begging to be bought. There was not a single other shopper in the complex; at least he knew that he was not being followed.

He had heard the police sirens echoing down the corridors of the arcade. There was no reason to presume that they had anything to do with him. He was about to turn into a side street when he saw someone being pushed into the first of two police cars outside Empty's block of flats. Jack nonchalantly stepped across the road junction, crossed back over Sitteen Street and walked around the arcade for a few minutes before getting back into the waiting limousine which took him back to the hotel.

CHAPTER TWENTY-THREE

Bees buzzed and chaffinches trilled in the apple trees; the orchard typified the rural idyll. Marcus shut the kitchen door of his Cotswold farmhouse and walked under the obligatory spreading walnut into a grassy paddock. The roughness of the old, greying oak encrusted with lichen pressed into his soft forearms as he rested on the orchard gate. He was in contemplative mood. When things go off the rails, they rarely jump back on. Just before he had come home from Mannington he had heard from Jack about Empty's possible arrest, and he was now evaluating all of the options. While he did this, Mother Nature all around him maximised the use of the daylight with summer just beginning. The sky was a milky blue and a low, warm sun threw the trunks of the trees into sharp relief. His mind had wandered off, but as he looked down at the cracked, dry earth at his feet, he was brought back to reality. There was no point in regretting past events, he told himself. What should Mannington do about the present and the immediate future?

Always tempting is the 'do nothing' option; it gives the illusion that you have made a conscious decision and hands the outcome to others, or just to Fate herself. Perhaps Mark Tanner would be released? Perhaps he would not say anything about meeting Jack? Perhaps it was all a big mistake? At the other end of the scale is the 'confess all' option; this meant telling Sir Cecil and putting all of HM Government's resources behind sorting it out. Pride would never let Marcus do this. In between these two extremes were the messy possibilities such as the 'let Jack investigate quietly' option, and the one that Marcus was beginning to favour; namely, the 'let Julian Prior-Jones investigate very quietly' option. Julian was a good friend of Jack's from the old days who also did not hold Sir Cecil in high esteem after a small incident which involved a drunken escapade with a couple of European ambassadors in Bahrain.

Marcus seemed to be being given advice by everything around him. The long-gone voice of his young daughter sellotaping a pear to an apple tree encouraged him into gentle deception. The yellow-eyed cuckoo with barred breast who used the orchard as its personal fiefdom suggested letting others do the hard work. However, the menacing 'kraark' of the grey heron flying back to its treetop roost warned Marcus not to underestimate Sir Cecil.

* * *

While Marcus was communing with nature, at Mannington tired eyes were scanning transcripts and photographs trying to find the *Ikiz 2*, or, at least, whether she existed. Periods and areas of search were widened, but the Black Sea, Eastern Mediterranean and Red Sea are huge expanses of water.

* * *

"Omar! You old … Jordanian!"

"I am not old, Julian."

"Not a bloody Jordanian either, come to that!"

"How can I help the British Embassy Attaché for Dirty Things?" The benign and smiling police sergeant leant back in his chair.

"If there were no dirty things, we wouldn't have jobs."

"You are right."

"Someone told me you had another stupid Brit in your cells caught with a case of whisky in the boot of his car. Don't touch the stuff myself," Julian added, rather unnecessarily as everyone knew that he drank gin at a rate which could threaten the long-term survival of juniper on earth.

"No. You are told incorrectly."

"I could have stayed in bastard bed. What time is it? Ten o'clock!"

"We have no British person in our cells."

"Glad to hear it. Glad to hear it."

"We have a person from Greekland."

"Greenland, did you say?"

"No. Greek. He is here and his wife and childrens are in their house with a policeman."

"Visa problems? Always the bastard same."

"No. Drugs."

"Drugs?!" Julian was not prepared for that.

"Yes. Very much."

"Just him and his family? Nobody else involved?"

"That I cannot say at the moment."

241

* * *

Jack bumped across the compacted sand towards a dozen villas. The development had absolutely no reason to be there and nothing had been done to the desert outside of the high garden walls – no road, no pavement, nothing. Clouds of dust billowed up behind the car. He found the inverted 'V' on the wall that indicated the number eight in Arabic and pulled up outside the villa. At least there was no shortage of parking space – about a square mile by the look of it. He pressed the entryphone button.

"Hello?" A fuzzy, metallic voice emanated from the speaker.

"James Melrose to see Francis."

"Hi. Fine. Come in."

There was a buzzing noise and a clang as the painted steel gate opened. Jack stepped inside to a patch of enclosed desert that was remarkably similar to the desert outside of the walls. He walked up to the big wooden door, which opened as he skipped up the tiled steps.

Francis proved to be tall and blond, with a '50s rock-and-roll quiff which occurred naturally without oil or hairspray. He had blue eyes and a demeanour which suggested that he had just got over a major trauma; confident but chastened.

"What can I get you to drink?" Big hands on thin arms waved towards the kitchen.

"A cup of tea would be fine, thanks."

"Oh, sorry, I don't have tea or coffee. I don't drink them myself. Water? Orange juice?"

"Water, thanks."

"Excellent." The hands were still in motion docking jumbos at their terminal gate or directing cars in a temporary car park as he walked into the kitchen. "Have you known Empty long?" Francis's voice was accompanied by the clatter of saucepan lids as he tried to remove a drying glass from the draining board.

"No. We met in London a while back. It seemed a shame not to meet him while I was in Riyadh."

"Of course." The conversation continued through the open lounge door.

"I tried to phone him last night but there was no reply," Jack prompted.

"He didn't say he was going out last night. He may have popped out to a cassette shop. They become a bit addictive at that price, and with nothing else to do …"

"Was he at work today?"

"No … but that's not surprising. Sheikh Faisal uses him on so many schemes … mostly at short notice."

Francis brought two glasses of water, placing them on the standard feature of all Saudi villas and flats – the smoked-glass coffee table. Jack reached across for his drink, accidentally touching the metal rim of the table. He was jolted by the shock of static electricity.

"One of the joys of Saudi Arabia," Francis apologised.

"How long have you been out here?" Jack asked.

"Five months."

"Why are you here in this villa while Empty lives in the centre of Riyadh?"

"No reason, really. I am halfway to the Nefud-al-aan site here and Empty needs to be nearer to the sheikh. But I expect it had more to do with where there was a space at the time of arrival." Francis added, "Empty sleeps here sometimes, and I sleep in his flat if I need to go into Riyadh."

Jack made a mental note that Francis must therefore have a key to Empty's flat … but how to borrow it?

"Randy's gone to Dammam." Francis was musing on why there was no reply at the flat.

"Who's Randy?"

"Randy Coleman is a Canadian who was at the flat for a few days."

Jack was getting no nearer. "Can I be honest with you, Francis? I'm a little worried that Empty has had an epileptic fit. You know he's epileptic?"

"Yes, of course, but he's been all right since he's been out here, I think."

Jack left the silence hanging in the air.

"I hadn't thought about that … he has been under a bit of stress lately, come to think of it."

Francis went to fetch another bottle of cold water, returning with a biscuit tin in his hand. It took the form of an English thatched cottage with roses around the door and doves on the roof; the rectilinear shape of the tin was better suited to a Saudi villa but that may not have been a bestseller.

"You've got me worried now." Francis had been rerunning some moments of the recent past involving Empty. "He makes jokes about everything so it's hard to know what he's really thinking. I am worried."

Not as worried as you should be, Jack thought to himself, imagining Empty in some Saudi jail. "I could, of course, call in on my way back to the hotel," he suggested. "I could telephone you from the flat," he added as a tempting afterthought.

"Yes, good idea. If he's not there, leave the key on the table by the telephone. I can pick up another one from work."

With that, Jack got out of the armchair and waited for

Francis to get the key. He came back quickly and wished Jack well in his errand.

"Please phone as soon as you know, won't you?"

"Of course."

Jack left Francis muttering on the doorstep; a scenario not unfamiliar to a Jehovah's Witness. He drove back into the city not knowing what he would find. Every minute that passed he regretted getting involved at the sharp end, but it was too late now. Why had Mannington not left well alone and stayed at the … whatever the opposite of the sharp end was? The stern? The blunt end? He was ashamed to admit to himself that he was more worried about the consequences for Mannington and him personally, than for Empty.

* * *

To the uninitiated, the noisy, long room with the overlapping queues of animated people from all over the world probably looked like the Tower of Babel had fallen over. There was no guidance and no logical or obvious system; in fact, not much to indicate that this was an Exchange House; an essential facility to anyone who wanted to change Saudi cash into, primarily, cheques. This applied to most people. People filled out white forms leaning on walls, on books; in fact, on any surface that was not moving or greasy. Everyone was asking questions; everyone was shouting replies or opinions, or shaking their head. Eventually they found themselves in a queue up to a grille, where the white forms were stamped and recorded. This pointless act appeared to give you the right to proceed to another zigzagging line across the centre of the vast room. At the front of this queue a bored Indian stuffed wads of riyals into a machine that counted them by flicking the notes at eye-blurring speed. There was no security grille. He stamped the white forms, securing one around the riyals with an elastic band. Another of the white forms was given back so that you could join a slower moving line which headed to a corner of the room. Several more Egyptians and Indians took the now-greying forms and typed out cheques on antiquated Adler machines. The large, multicoloured cheques were cheapened by the crude, misaligned typescript pronouncing '1,652 – 20 Pds. Stg' or '3,324 – 30 US Dlrs.' It paid to watch your name being typed because mistakes could not be rectified afterwards.

Clutching his multi-franked form, Empty had joined the final queue heading to the manager's desk near the door. Each person's eyes followed their own cheque's progress from the typewriter around the periphery of the room, crossing various tables and acquiring various signatures. Empty needed the final manager's signature before he could cross the street and post this next cheque back to England. The manager certainly tried to add interest to what must be one of the most tedious jobs in Saudi Arabia. He got up and walked around for no apparent reason. The queue lengthened. He shuffled the cheques so that they didn't match the order of the people in the queue. And then, finally, he turned his signature into a calligraphic extravaganza which he performed with mechanical arm movements that sped up, slowed down, sped up, paused and ended in a flourish. The result looked like the wiring diagram for a small power station.

Empty handed over his now dog-eared form in exchange for the cheque. The first time he had visited he had made helpful comments and suggestions at every stage, including asking the manager why there were no free pens like at Barclays back home. That visit had taken over half an hour, to the annoyance of those behind him. Today it had taken twenty-five minutes to change his wad of riyals into a sterling cheque because he had kept quiet, mostly by actually biting his lower lip. Why did they make everything so complicated?

He was heading for the bright sunlight of the main door when he heard the sirens. Across the street, armed police were running into his block of flats, shouting at each other, their cars blocking the road with red and blue lights flashing. The queues in the Exchange House knitted together as people pressed for a better look at what was happening. Empty put his cheque in his pocket and found a discreet place from which to watch but not be seen. He tried to join up all of the dishdashas and djellabas before him into an enclosing wallpaper, but failed. His heart thumped and his mouth was dry. Had Sheikh Faisal called the police? Had Empty asked too many questions about the library, or been overheard recording his call to Jack, or … it did not matter, he was in big shit. He pulled the cheque back out and looked at it. He may need to change it back into riyals. It was clear that he could not go back to his flat.

Moving against the swell of humanity eager for a look, Empty made his way down the side of the Exchange House to the quiet of a recessed door. To his great relief, there was no one to be seen, if you excluded the goat tethered in the back of an old sheikh's pickup. Two sacks of riyals tied with a cord leant against the cab's rear window. Empty was mesmerised by them. Strangers in his head, all speaking in his own voice, urged him to take a sack (after all, he was a fugitive now and would need money) or not to take a sack (and to make his way to the British Consulate and hand himself in).

The sun beat down relentlessly. The sirens wailed. The goat was the only witness to Empty's decision. Its pale, penetrating eye followed him away from his flat down the side road. Its mouth chewed absent-mindedly as if rehearsing some speech. *Why are the most momentous decisions of one's life always made on the spur of the moment?* it might have been saying. Then again.

CHAPTER TWENTY-FOUR

From the elevated soundproof translation booth, the conversation was distant but also immediate coming through the headphones. He could see nothing but the conference floor beneath him and hear nothing except the repetitive witterings of the delegates in his ears. There was no escape from this aural and visual tedium.

As a hand came down on his shoulder, Jack jumped. He pulled off the headphones to find Julian Prior-Jones beaming at him.

"Why, you …!"

"Listening to the football results? How are the Arsenal doing?"

"Losing to Riyadh Rovers, by the sound of it," Jack replied.

"How are you, you old bastard?"

"I'm fine. How are you?"

"Never thought that you would dirty your brogues with desert dust again. I thought that your feet were firmly on the rungs to heaven or Century House, whichever is higher?"

They both were both reasonably happy that they could talk freely in the small soundproofed booth.

"Any news of our man?" Jack asked.

"Just enlighten your old mate a bit further on the 'our', could you?"

"In this instance, 'our' means my place, not London, if you see what I mean."

"And 'my place' means Cheltenham or just outside it?"

"Just outside it."

"Really? There's a bastard turn-up for the books." Julian rested his large backside on a corner table designed to take a small control unit and microphone.

"Any news? Just between you and me?" Jack persisted.

"No idea where he is. He's not in jail, if that helps."

"Are they looking for him?"

"I'm not sure."

"Julian, it would be seriously embarrassing for me personally and HMG generally if he was to be … interviewed."

"I gathered that from your call. I have to say that I think it might be the chap across his landing who has been locked up."

"What for?"

"Growing a few too many houseplants in his spare bedroom and smoking the bastard clippings."

"Our friend is not involved, is he?"

"The police are not looking for anyone else but they may well speak to all Europeans in the block of flats."

"Are there many?"

"Just our friend."

"Ah." Jack stared down through the glass at the ring of tables with a forlorn flower display trying to fill the hole in the centre. Apart from an occasional hand movement, little activity could be seen from the delegates. "I have a key to his flat. I was going to pop around, have a look, you know?"

"Not a brilliant idea, old friend. Let me have a butcher's. I know the policeman in charge if anything happens. And, worse comes to worse, I can claim DI, which you cannot."

"That's kind of you. I have no idea what sort of immunity I have with this delegation. None, I expect."

"Shall I leave him a note in the flat?"

"Good idea." Jack took out a small pocket diary and flicked through its pages. He scribbled on the writing pad before him and tore off the sheet.

"'Please phone Jack ASAP on …' what number's this?" Julian read out aloud.

"It's a recorded-message service in London. It is not connected with me in any way. By the way, he knows me as James Melrose, should you bump into him."

"What does he look like?"

Jack gave Julian a brief description.

"I'll go round to the flat now. When are you back at the hotel?"

"I'll leave now, as well."

"Aren't you meant to be translating this rubbish?" Julian nodded through the window.

"No. I'm meant to be picking up trends, listening in foyers, you know?"

"Spent my bastard life hanging around foyers. See you at your hotel in an hour."

* * *

Ross Smith leant against the back of his chair in that way used by people to distance themselves from a subject while looking for an answer. He folded his arms behind his head awkwardly and sucked in the air around him. Inspiration was in short supply. The *Ikiz 2* existed, and still existed. He knew when it was built, where it was built, how much it cost and who owned it. He did not know where it was now, when it last set sail and where it was going. The thing that was testing his mind the most was why it was not registered as setting sail about the same time as the *Ikiz 1*. They had the dates and information from the other sources. There was no trace on the satellite photographs and no record at Trabzon or any nearby Turkish port. He rocked forwards towards his monitors, trying to recall the data on the *Ikiz 1*. When, and from where exactly, did she sail? He needed to remind himself. The image of the *Ikiz 1* taken some weeks before scrolled down on one of the screens. It was in the eastern Black Sea near Sukhumi. Where was her twin? Where was her identical twin?

It came to him in a flash. On the next monitor he called back up the image of the ship he and Marcus had looked at while she was sailing in the Sea of Marmara. Something was different. On closer inspection, several things were different. Which was which? What Mannington was calling the *Ikiz 1* was filmed, as predicted, being loaded in the eastern Black Sea. Between Trabzon and Istanbul the *Ikiz 1* disappeared and the *Ikiz 2* appeared. The *Ikiz 2* was followed across the Mediterranean, stopped by the frigate, found to be clean and allowed to deliver its carpets to the Red Sea Villas. So, where did the *Ikiz 1* go? Did she hide along the Turkish coast, or in Haydarpaşa port at Istanbul? If so, where was she now? Or did she sail through that first night so that she was long gone when Mannington picked up her sister ship sailing in full view?

"Very clever. Very, very clever," Ross whispered to himself. He called Marcus and told him. The rest of his colleagues were given the task of checking the two main theories: was the *Ikiz 1* behind, in which case she could still be stopped; or was she in front, in which case she had already unloaded, and, if so, where? The Red Sea Villas or somewhere else? So many questions and so little time.

* * *

Julian Prior-Jones parked on Sitteen Street and waddled along the pavement, mopping his brow. In his other hand, he carried a long brown envelope containing an embassy questionnaire; a load of boring but uncontroversial questions about your job, predicted length of stay, UK contact telephone numbers and so on. It was his standard excuse if ever stopped while contacting a British national: 'I was just getting him to fill in our questionnaire.'

The sweat had penetrated his buff linen jacket down the centre of his back by the time he reached the gatehouse outside Empty's block of flats. "*Marhaba*," he said to the doorman sitting in his murky hovel. A waft of paraffin overpowered every other smell. Julian asked the doorman if Mr Tanner was at home, but this elicited absolutely no response. He did not appear to have seen him come or go, which was surprising as Empty would have needed to have walked within a yard of him to get in or out.

Julian trudged up the marble stairs, eschewing the lift. He wanted the maximum time to see what was happening on Empty's floor. 'Nothing' fairly summed it up, if you excluded a trail of ants carrying the dismembered parts of a cockroach. Julian paused before ringing Empty's doorbell, listening for activity behind the four heavy front doors surrounding him.

Nothing. He turned around, tapping his brown envelope, looking as if he was begging help from someone watching through their spyhole. Nothing. He put the key in Empty's door and stepped inside, leaving the key in place. He would always say that that was how he had found it. Julian walked along the internal corridor, expecting to be hit or grabbed by waiting policemen. Nothing.

"Hello? Mr Tanner?"

No one was around and no one had followed him in. He took the key from the door, shut it and flicked the deadlock. The first thing he did was to place Jack's note on the coffee table. He snapped his hand back from a jolt of static electricity off the chrome frame.

"Bastard thing," he cursed quietly.

Empty's belongings were few and far between. The contents of two suitcases do not fill a large flat. Julian went through the drawers in the bedroom, through the pockets of a jacket on the back of a chair, and through Empty's briefcase, but found nothing. The bathroom and kitchen likewise offered nothing of interest, so he returned to the lounge. Next to the telephone was a pad, and on this he found a note. It read, 'Amira (Mohammed is her father)', and gave a Riyadh telephone number. How did Empty know an Arab woman? Who was she?

Julian was relieved to find no illegal plants growing in the spare bedrooms, and left as nonchalantly as a short fifteen-stone man can, flushed in the face and needing a gin and tonic. He did not know what to make of Mark Tanner's absence. He obviously hadn't been to the flat for a while. The milk in the fridge was days old and the dust lay too perfectly across the glass tables. Yet he hadn't been picked up by the police, so where was he?

When Julian reached Jack's hotel, he telephoned the number on Empty's pad to establish Mohammed's identity. This was easily done, and he passed on all of the information to Jack before making excuses to return to the consulate, where he intended to top up his quinine levels, helped by a tincture of juniper.

* * *

Despite his large hands, Quentin White was adept at using his keyboard. He had the workstation next to Ross and had been given the unenviable task of flicking through the satellite images of the Suez Canal, looking for the other *Ikiz*. After a few hours he felt like screaming at the sight of yet another tanker or container ship. Quentin, however, was the favourite in the betting ring that had developed on the 'Arab' floor to be the first to spot the boat. It was argued that the Suez Canal represented a pinch point through which it must sail. He had countered this by suggesting that the Bosporus or Dardanelles were far more likely and had less traffic.

"If she travels only at night, we'll never see her, will we?" someone asked.

"Would she need to stop for anything?"

So the speculation and ideas flowed.

"Is there any shipyard or repair shed under which she might be hidden for a while?"

"No idea."

"What about the Suez Canal? They must have records?"

And so it was almost a dead heat one hour later when Quentin shouted, "Eureka!" and an anonymous voice across the room, searching the Suez Canal logs, came up with the days and times of entry.

"Before or after?" Ross was standing up.

"Before," Quentin replied.

"Right! Quentin, you follow her southwards using SATINT, and Tony, you follow her back in time across the Med. Find out if she stopped or linked up with any other ship – or should that be boat? I never know the difference."

The hum of excitement and expectation even exceeded that produced by the electronics. Marcus could no longer sit in his office waiting for updates. He prowled among the workstations, scanning screens and reading logs. As another cry of success went up, he would saunter over to peer down upon the ridiculously small vessel that was the focus of the entire room. But in his mind's eye he was not seeing a Turkish trawler; it was Sir Cecil's face. A face fighting to keep control as Marcus explained the new situation.

"She's approaching the Red Sea Villas!"

The weight of interest within the room moved to Quentin. A few minutes later a voice called out, "She didn't stop at Istanbul!"

"She's gone past the Red Sea Villas!"

This last call surprised everyone, and the euphoria was tempered as people extrapolated as to where she might be going.

"Jeddah?"

"No! Surely not."

"Yes if the stuff is going to the so-called library."

"Yemen?"

"Oh, Christ, I hope not!"

"The Emirates?"

"Never."

Nobody dared say Iran or Iraq, but the possibility passed through everyone's mind in the following silence.

Little happened for almost an hour, and the time began to drag.

"I hope she pulls in soon," Quentin prayed quietly to himself, but was overheard by Marcus.

"Why?"

"Because we'll run out of satellite coverage. It begins its spiral to the South Atlantic."

"Oh, great! Then we'll have twenty-four hours of useless pictures of the Sahara and the Amazon rainforest." Marcus went off to top up his caffeine level. "Where is she now?" He was back, sipping coffee from a plastic cup.

"I've scrolled forward. She's off Qatar. Halfway up the Arabian Gulf."

"But still out to sea?"

"Yes."

"And how much more satellite time?"

"Half a day's worth."

"Jesus."

Ross was trying to compile a report in parallel with all of the search activity, knowing that Marcus would require it immediately. It had just been established that the ships had been switched at Samsun on the north Turkish coast. The *Ikiz 1* had sailed through the next two nights while the *Ikiz 2* had dawdled in daylight, attracting all attention.

"I've run out of coverage," Quentin proclaimed to the room.

"Damn!"

"But the good news is that she has stopped."

"What do you mean, 'stopped'?"

"Moored. Anchored."

"Where?"

"Just offshore of the Sabaramco oil terminal."

* * *

Empty was feeling alone and exposed. Why were the police looking for him? Was it for spying? Was it for associating with Yiannis the Greek? Or both? He couldn't risk going back to his flat or his places of work; it began to dawn on him that he had nowhere to go. And who could he trust? So many of his acquaintances and colleagues seemed interconnected. In fact, he couldn't think of anyone he knew whom he had not met through work.

Then there was the small problem of his passport (or, rather, the lack of it) and an exit visa (or lack of it). How could he leave the country?

His immediate problem was finding a place to sleep. That first evening he had walked a few blocks away, looking for inspiration, when he had passed a new unlet office development. Major building works looked complete but they were still in the fitting-out stage. He squeezed between two lengths of chain-link fence that were more to keep out goats than people, and walked around the back. There were no vagrants and no burglary in Saudi Arabia, which made entering a back office very easy; the doors were not even locked. He gave the lifts a miss and crept up the stairs, fearing that there might be someone around. The first big room he entered had a bare concrete floor and would have been more than uncomfortable, and reminded him of the prison cell that he would be occupying soon if he did not work out what to do. The next room was more promising as it contained a dozen or so rolls of dark red carpet, some barely used. He arranged them into a sort of low throne configuration that resembled an Ottoman majlis. The smell of new wool carpet was strangely reminiscent of his childhood, and Empty ended up falling asleep almost immediately with one arm wrapped around a large roll. It was a poor substitute for Dawn but proved very tolerant of his night-time mutterings.

He woke at first light because of the lack of curtains or blinds, and freed himself from what now resembled a collapsed log cabin. What now? The British Consulate seemed like a good bet initially, but how would they get him out of the country? Stories of fugitives holed up in embassies for years made the idea unappealing. It might seem like the safe option, but was it? What about his new friends and colleagues?

After a few minutes pondering this, he decided not to contact any of his non-Arab friends as it would only compromise them and there was nothing that they could realistically do. They would be the first people the police would visit and interview; better that they knew nothing. So, which of his Arab friends could he really trust? Kamal seemed the most likely but Empty did not want to put him in an intolerable position. The list was getting shorter. Actually, there was only one name left – Amira. Would she help him? Probably not, and this was not England; he could not just telephone her or knock on her father's villa gate. And yet, the idea would not leave him.

He boarded a bus displaying the yellow diamond symbol that signified its route, paid his riyal and joined the manual workers on their early morning commute. After breakfast in an over-lit doughnut and milkshake diner, he made his way to the souk where shutters were being raised, goods were being spread on the dirt and feral dogs were stretching themselves awake. The Bedouin did not bat an eyelid as Empty bought a beaten face mask and a black abaya. Together with the male headdress, or *ghutrah*, these represented the only items expat workers could take back as souvenirs or gifts. Ironically, most of the red-and-white patterned cloths were made in Yorkshire. The Bedouin would have been a little more surprised to see Empty emerge from behind a rusting shipping container wearing his recent purchases. Only his brown eyes and hands remained uncovered.

He timed to perfection the approach to his offices, such that he was not required to hang around for too long before the Chevrolet drew up outside, driven by the Filipino chauffeur. Amira emerged, draped in black, to be met at the car door by another figure in black.

"Amira, it's me, Empty. I need your help. Can we get in the car? I'll explain later."

Whether it was because she did not have time to think about the consequences, or was just stunned, Amira opened the car door and got back in, quickly followed by Empty.

"Where's my mother, Tommy?"

"At Sheikh Mustapha's villa," the chauffeur replied, finding it difficult to take his eyes off the rear-view mirror.

"And my father?"

"He is in Jeddah today."

"Could you take us home, please?"

The two 'women' stepped out of the station wagon into the ladies' entrance of Mohammed's sprawling villa. Amira walked through first, establishing that none of her sisters were around. She beckoned Empty inside.

"Are you in trouble?"

"Big trouble, but I'm not guilty of anything. Honest."

He majored on the Yiannis drugs angle in preference to the

espionage side of the situation, saying only that he thought that Sheikh Faisal may be involved in some bad things. She listened generously but told him that there was nothing she could do and that he would have to leave very soon. He asked her a whole series of questions starting with the Mumtaz Building, and she reassured him that it was a harmless organisation but that it preferred to keep quiet about what it was doing. Her father and many of her uncles and friends were involved.

Empty was reassured. "Who can I trust, Amira?"

"Kamal ... and my father, so long as it does not involve Sheikh Faisal. Empty, you must realise that almost all of the 'Arabs' you are working with are Palestinians, including my father. They were all born in Bethlehem or Gaza and have adopted another nationality. Your Jordanian, Syrian, Iraqi and Lebanese friends are all tied together by a common bond. Even Sheikh Faisal has a Palestinian mother and a Saudi father. They are all supporters of the PLO. Sheikh Faisal has given fortunes to them."

Empty was busy listening but wondering what this meant for all of the projects on which he had been working. "How can I get out of Saudi?"

"I have absolutely no idea. I am so sorry. I know that you are a good man."

"I cannot use my passport. I don't have my passport," he corrected himself. "I cannot get an exit visa without Sheikh Faisal. I am stuck."

"I can see that."

He stared around at the beautiful lounge. Being caught there would probably mean life imprisonment for him or worse, and probably the same for her. "Could Kamal help me? Would he?"

"He likes you very much, but what could he do? Don't you have any other British friends who could help?"

Randy Coleman sprang into Empty's head. "How could I get to the Sabaramco compound?"

"On the east coast?"

"Yes. Dammam."

"That's five hours' drive away."

"I know."

Amira stood up, and Empty thought that she was going to ask him to leave.

"It's Tommy's day off on Friday. What if I asked him to drive you there in one of our smaller cars?"

"Would he do it? Can he be trusted?"

"Yes, he is also a good man. I have helped him in the past and, anyway, I will pay him."

"Don't worry, I can pay him."

"Wait here."

When the arrangements had been made, he kissed one of the most gorgeous girls on earth goodbye. They would never see each other again.

* * *

Outwardly calm and confident, inwardly bubbling and confident, Marcus Billingham had to stop himself rehearsing his meeting with Sir Cecil in London later. He looked upwards at the ceiling of the lift to relax his neck muscles. His eyes dropped down to the notice warning him not to panic in the event of a fire and not to use the lifts. A strange place to put such a sign.

Harry Mumford, Mannington's Chief Liaison Officer for Soviet matters, was waiting for Marcus outside his room.

He looked like Dracula on a bad day and Ray Reardon, the snooker player, on a good day. Today was a good day, and he had a benevolent if puzzled look on his face under his slicked-back black hair.

"You look as if you've lost a fiver and found fifty pounds, or is it the other way round?" Marcus asked.

"I don't know what I've found."

They stepped into Marcus's room.

"Well, I've had an excellent day so anything you have found is a bonus."

"It's the only thing we have found from Bag Day. Anyone else found anything?"

"Do you know, I haven't even asked. We've had such a success on the *Ikiz* front that I put Bag Day right out of my mind."

Bag Day was the brainchild of Hamish Dawes' predecessor at the Vetting Department. He had suggested that, unbeknown to anyone at certain embassies abroad, the confidential shredder would be replaced for a day; to all intents and purposes it looked and sounded the same. The mass of paper would be collected up and brought back to England in the diplomatic bag. The vetters would check that embassy staff were not up to anything they should not be. Once Vetting had finished with the day's collected paperwork, it would be passed to Mannington, who would check that valuable information was not being thrown away and that they were fully aware of everything going on at the embassy. Bag Day moved around the world – Paris today, Tokyo next week and so on. Three days earlier it had been the turn of Moscow.

"What have you found?"

"Have you ever heard of Project Canute?"

"Don't think so … although I have a faint recollection of something."

"Nobody else seems to. This is a piece of paper from the shredder."

Marcus scanned the list of high-ranking Soviet politicians, generals and key individuals. Next to each name was a long line of numbers and asterisks. "No idea," he said. "I don't suppose that this is someone working on their own?"

"I don't think so. This is the other piece of paper … the cover sheet."

Marcus read the words 'SIR CECIL MACKAY: EYES ONLY: DIPLOMATIC BAG.'

CHAPTER TWENTY-FIVE

It is not just in bad movies that logic goes out of the window. Would you pick up a blood-stained knife found next to a corpse, thus putting your fingerprints all over it? Who knows? And in Empty's situation, would you have dressed as an Arab man carrying a briefcase, based on the premise that the police were looking for a Westerner? Having contacted Amira, he was greatly relieved not to be dressed as an Arab woman. Even greater relief came from the punctual arrival of Tommy driving Mohammed's Datsun estate.

"It's great to see you, Tommy." Empty opened a rear door and slipped inside.

Tommy's eyes beneath his spiky black crew cut showed a little surprise, but then he had seen Empty dressed in a shirt and tie, as an Arab woman, and now as a Saudi man complete with sunglasses and a pack of Marlboro cigarettes.

"Do you know the way to Dammam?" Empty asked. "Actually, 'Do You Know the Way to San Jose' does sound better. In fact, I wish you could take me to San Jose."

"Dammam, right?" Tommy was looking back at Empty in the rear-view mirror.

"Yes, the Sabaramco compound."

Empty settled back into his seat, relieved to be cocooned in a moving vehicle and hidden behind dark sunglasses. Even the presence of Tommy gave him some reassurance after the tortured loneliness of the last couple of days. He opened an American newspaper and began the five-hour journey eastwards across Saudi Arabia. He read for twenty-five minutes. He looked out of the window for five more. *I spy …* he thought to himself, but quickly stopped that train of thought.

"I probably owe you an explanation," Empty began, feeling a bond between one expat and another.

"No need."

"I just want you to know that I am … in disagreement with the Saudi authorities. I am not a murderer or a rapist. OK?"

"Sure thing." Tommy over-corrected the wheel, having been lulled into a false sense of security by the power steering and cruise control.

"All I want to do is get out of this country."

"I understand."

"I just need an exit visa, that's all."

The long silence that followed emphasised the enormity of the problem encompassed by 'that's all'.

Up to this point, Empty had managed to keep his spirits up, but the silence in the car and the monotonous brown moonscape out of the window gradually began to depress his mood. "Tommy, how do you cope out here?"

"I just drive," Tommy replied in his Spanish-American accent.

"But don't you think about things? Don't you think about your family back home?"

"I just drive. I am on a long journey in my car from Manila to Riyadh and back to Manila, and every day I am one day closer to Manila and my family."

"That's a great way to cope. Keep it simple, eh?"

"We are just on a car journey." Tommy lifted his eyes to the rear-view mirror.

Unfortunately I have just run out of petrol, Empty thought to himself, but he said nothing.

After what seemed like ten hours, not five, a mirage of date palms appeared. Ten minutes later the floating apparition settled on the surface of the desert behind a long, high wall. A frightening bronze sculpture symbolising the world forested with oil derricks dominated the main entrance. It looked like one of those huge Second World War mines washed up at the seaside. A bored guard did not look up from his television as they cruised through and up the central avenue into the complex.

"We're looking for Block 6 on Amsterdam Road, which is between Rhine Street and Danube Street." Empty leaned forward.

The north/south streets were named after European rivers and the perpendicular roads after European cities. All of this was lost on Empty, Tommy and ninety-nine per cent of visitors to the compound.

"Where's Amsterdam Road?" Tommy asked a German-looking man in a short-sleeved white shirt waiting for the internal bus service.

"Immediately south of Stockholm Road."

Still they missed the planner's cute idea.

Block 6 looked much like Blocks 5 and 7. Amsterdam looked much like Paris, Madrid or Rome.

"I'll wait an hour, then we should leave," Tommy said.

"Thanks."

At that moment, Empty could not conceive of getting back in the car and being driven another five hours to Riyadh. His nerves were so frayed that he was operating in a fuzzy haze. He walked up the path through the manicured grass, approached the external door and pressed the button marked 'Coleman'.

"Hi, who's there?" The faux-Canadian drawl oozed out of the entryphone.

"Empty."

"Oh, hold on. I'll be down in a tick." The English accent segued seamlessly as the pretence was dropped.

* * *

"That explains why Sheikh Faisal telephoned me asking if I had seen you." Having listened to Empty, Randy was not sure if he was more amazed at his account of recent events, or seeing him dressed as a Saudi man.

"Randy, I need help. I need a couple of favours."

"Fire away."

"Have you got a spare passport, preferably with an exit visa, that I can use?"

"I have a spare passport, but it doesn't have an exit visa and, sadly, it doesn't have an entry visa either, and the photograph does not look like you."

"But apart from that, the answer is 'Yes'?"

"Can't you get your own passport?"

"No, Sheikh Faisal has it."

Randy screwed up his face and let out a long sigh.

"I think that I have no choice but to try Plan B," Empty

confided, stretching out his thin legs from under his long white dishdasha.

"I'm glad that you have alternative plans."

"If I tell you that Plan C is to panic and Plan D is to commit suicide, you'll realise the importance of Plan B."

"I hope that it doesn't involve smuggling yourself aboard oil tankers at Jeddah or cattle-fodder lorries heading back to Baghdad?"

"No. It's worse than that … but I might make those ideas Plans C and D. I think they're an improvement."

"What's Plan B?"

"I'd rather not tell you. What you don't know, you can't be done for."

"What was the other favour?"

"Can I use your telephone? Don't worry, I'm not phoning Dawn. I want to call my brother, and also a … shall we call it an answering service?"

* * *

Marcus stared at the cream-coloured telephone on his desk. Where would it all end? Was the Orwellian nightmare already here? Computers would only become bigger and faster, and what might they do? As it was, he could listen to practically any telephone conversation in the world if he wanted to. Admittedly, he was in a very privileged position, but who was listening to him? George Orwell had been frighteningly accurate; 1984 was only eighteen months away. There was a certain irony to the fact that the person most likely to be tapping Marcus's phone was Sir Cecil. It may have been the thought of 1984 that made Marcus think of rats, or then again …? What was Sir Cecil up to in Russia?

After checking, Marcus could find absolutely nothing on Project Canute. Actually, this was not quite true. He had found a Project Canute but it was from five years ago and long finished; a boring, low-status, almost administrative idea about the avoidance of duplication. This was clearly not what Sir Cecil was calling Project Canute. Marcus was deep in thought about the straightforward simplicity of the stand-off known as the Cold War; the USSR against the West. Again, ironically, he was not far away from the new Project Canute, but he would never get any closer; he was not one of the six people who would ever know about it.

The telephone suddenly rang, snapping him out of his reverie.

"Marcus?" the Foreign Secretary began.

"Yes. Thank you for calling."

"I hope that this does not involve Turkish trawlers?"

"Well … I'm afraid it does."

"I give you ten out of ten for perseverance, but nought out of ten on the job-preservation front."

Asking the Foreign Secretary to call back was not the normal way things were done. Marcus cut straight to the chase. "They were very clever. There were two ships. '*Ikiz*' means 'twin' …" He explained the recent discoveries in a series of staccato sentences and finished by asking for a private meeting. He wanted to ask the Foreign Secretary about Project Canute, but could not risk it over the telephone. The latest developments on the Zugdidi affair should get him his meeting. If Sir Cecil was listening, he could do little about it.

"Why did you not want to go through the normal channels?"

"There are certain complications about all this that I would like to discuss with you personally." Marcus was speaking slowly and calmly, avoiding any emphasis or innuendo. *Please say yes. Please do not ask too many questions. Please do not demand the presence of Sir Cecil and his cronies at the meeting.*

"When will you know where the second ship has docked?"

"In the next few hours."

"I can see you before a dinner appointment at eight tomorrow evening. Come to my house in London."

Marcus stared at the telephone long after the call had finished. He was not sure whether he wanted Sir Cecil to hear that conversation or not. He was being neurotic, but, then, wasn't that part of the Orwellian nightmare?

* * *

A few miles from Mexico City, the irony of the framed photograph of Queen Elizabeth and Prince Philip, taken in the 1960s, was clearly lost on its present owner. He was Colombian, and had bought the whole estate, lock, stock and barrel, from an old Mexican family who had enjoyed the visits of British royalty to play polo thirty years earlier. The converted sugar mill, now engulfed by ficus trees and climbers, was a discreet base for an arms dealer as it gave easy access to North, South and the rest of Central America. The faded glory of the estate, with its black-stained concrete and peeling paintwork, was of no concern to him; it was just a transit point, somewhere to sleep.

Rhys, one of the advance SAS team, peered through the window at the high ceilings, the whitewashed walls and the suits of armour; these he could accept. The old painted fairground horses impaled on poles spiralling up the central staircase, he could not come to grips with … but he was not here for his opinion on 1980s Mexican interior design.

Rhys retreated silently around the edge of the garden and hid behind the pillars of a small, overgrown aqueduct which had once channelled water to the mill. The tendrils of forest trees engulfed the old volcanic-stone walls and structures like octopus tentacles. The tree canopies created a steamy and gloomy shade. He retreated further away from the house, gently approached some free-ranging chickens to avoid any outburst of squawking, and tucked himself behind a rusting iron cog of enormous proportions which sat underneath a stone arch.

A dirty green Range Rover crunched along the driveway of crushed lava to the back of the hacienda. While Rhys watched the Colombians return, the remaining three of his team were checking out the old stone vault which they had watched being emptied and prepared the day before. Old piles of sacks, a 1960s Jaguar on blocks, abandoned air-conditioning units and a long, rolled conveyor belt had all been pulled out and the concrete floor swept clean. There had been a dog – an inquisitive, overweight Dobermann – but this had been eliminated by Rhys to avoid any complications later. The movements of the lethargic Mexican peasants as they cleared out the arched vault had been watched closely by the SAS team; although spotting any movement in these underpaid and apparently drunk locals was often difficult, especially after they had discovered how comfortable the piles of hessian sacks were.

The arrival of the Sparrowhawks was something of an anticlimax. Four six-foot-long crates were lifted from a small lorry and positioned like coffins on the floor of the vault. The security category went from non-existent to Level 1; this involved the locking of the large double wooden doors. If security was lax, the missiles would not be here long. This was more of a chink than a window of opportunity. The good news was that the wooden crate lids were held down by six large screws; the bad news was that Mitchell de Jong, escorted by Joe and his colleague, would not arrive for four hours. Mitch, Joe and Marco had flown into Mexico City from Miami on a scheduled flight. It was an uneventful trip, exactly as it was meant to be. Joe and Marco were unarmed but in the one-in-a-million event that a mugger had tried anything he would have lost the use of his arm long before he could enter Mitch's personal space. When Rhys and his colleagues had flown in illegally from Belize two days previously they had brought with them the replacement detonators and a selection of weapons. Joe and Marco would be given some of these when the three of them were picked up by a driver outside the airport.

The car journey out of Mexico City lasted almost two hours and they were still not in virgin countryside. Mitch became ever more tense and craved for it all to be over as quickly as possible so that he could get back to his desk, laboratory and classroom in Portsmouth. They passed through a beautiful wooded landscape of volcanoes and deep gorges, but this failed to lighten his mood. He got out in silence as they arrived at a small farmhouse about three miles from their target: the hacienda and sugar mill. The sweat oozed from every pore; in Mitch's case this was more from nervousness than the high humidity. They grabbed their bags from the back of the car.

"Let's get a cold beer. Rhys promised to stick some in the fridge." Marco was first up the path. "Cheer up, Mitch. It'll soon be over."

A couple of minutes later, Mitch was staring in the bathroom mirror at his drawn face illuminated by the stark blue-whiteness of a short fluorescent strip light. He thought that he looked at least ten years older but he couldn't decide whether this was from fear of the task ahead, or disbelief at the bare wires hanging down near the basin taps and the size of the cockroaches that scampered noisily across the bumpy blue-and-white tiles to the rusty grating in the middle of the bathroom floor. While he was unpacking his toothbrush and shaver, his two co-travellers could be heard laughing in the kitchen, clinking bottles and looking for lunch. Compared to storming embassies or hiding in an attic on the Falls Road shitting into a bag, this was a holiday.

All Mitch could hear that evening as he followed Joe and Marco in single file down the track was the flat, harsh sound of a mariachi band playing below them in the valley, perhaps a mile away. He would never know that they sound even worse close up. An occasional firework lit up the sky to their right, throwing the trees into silhouette. There was a smell of rotting fruit in the night air that began to smell more like rotting flesh. Mitch would never know that Bella the Dobermann was twenty yards to his left.

The doors to the vault opened relatively quietly but two bats – or, more likely, roosting birds – clattered out of the lianas and ivy. Mitch managed to overcome his fears when the rhythm and repetition of his task kicked in. Unscrewing and replacing the detonators in every missile took almost half an hour. Once the glue was set, there was no way of replacing them without blowing up everyone and everything around. Joe and Marco replaced the crate lids and ensured that everything was left exactly as they had found it. Mitch suddenly felt relieved as his task was completed, and safe knowing that he was protected by Joe and Marco nearby and Rhys and the team outside watching the house.

Mitch would never know that the whole vault was ready to explode, having been wired by Rhys shortly after the Sparrowhawks had arrived. He had placed enough explosive to open up a new link from the Atlantic to the Pacific that would rival the Panama Canal, just in case Mitch failed or the mission was compromised. Mitch would never know that these missiles were not leaving this vault unless irreversibly sabotaged. There was lot that Mitchell de Jong would never know.

If HMG could sabotage the Sparrowhawks, all well and good. If they might sink an Argentinian warship when fired, all the better, but under no circumstances were the four missiles going to end up being fired at British troops, planes or ships. If the Mexican adventure had failed in any way, the vault and its contents would have contributed to the high level of pollution over Mexico City.

* * *

"But don't we have anyone at Sabaramco?"

"No. We used to, but not now," Robin Mills replied.

"Surely it's the perfect cover?"

"I'm sorry, Marcus, but we do not have someone everywhere we want at all times."

This was not how Marcus had wanted the telephone conversation to run. In his head it had gone something like, "Hello, Sir Cecil … Yes, there is a Turkish ship … No, no, apology accepted." Instead, he was discussing why we had no person on the ground in Sabaramco with Sir Cecil's number two, Robin Mills. At least Marcus had already told the Foreign Secretary, so Sir Cecil could not score any points or manipulate the story. Still, a little humble pie should have been on the menu. He didn't bother to ask why there was no longer satellite coverage over the Gulf; he already knew the answer.

"We need to establish if the second *Ikiz* went into Sabaramco's port, went past it, or is still sailing north."

"Marcus, I know. We will pull out all of the stops. HMS *Majestic* is not far away in the Gulf; we are checking with her captain. We have someone talking to the harbour master as we speak … we are back to old methods, I'm afraid."

"We have the records from Kuwait. The second *Ikiz* is not there. She is either in or near Sabaramco, at sea, or in Iran or Iraq."

There was a silence because neither Marcus nor Robin could really contemplate the last two possibilities.

"Marcus, I'm truly sorry that you did not get the right *Ikiz* the first time. It would have been good for Mannington and good for the Service." Robin sounded almost contrite. The word 'Service' neatly encompassed Marcus and Sir Cecil. "Sir Cecil feels the same way," he added.

My ass he does, thought Marcus, but he let it ride. "I hope the mistakes of the past won't divert from the importance of finding this bloody ship?"

"Marcus, I give you my word that everyone here and around the world who can help to find this ship is working flat out to do so. Trust me."

People should never say that.

* * *

Cherry Prior-Jones had either heard or imagined it all before. She always appeared so innocent, as though butter wouldn't … just wouldn't. In fact, she knew more rugby songs than the

Llanelli front row. She was sat in her lounge wearing a sort of striped kimono resembling an ex-*Punch and Judy* tent, cradling the telephone to her ear under a neatly trimmed pageboy haircut. Thirty-five years of marriage to Julian had prepared her for almost anything; perhaps involving butter and the Llanelli front row. She had lost track of how many drunk businessmen she had put to bed or doting Arabs who had sent her flowers and offered to buy her for a hundred camels. She often fondly remembered her time at Oxford with Julian … passionate days. They had put on about ten stone between them … literally between them. Since then, passion had been replaced by pragmatism. Mr and Mrs Bouncy Castle. At least no one was likely to get hurt. Julian still drank, he still cared desperately, and he still conned just about everyone into thinking that he was a complete idiot.

Julian flicked off the air conditioning in the lounge to reduce the noise temporarily. "Cherry, darling, here's the number. Her name's Amira. Bit sensitive. You know, tiptoe through the proverbials. Softly, softly, catchee whatsisname."

"I know."

"His name's Tanner, Mark Tanner, but she knows him as Empty. God knows why."

"Because of his initials, I expect."

"Well, of all the bastard … you are quick, like a hot knife through butter."

Huda, Amira's sister, answered the phone. She listened carefully to Cherry's request to speak to Amira. "She is with her aunt. She will return tomorrow, Insha'Allah."

"Could you ask her to telephone me?" Cherry gave the number and tried to strike a balance between keenness and nonchalance. "She doesn't know me but we have a mutual friend."

"I will tell her. Goodbye."

Cherry replaced the brown receiver on its cradle. "She will telephone tomorrow."

"M. T. Who'd have guessed, eh? I wonder where he is?"

CHAPTER TWENTY-SIX

Sheikh Faisal was being watched as he was chauffeured in a white Mercedes down the long drive of his principal villa in Riyadh. The enormous gates swung open and the car swept out onto the main road.

Empty had concealed himself in the whitewashed bunker which served as the irrigation and swimming-pool control room. He emerged and waited until the rotating jets began spraying the lawn before he slipped, in the half-light of early evening, up the steps into the main building. The air-conditioning units provided cover for his footfall once inside but prevented him hearing if any of Sheikh Faisal's domestic staff were around. In his red-and-white headdress, long white dishdasha and dark glasses, he was unrecognisable.

In a few quick strides he was through the lounge and into the sleeping area. The consequences of what he was doing did not bear thinking about in a strict Muslim country, and he realised that his whole body was shaking. A noise startled him but it was only the automatic aeration unit in the tropical fish tank. He tried to calm down by reassuring himself that 'stealing' your own passport back was not stealing.

He rifled through the drawer where he had seen Sheikh Faisal throw all of the passports. There were half a dozen dark blue British passports, most bulging with stamps and affixed visas. He found his own. It didn't have an exit visa but he would need it if and when he ever got out of Saudi Arabia. There was a resemblance between the young scarecrow staring out of the photograph and the terrified man holding the passport today. He remembered the trip to get the photograph. He had been adjusting the stool in the booth when the flash had gone off, catching him by surprise. Would he ever see the Woolworths in High Wycombe again?

But Mark Tanner was not finished in Sheikh Faisal's bedroom. He had crossed a line and there was no going back. Whatever it took to get home, he would now do. Opening the next drawer, he found the sheikh's own passport. *You may as well be hanged for a sheep as a lamb*, he thought to himself … and hadn't he eaten enough bloody lamb at midnight in the adjoining lounge while watching *The A-Team* and *The Dukes of Hazzard*? He put both passports into his pocket and paused only to take the almost transparent, thin black cloak with exquisite gold edging that was hanging on a coat hanger from a wardrobe door. He retraced his steps and slipped out of the villa.

The route he took across the garden was mathematically chosen to avoid the pop-up sprinklers that were on their nightly cycle. He made it to the side gate but forgot about the sensor which turned on the security lights. He took his chance and ran through the gate into the roadway. If anyone could have seen his frightened face, he now resembled his passport photograph.

* * *

The policeman stood out like a sore thumb in front of the London plane tree. If there was one place on earth where standard-issue Army camouflage might actually work, it was in front of the peeling green, cream and grey of the plane bark. But no, he was wearing his dark blue uniform like all British policemen; only the gun resting across his arms differentiated him. Since the Falklands War had begun, the Foreign Secretary had been given increased round-the-clock protection, especially at his Kensington home. Despite heightened tensions, it was difficult for the policeman to keep alert when the most exciting event in the street was the bin collection on Tuesday mornings.

A voice in his earpiece had warned him that Marcus Billingham was arriving in his chauffeur-driven car just before 8pm. Various forlorn-looking members of the laurel family nodded in the breeze behind the heavy black railings, like animals in a zoo displaying early signs of madness.

The massive, glossy white door opened to reveal a high hall bathed in a warm yellow glow from various table lamps.

"Marcus. Come on in. I can only give you half an hour. Let me show you round the house."

So don't waste time showing me around the house, Marcus thought to himself.

They spiralled up a central staircase, grabbing cursory glimpses of a few rooms. At the top of the house they stopped in a small attic lounge which had been part of a bed-sitting room arrangement used by the Foreign Secretary's mother.

"Sorry about the whistle-stop tour but I wanted to talk in a room where I am reasonably confident that we are not being bugged."

"Do you think you are?"

"I have no idea but I wanted to say a couple of things to you which I definitely do not want to be heard by others, friendly or otherwise."

"That suits me too."

"As you asked for the meeting, you fire away first."

Marcus explained the results of Bag Day in Moscow and his worry that Sir Cecil was either concealing key information from Mannington or involved in unthinkable liaisons.

The Foreign Secretary raised his hand gently from the sideboard on which it had been resting. "Well, this all ties in with what I wanted to say to you. Yes, I do know about Project Canute, and we have kept it strictly to six people. Firstly, let me reassure you that it is above board. Well, actually, it isn't above board but let's steer clear of semantics. Secondly, let me ask you to destroy all trace of it from your records at Mannington and not to pursue it in any way."

Marcus was confused. He ran Mannington: the Collation Unit. He was meant to have access to everything so that it could be collated, and patterns and links could be established. There were not meant to be any secrets to which Mannington did not have access. The Secret Services worked on a need-to-know basis, and Marcus's unit needed to know everything in order to function.

"No … I can see what is going through your mind, Marcus. Let me tell you that this is a one-off; in fact …" the Foreign Secretary paused to reflect, "this is the only one-off that I am aware of, and you have nothing to fear. If it comes off it will have the very greatest rewards for us at absolutely minimum risk. It is Sir Cecil's baby and I must reassure you that, spiky as he may be, he has been and is achieving exceptional results."

Marcus realised that he was holding his breath. "Surely Project Canute must impact on some other area of intelligence in some way?"

"No, it is absolutely stand-alone. That's the beauty of it. That is why we are keeping it so well hidden … well, until Bag Day unfortunately brought it to a wider audience."

"OK, but is there a chance that, through ignorance or bad luck, we or others like us might mess up Project Canute or … things relevant to it?"

"No," was how the Foreign Secretary began, rather unhelpfully. "Marcus, I would like to discuss so much in detail with you but I only have twenty minutes, and so you must accept a shorthand version. Please don't interpret my brief remarks as overcritical or rude. I am up to my ears in it at the moment; in fact, I don't expect that any Foreign Secretary has been busier since 1945. Firstly, I have the Falklands; it's been almost unbearable waiting to hear that the bloody *Ark Royal* or *Canberra* has been hit. I don't want to tempt fate but, as you know, I think that we have achieved sea superiority. Secondly, as you also know, we have sabotaged the Sparrowhawk missiles in Mexico. Thirdly, a certain Mr Geoffrey Prime, arrested for paedophile offences last week, looks as if he has been passing GCHQ's secrets to the Russians for the past fifteen years. We shall find out more next Tuesday when he is interviewed by Special Branch in Gloucester Prison."

As if on cue, a police car sped down the road below them, its flashing blue lights passing rapidly across the attic ceiling.

The Foreign Secretary continued. "You will understand, therefore, why I am keen that Project Canute stays under wraps, and why I would prefer that any internecine rivalry between London and Mannington is minimised."

Marcus nodded but didn't speak as the Foreign Secretary was in full flow.

"Computer and satellite involvement in the Security Services is increasing at an incredible rate; you know that more than anybody. Sir Cecil is heading for retirement. We will be re-elected after a successful Falklands War. You know that I hold you in high regard … so your future is more than secure. Please don't press me at such a critical moment on internal management restructuring."

"You have my word that I will do nothing to antagonise London, and you have reassured me on Project Canute." Marcus was regretting more and more asking Jack to get Mark Tanner involved. He prayed that he would be found before the Saudi authorities caught him. He prayed even harder that the second *Ikiz* would be found soon and its cargo neutralised.

* * *

In the end, Sir Cecil's men had decided not to approach the Sabaramco harbour master at Dammam direct. If you were importing something dubious into Saudi Arabia and had chosen a port on the east coast, you would have ensured that the harbour master was very well paid and turned a blind eye to your activities. Instead, they had a 'friendly' Arab, purporting to be a Turk, ask a British dock worker whether a Turkish boat had arrived because one of his family was on board. This inquiry elicited the vital information that the second *Ikiz* had arrived and left. In fact, the dock worker had helped with the unloading of the furniture and carpets himself, operating one of the forklift trucks. As he remembered it, the only unusual aspect was that the cargo had been given special clearance because it was bound for the new Turkish Embassy in the Diplomatic Quarter now under construction in Riyadh.

Back in London and Mannington, they weighed up the likelihood that furniture and fittings for a new embassy in Riyadh would be sent past the port of Jeddah, where the existing embassy was located, around the Arabian Peninsula to Dammam. This just extended the journey by a few unnecessary days. None of the new embassies in the Diplomatic Quarter in Riyadh were even finished, and the arrival of a few carpets and wooden balustrades seemed a bit premature.

"Fishy. Too fishy."

Ross and his colleague were discussing the latest findings while pouring themselves a coffee from the Cona jugs steaming away on the hotplate. A large grey computer cabinet about the size of a wardrobe was being wheeled on a trolley towards the lift. They both stopped talking about Saudi Arabia as the trolley passed by, even though they knew the men, who were Mannington computer maintenance staff rather than outside contractors.

"Another one for the scrapheap?"

"We only brought this in last year. The new one's even bigger."

"Bigger and better?"

"Well … faster, anyway. It doesn't have reels."

"God help us."

The grey cabinet disappeared around a corner towards the lifts to be taken back to a special unit at GCHQ where computer hardware was assembled or dismantled. New equipment was tested there before being transferred to Mannington by their dedicated staff. The same two men appeared every few days on each floor, moving computers and monitors in and out. It was not an ideal system.

"When's Jack back?"

"A few days' time, I think," Ross replied, concealing his dread at all the professional and domestic consequences that would then occur, turning his world upside down.

* * *

In Great Witcombe, Victoria was also counting down the days to Jack's return on her kitchen calendar. Meticulous black lines crossed out every passing day. She was still watering the flowers he had sent her on her windowsill which were now, strictly speaking, past their aesthetic best, but there was no way that she was going to throw them out. Until he returned, she had no way of contacting Jack. The flowers, fresh, dying or dead, represented that last contact and, even more than that, they were an affirmation of his love. She had convinced herself that everything was going to work out.

At GCHQ she was not in a position to find out what was happening with the *Ikiz* ships. She was in enough trouble for having an affair with Jack without being caught looking at transcripts outside of her remit, even if she could gain access to them.

* * *

Sixty miles east in High Wycombe, Dawn was making a cup of tea. The strain of the last few months was beginning to tell on her face; she looked pale and drawn. A phone call from her brother-in-law had improved things. Mark was alive and well. She stirred in the sugar while staring out at the rooftops below her. At least she had a view to occupy her.

"Does that dress still fit you?"

"Yes." Her eldest daughter was adamant.

"Are you sure?"

"Look." She tucked the dress under her chin and let it hang down in front of her.

Well, at least the children were occupied. They were busy carrying piles of folded clothes from a chest of drawers, ready for packing in the two big suitcases sprawled across the central kitchen table.

"Are we going to Florida?"

"No."

"Are we going to France?"

"No. We are not going anywhere beginning with 'F'."

* * *

"It's because there are no fireplaces," Julian was in full flow.

"It has more to do with the fact that the windows don't have clear glass. It turns every room into a cell," Cherry was standing her ground.

"They *are* bastard cells!"

"They have no orientation, no focal point except for oversized televisions … to go with all of the other oversized furniture."

"If you put a decent fireplace and mantelpiece on that wall it would make all the—"

The discourse on why rooms in Saudi Arabia do not feel cosy was brought to an abrupt end by the telephone ringing.

"Cherry Prior-Jones."

Julian stood in Falstaffian pose with arms akimbo, waiting to learn the identity of the caller.

287

"Oh, Amira, thank you for calling back. I know that this is a bit unusual but I am a friend of Mark Tanner and I wondered if you know where he is?"

Julian waddled nearer to the side table in order to read anything that his wife wrote down.

"No, I work at the British Embassy but I am nothing to do with any police. I just want to help him if I can."

Why had Amira asked about the police? Julian was a bit concerned about that, but it sounded as if she might know where Empty was.

"No. I understand that … of course … I realise the dangerous position you are in … that would be really helpful … no, no, I won't mention your name to anyone."

Julian looked down at the notepad as Cherry wrote down the name of Randy Coleman at Sabaramco.

"Amira, thank you so much, and if you hear anything from Mark or if he needs help, please give him my name and number … yes … thank you. Goodbye."

Five minutes later, Julian was telephoning Sabaramco, and five minutes after that he was speaking to Randy Coleman.

"Hello. Good to speak to you. This is Julian Prior-Jones from the British Embassy in Jeddah – well, I am in Riyadh, actually."

It was Cherry's turn to listen to one side of a conversation.

"No. Don't panic … yes, yes, I know that you are Canadian."

Randy had obviously assumed that his casual attitude to nationality and the ownership of passports was catching up with him.

"No, nothing is wrong … well, nothing to do with you, it's just that, well, I wondered if you had seen Mark Tanner over the last couple of days? We thought that he might be in a bit of trouble and need our help." Julian was perched on a small stool that was not visible under his ample frame. He looked like a dancing Cossack as his arms crossed in a strange movement, transferring pen and paper while pinning the receiver against his shoulder under his tilted head. "Really? No … don't worry. No names, no pack drill. Mum's the bastard word and all that."

Randy was conveniently forgetting that Empty had asked him for his spare passport, and also failed to mention that he had used his phone to call his brother.

"Thanks, and can I give you my telephone number here in Riyadh? Great."

Cherry looked at her husband's resigned expression as he said goodbye to Randy Coleman.

"If he's a Canadian then I'm a Dutchman. Still, he says that this Tanner chap did visit him but is now back in Riyadh and he doesn't know where the idiot is."

"So, back to square one?"

"More likely 'Go directly to jail. Do not pass go. Do not collect your bastard two hundred quid.'"

* * *

At that precise moment, Empty was, unknowingly, not far from the jail in Riyadh, using a public telephone exchange where expats could book calls locally or internationally. He was spending considerably more than two hundred pounds on his Barclaycard, having booked a British Airways flight from Jeddah to Heathrow for the following day, Monday 7th June, using his own name. He had not booked the domestic flight which would take him from Riyadh to Jeddah.

With all of his possessions in a briefcase, he pulled his sunglasses down over his eyes and stepped out into the glare; just another Saudi going about his business. After an early meal of *Gomen Wot* with rice and injera bread in an Ethiopian restaurant, he walked about half a mile to his fellow language student's flat. Kamal would not be expecting him. Kamal would not be expecting him dressed as a Saudi man. Kamal would not be expecting him dressed as a Saudi man with green teeth from the spinach stew.

CHAPTER TWENTY-SEVEN

Dawn was rising in High Wycombe … literally; it was very early Sunday morning. The route from bedroom to kitchen was even more circuitous than usual with two large suitcases overhanging the central table. She was about to fill the stainless-steel kettle from the tap when she was distracted by a sharp blast of Morse code coming from behind the closed orange curtains. She only knew of one person daft enough to be that many floors up at this time of the morning, tapping at her window, and he was in Saudi Arabia. She drew the curtains and stared for a split second into the dull black eyes of a carrion crow that tumbled into a glide down across the rooftops, half replete on a breakfast of putty pecked from the window frame.

Dawn had some difficult decisions to make over the next twenty-four hours. That she had had enough was not in question. The flat was too small and she was fed up with the penny-pinching. Tomorrow she was leaving for pastures new (well, 'pastures' was a misnomer, perhaps). She poured out a bowl of cornflakes, paused and proceeded to pour some more. The pyramid of pale orange flakes made the addition of milk an interesting problem. Why had she been so greedy? Because years of parsimony had made it impossible for her to leave a half-full packet of cornflakes (and she could not take them with her). Between munching mouthfuls of cereal she wrote lists; her priorities for packing, and those of the children. Compressing your family's belongings into two suitcases is almost impossible, and a bizarre logic begins to apply (no room for her wedding dress but space for the deflated Saudia Boeing 747, for example). At least she would not need Empty's remaining clothes. She had decided to leave some cardboard boxes full of stuff outside the door of her neighbour, Yolanda, the Polish lady. She would find use for the contents of Dawn's larder – the half-empty jars of peanut butter, the tins of custard powder and the small boxes of cereal. As in so many households, the miniature packets of Coco Pops were well past their use-by decade.

She was finishing her last soggy mouthful and writing the very last item on her definitive list just as the children emerged from the bedroom. Could such unique and perfect timing be an omen for the next twenty-four hours? The surprise visit from Empty's brother had set in motion a series of actions with little time for thought or reflection. With mixed emotions, she poured the children enormous bowls of cornflakes.

"Why have you filled the bowl so much?"

"Leave what you don't want."

They were all leaving tomorrow.

* * *

292

Not a million miles west up the A40, Victoria was also having breakfast. She, too, avoided the Coco Pops, favouring a jar of honey of indeterminate age which had separated into several layers ranging from crystalline to liquid. Her kitchen table, however, was dominated by something else well past its best: the wilting flower arrangement from Jack, now over a week old. Like the Buddha's tooth in Kandy or the bones of saints in Santiago de Compostela, the carnations and lilies had assumed another level of importance. They were well on their way to achieving the status of relics, soon to be pressed between paper and brought out on important anniversaries or at moments of weakness. To Victoria they were the winner's laurels, proof that she had succeeded. The flowers confirmed Jack's intentions.

She was not sure why he had delayed his flight back by a couple of days. Presumably something to do with this *Ikiz* affair was preventing his return now that the OPEC conference was over. She could wait. After all, the flower arrangement was proof that she was not deluding herself.

* * *

Across the valley in Cheltenham, Sarah was staring at two children stirring the breakfast in their bowls, turning the milk a sickly chocolate brown. There had been nothing else in the cupboard as neither she nor Ross had made it to Sainsbury's. He would very soon be several floors under the Cotswolds and unlikely to see the light of day for a week. The disturbing idea that she had exchanged one workaholic for another slipped along the interface between her conscious and subconscious and was gone.

Ross drove across the Cotswolds in a summer morning sunlight which gave sharp definition to the natural stone walls and the rolling topography of the dry valleys. He had noticed that his affair had made him more emotionally aware – or, then again, was appreciation of the landscape a diversion therapy so that he did not need to think about the hurt he was causing? His tyres began a rhythmical click as they passed over the cat's eyes in the middle of the road. He kept the car on this line and allowed the tick, tick, tick to bring him back to the present and to more immediate problems.

He drove into the cold artificial light of the hangar at Mannington and parked his car. Only his eventual meeting with Jack loomed on the horizon. He picked up his card and descended in the lift. Along the corridor, he meandered around the traffic cones towards his workstation. Only a pair of maintenance man's legs hanging down from a hole in the false ceiling broke the routine.

Two items caught his eye as he clicked down the priority list while rocking back and forth in his chair, trying to settle into a comfortable position. The first was a re-evaluation of all potential missile sites in Saudi Arabia, fanning out from Dammam westwards towards Riyadh. The Middle East section had gone back to square one, assuming nothing and looking for any building works that could be a theoretical location; the sewage farm at Nefud-al-aan had come out top of their list.

The second item was a copy of the transaction which booked Mark Tanner on the British Airways flight from Jeddah to Heathrow on Monday 7th June … tomorrow. Ross pulled himself upright. How was Mark Tanner going to get to Jeddah?

He checked the domestic flights in Saudi Arabia and found nothing. Mark Tanner must already be in Jeddah – or, perhaps, driving or being driven there. Marcus must let Jack know. Jack may be able to head Mark Tanner off at the pass before the Saudi authorities or anyone else got to him. Did Mark Tanner really think that he could simply fly out of the country?

* * *

There was a strange atmosphere at Riyadh airport. It was not just the smell of spicy sweat and the laughter from the Pakistani hordes scattered across the marble floors. Similarly, it was not just the fuzzy, guttural announcements in Arabic that were no more comprehensible on the second time of hearing as they echoed off the stark walls of the huge hall. There was an end-of-term feeling to the proceedings.

Today was the last day for the 'old' airport. Tomorrow a 'new' airport outside of Riyadh would open, providing the level of national and international facilities a modern capital city should expect. It would be the largest in the world (mainly because the airport perimeter fence had been put right out in the desert, enclosing a vast area of nothingness); it was good for marketing and massaged a few egos. With its open desert setting, the newly constructed complex really did look like the architectural model which sat in the Ministry building on Airport Road. Rapidly expanding Riyadh had strangled the 'old' airport, and the noise that it generated was unacceptable to the hundreds of thousands of residents under the flight path and nearby. It was rumoured that the 'old' site would be turned into an airport for private planes, a military airport, or possibly redeveloped as a business park.

It was into the 'old' departure hall that Empty walked that Sunday, dressed as a fifty-five-year-old sheikh in black robes with gold edging. With his hair hidden under his headdress, sporting dark glasses and with only parts of his tanned face showing, he could just about carry off the disguise. He was sweating profusely and walking a few paces behind Kamal, who carried a small suitcase and some papers. Empty was trying to control his shaking, although ironically it added to the overall impression of infirmity. He knew that this was make-or-break time. Either he would escape from Saudi Arabia or they would put him in jail and throw away the key. For some reason, probably because he was thinking of Dawn, he remembered the pen with brown ink which had caused all of the trouble when he had first arrived into this airport what seemed like years ago. If only they had turned him around and deported him at that point.

He pulled himself back to the present, concentrating on looking and acting older, less mobile and … deaf. How do you act deaf?

Kamal walked up to the desk and bought a first-class ticket to London Heathrow on Saudia. He paid with a wad of dirty blue hundred-riyal notes held tightly by a red elastic band. He explained that his boss, Sheikh Faisal, was deaf and may need help to board the plane. The smartly dressed ticket seller was a Palestinian from Damascus who recognised Kamal's accent, and they exchanged a few pleasantries on the uneven distribution of wealth in the world. He encouraged Kamal to hurry to the check-in desk as the flight was soon to be called. Kamal and Empty had purposely left it to the last minute. In fact they had left it later than intended because a sandstorm had thrown the traffic of Riyadh into a dull red confusion where headlights were of little value and pedestrians could hardly breathe even through several layers of cloth.

Kamal escorted his shuffling 'master' to the first-class check-in desk, where Empty made a very passable impersonation of a deaf Arab loudly clearing his throat; this was more down to a dry, nervous mouth exacerbated by lungfuls of red dust than to theatrical skills. He wanted to go to the toilet, to run away, to stick his head in the sand, to wind back the clock … he wanted to do anything but stand in this place.

As at all first-class check-in desks in the Middle East, 'his' passport was given only a cursory glance by the Egyptian official. Another high-ranking Saudi flying first class out of his own national airport. The official was keen to get Empty's small suitcase onto the conveyor and off to the plane. He was even keener because this would be the last passenger he would check in before he moved over to the wonderful new airport tomorrow.

Empty had been so busy squeezing his buttocks together and avoiding everyone's gaze by staring at the belemnite fossils in the grey marble floor that he jumped when Kamal pushed the passport into his hands. It all looked very authentic.

Within half an hour he would be on that TriStar, leaving Saudi Arabia. He did not care if he was sat next to a dozen hooded falcons or a dozen drunk expats (although the chances of that happening in first class were infinitesimal). He had not given a second's thought to the luxury that awaited him on board. All he had to do was keep up the disguise; it was all part of his plan, just like booking the Jeddah-to-London ticket in his own name on his credit card had been a key part of the deception.

He did not dare think about the next thirty minutes. He was counting repeatedly in his head from one to ten in Arabic.

This was not part of the disguise; this was self-control. It was a new form of wallpaper.

Kamal handed the boarding pass to the official, repeated the explanation that his employer was profoundly deaf, and asked that he be escorted to the plane. Kamal leant forward to kiss Empty on both cheeks, whispered goodbye under his breath and walked away across the hall. His friend would never understand why he had agreed to put his own freedom at risk to enable him to escape.

* * *

With however many billion people there are in the world, it would be the understatement of all time to say that quite a lot is happening at any split second. We are, of course, blissfully unaware of the synchronicity of these myriad events. Maybe, occasionally, we find out about some of the most notable through the media and work out what we were doing at that time. Just like Lee Harvey Oswald, we all remember what we were doing when President Kennedy was assassinated in 1963.

Mitch de Jong had been a junior technician stood in a workshop in Fareham when he heard the news from Dallas on the radio. Joe, long before he ended up in the SAS, had recently joined his regiment and had been in a Hercules learning how to parachute over Salisbury Plain.

Half past two in the afternoon of Sunday 6th June 1982, however, may not be lodged in all of our memories. Mitch was back in his house in Portsmouth, still going over everything in his mind as the reality of his recent trip to Mexico began to sink in. He was sanding down the floorboards in his new kitchen, having ordered the industrial machine some weeks before, and it was costing him a lot of money. The noise, dust and vibration, coupled with the physical exertion, were probably what the doctor would order.

At that exact moment, Joe was at home near his base in Hereford. He was drinking coffee and reading the Sunday papers. A Chinook helicopter thumped somewhere overhead; the locals must love having the SAS around. Joe was surprised that the Mexican adventure had passed off so easily. In fact, he couldn't think of a single other foreign mission that had gone according to plan and had not had the odd hairy moment. He was coming to the end of his Special Ops career but was still 'on call' given the Falklands War, with the likelihood of a noisy and uncomfortable slog down to Ascension Island in a Hercules to look forward to next week.

In the South Atlantic, at that same moment, it was a grey morning. HMS *Fearless* was at anchor, facing Fitzroy Sound. To starboard lay HMS *Plymouth* and HMS *Intrepid*. Two harriers in silhouette drifted across on patrol; they were flying in the band of light being squeezed to the horizon between dark, heavy cloud and the dull black land. Over that horizon the ARA *Santa Rosa*, an Argentinian destroyer, was also at anchor just outside the Total Exclusion Zone. Manuel Alvarez was one of six naval conscripts carrying the first Sparrowhawk missile towards its firing cylinder. If asked, he would not have known where he was when Kennedy was assassinated, for he had been just entering the world at the Hospital Militar Regional in Comodoro Rivadavia.

The explosion killed Manuel and his compatriots instantly. The whole midships became an inferno, and a towering cumulonimbus of black smoke powered upwards through the low cloud ceiling, where it merged to be scattered later as raindrops across the Atlantic Ocean.

CHAPTER TWENTY-EIGHT

Mark Tanner was having to go very deep inside his head to find his last dregs of sanity. He had given up counting in Arabic and was now feeding grey beads through his fingers, reciting nursery rhymes repeatedly in his head. His flight had been delayed, so far by five interminable hours. The sandstorm had become a dust storm. A dense red mist had turned the world into a Martian nightmare. Through the glass of the large window at his departure gate, he could barely make out the low-clipped *Dodonaea* hedge only a couple of metres away across the gravel. The dry fog seemed to dissolve the light, and dusted every surface with a rusty-red matt powder.

He was in no man's land; through passport control but not out of the country. To make matters worse (as if matters could be made worse), the facilities at the departure gate could at best be described as primitive – this was an old airport. The word 'facilities' also flattered a wall-mounted telephone which only took coins and only made domestic calls, single male and female toilets, and a bar which only sold crisps and soft drinks. Nobody had access to any lounge and, because the rest of the airport was now closed, nobody could leave the gate to re-enter the main airport. At a moment that was hard to distinguish from any other, the man behind the bar collected the remaining cans and packets of crisps, emptied the till into a bag and walked back towards passport control pushing his sack trolley.

"Where the fuck's he going?" a disgruntled Brit said to a friend in exasperation, and Empty had to summon all of his self-control not to make some flippant comment and give the game away.

"He's just fucked off."

"He's closed down for good. This is now the last fucking flight out."

"You got any coins left? I'll phone Sulaiman and get him to call Belinda. Shall I get Belinda to call Theresa for you?"

"Yeah, we don't have many coins. Who uses fucking coins in Saudi Arabia?"

"This is fucking ridiculous!"

You do not know what 'fucking ridiculous' means, thought the beleaguered man with the grey prayer beads whose situation had redefined the word 'ridiculous'. But Empty could not risk speaking. He could not walk about, read, shop, use the telephone or any of the other gradually diminishing facilities. With a growing sense of alarm, he considered how many of the more general airport facilities were being closed down for good. The luggage loaders? The firemen? Air traffic control? What if they cancelled the plane? The prayer beads became warm from the friction and his sweaty hands.

But wait a minute – the incoming plane had already landed

when he was checked in by Kamal. They would have to fly this plane back to England anyway, wouldn't they?

* * *

The good news for Jack was that he was finally on his way home after the Geneva/Riyadh round of conferences. Actually, the really good news was that he was going back to Victoria with only a half-guilt given Sarah's own actions. The bad news was the breakneck speed at which everything had had to be done after receiving the call from Marcus. Saudia was the only airline that flew out of Riyadh, so Jack had had to book an internal flight to Jeddah from Riyadh and then a British Caledonian flight back to London. This was actually the favoured route among Brits who couldn't wait a few more hours for a drink and were prepared to fly via Jeddah just to drink on British Caledonian once in international airspace over the Red Sea. The Jeddah-to-London flight was the one booked by Empty in an attempt to fool everyone into thinking that he was going to fly back this way.

Jack was not a spy in the field and so he was having to learn new operational skills fast. He needed to get to Empty before the Saudi authorities, who would surely pick him up as soon as he checked in. At least Jack knew what he looked like. At Jeddah airport he had spent a few minutes selecting the best vantage point from which to spot Empty however he arrived from Riyadh. Was he coming by bus, taxi, hire car? Was a friend driving him and dropping him off? Was he going to book the internal flight at the last moment? Perhaps he knew that the old Riyadh airport was closing down and had chosen to travel overland? From his elevated position, Jack could see domestic arrivals and the bus, car and taxi drop-off as well as international check-in. For good measure he could also see the vast, permanently tented Hajj Terminal, which looked like a tray of meringues baking out in the sand.

If Mannington knew that Empty had booked the Jeddah-Heathrow flight, so did the Saudis. Where were they? Jack could not see anyone acting suspiciously – but they wouldn't anyway. He scanned the Lowry-like scene below him, with everyone hurrying in all directions through the echoing concourse, for anyone acting suspiciously. Would they use soldiers? Airport officials? Uniformed police? Plain-clothed undercover police? Were they watching on surveillance cameras or from behind one-way glass?

Jack decided to check in his luggage and return to his vantage point. He was boarding the plane whether he made contact with Empty or not, but would go through security towards the gate at the last moment. Flicking open his passport, he stared at the elaborate three-month multi-entry visa. What some people in Saudi Arabia would pay for that …

Four soldiers strolled into view – two emaciated individuals with trousers that revealed most of their socks, and two corpulent types whose tunics did not reach their leather belts. They took up positions around the hall, looking suspicious to Jack.

Ironically, Jack had been a little nervous on arrival at the airport, but as his departure time fast approached, his desire to leave outweighed his desire to find Mark Tanner. What could he do anyway? Advise him to hand himself over to the British Embassy in Jeddah? How would that help now?

Jack had been out of substantial contact with his Mannington colleagues for long enough that he did not know whether the *Ikiz* was a wild goose chase of the first order. The day before, he had heard back from Francis at Nefud-al-aan. He had kindly, on some weak pretext, checked out the sewage-farm area of the site while doing a rescheduled 'regular' inspection. He had only had access to the outer area but found enough items marked 'MUMTAZ' that Jack had realised that this was a backup facility for the main new 'library' in Mecca. It was a secret location, but a rather harmless hidden, secure one for what was probably a very expensive cataloguing endeavour.

The final call for the London flight flicked down on the display board; each row of white letters on black clicking and clacking as they tumbled and cascaded down the display. Jack picked up his hand luggage, gave one more desultory glance around the place and walked slowly towards the gate. Perhaps Empty had slipped through and was already there?

* * *

Empty was still at a departure gate, but not the one in Jeddah. While a red haze still hung low, he had watched the percentage of blue sky increase over the last hour. His fellow travellers had all found their own least uncomfortable position and were in various states of sleep, half-sleep and daydreaming. This tableau came to life expectantly as two officials walked along the edge of the room to the desk by the external exit.

Empty did not need a translation of the heated exchanges in Arabic between irritated passengers and the disinterested airport staff. He could see from their actions that they were preparing to board. This was confirmed when a transfer bus drew up outside, blocking the view of the runway and throwing up a cloud of red dust which billowed around like illuminated dry ice at a '70s rock concert. Staring out of the window while speaking into a wall-mounted telephone, one of the uniformed men garbled those over-repeated instructions which are impossible to understand in any language.

Empty began to sweat again. He was meant to be deaf; that was part of his cunning plan. So how would he know when they were calling first class? The idea had been that some helpful official would escort him to the plane, but by now they would have forgotten any instructions, or the support staff would be at home enjoying a morning coffee and looking forward to working at the new airport. He looked across at an immaculately dressed sheikh who had been sat with his wives and retainers in a cluster in the far corner. Surely he would be travelling first class? On a cue which meant nothing to Empty, about a dozen people – all Saudis, including the well-dressed sheikh – stood up stiffly and made their way towards the desk. Empty stood up too and kept telling himself to act like an older man, which proved not to be difficult as his back ached, one leg had gone to sleep and his full bladder was causing him to lean forward at the waist.

Never had dusty air smelled so good. Never had boarding a bus felt so good. It was the best morning in the world. He kept his gaze out of the window, waiting for the build-up of engine noise and the swish of the doors closing. The bus skirted the airport buildings towards the only Saudia TriStar parked out on the tarmac; in fact, the only large plane parked out there. They were just passing an almost-finished new hangar which, a large sign proclaimed in Arabic and English, would be a new aircraft-servicing facility. *Why not build it at the new airport?* Empty was thinking to himself. Several men were stood at the black, gaping entrance with its huge doors rolled open. Empty thought that the large balding man looked like Ibrahim. It *was* Ibrahim! That was his distinctive two-tone green Chevrolet. Empty recognised several other men who worked for Sheikhs Faisal and Abdullatif. *How strange.*

At the top of the steps at the front of the aircraft, he did not hear what the stewardess asked him because he was miles away, wondering what he had just seen. She reached for his boarding pass and ushered him to his seat, which resembled a small settee. The wide, cushioned armrests themselves looked more comfortable than some of the seats he had travelled in before.

He immediately got up to use the lavatory, and returned having overdosed on the complimentary cologne. *I might as well enjoy this luxury*, he thought to himself as the relief of escaping Saudi Arabia washed through his body and his bladder resumed its usual shape. It looked as though the seat next to him was going to be unoccupied, but that didn't matter as he could hardly reach it. This was the life! It also looked like he had his own stewardess. This was going to be wonderful. He fastened his seat belt.

Immediately after take-off, he looked out of the window and saw the burnt-out Saudia TriStar just off the end of the runway; it was fenced off while investigations concluded into how the 301 people on board had lost their lives in 1980. This was the last thing Empty wanted to look at as he sat in a Saudia TriStar. It brought his mood back down with a bump, and he tried to focus on the palm-tree-and-crossed-swords logo that was all over the inside of the aircraft. Someone nearby was speaking Arabic but changed to English.

"Excuse me."

Empty's heart leapt and he grabbed the armrest. He looked up to see the smiling air hostess holding a small brass pot.

"Would you like some cardamom tea?"

"No thanks. It makes me fart."

Her smile quickly disappeared from her eyes, leaving a rictus grin. Whether she was trying to place this sheikh's accent, marvelling at his command of English or calculating how many miles were left on the long flight to London, we will never know.

* * *

Inspector Nick Forbes of the Heathrow airport police looked across at the telex machine in the corner of the room. It had burst into life and was spewing a stream of pre-punched paper into the wire basket.

When it had finished, a sergeant tore off the long outpouring and held it in the style of a town crier before him. "Ever heard of a Mark Tanner?" he asked.

The inspector was staring somewhere into the middle distance of the office across typewriters and filing trays. He shook his head. The name rang no bells.

"He's landing on the Saudia flight at three o'clock this afternoon."

"From where?"

"Riyadh." The sergeant read further down, allowing the message to concertina into its pre-folded shape. "Well, that's interesting … wait a minute … where did this telex come from?" He began scanning the top and bottom of the telex.

Nick Forbes, having failed to recognise the name, waited for the sergeant to give him more details.

"He was meant to be on a British Caledonian flight from Jeddah today," he read on, "booked in his own name, but he's pinched the passport of his Saudi employer and has managed to get on the London flight from Riyadh."

"So he's a Brit, is he?"

"Yes; they give his own passport number and the one for the Saudi passport he's using."

"What's he done, apart from steal a passport?"

"Doesn't say." The telex machine clicked into action again and the sergeant tore off the next message. "He must have done something wrong because this is from the Foreign Office."

Nick Forbes stood up and, in a subconscious movement, cleared a space on his desk immediately in front of him. He reached out for the telexes, realising that an ordinary day had just got a lot more interesting. "They want him met at the plane door and held ready for extradition back to Saudi on the next available plane. In fact, they want him on the same plane when it returns to Riyadh after its turnaround."

Two telephones rang almost simultaneously. Nick Forbes' day was about to get a lot worse, and his was not the only one.

CHAPTER TWENTY-NINE

It was the middle of June and Empty was mesmerised by a gecko which had materialised high up on the whitewashed wall above the heavily barred window. This one was paler and pinker than his old confidant Echo, but he knew that over the next few years they might become good friends. There was blatantly no rush to christen him, but not too many words rhymed with 'gecko'. 'Decko' was the bookmakers' favourite on account of the lizard's beady eyes. Empty's father had always used the expression 'have a decko', meaning to have a good look at … or perhaps he hadn't, come to think of it. Thoughts of his father threatened to take Empty's mood downwards, so he snapped back to the present. Was it really only ten days since he had been sat in his lounge watching Echo? It felt like several lifetimes, several light years away.

None of this would have happened if he had not volunteered to go to Saudi Arabia. What had been wrong with irrigating the greens and fairways of the Home Counties?

Why had he agreed to meet James Melrose? Who did he think he was, snooping around every building site in the Arabian Peninsula for … the Foreign Office? MI5? MI6? He didn't even know who he'd been doing it for, and was James Melrose for real? Empty realised that he was too gullible, too loyal and too eager to please. Even during the forty-five-minute stopover in Geneva on the flight to London, he had left a final telephone message for James telling him that the new aircraft facility at the old Riyadh airport was worth investigation. Still, he would never visit a building site again.

Years in a Saudi prison did not appeal to him. He was a creature of the great outdoors; he did not like walls … or wallpaper. Wallpaper – there was a novelty! The chances of him seeing Regency Stripe or wiping down the kitchen walls with the pattern of a Greek basket overflowing with grapes were nil; absolutely nil. Would Her Majesty's Government even try to get him back? The process would be long and drawn-out; imagine all of the forms to be filled in – in brown ink? He shivered at the thought as the memories flooded back.

That was why he had hatched the plan. One of the advantages of being a daydreamer is that you explore so many scenarios for any situation, ranging from the likely to the improbable. When the latter happens, you have already navigated the shoals and reefs. Even if Empty had waited, he knew that Sheikh Faisal would never have given him back his passport (with or without an exit visa). So where could he have obtained another one? Randy Coleman had been another possibility. If there was one man who knew how to live under the radar, it was him. However, the photo in Randy's spare passport didn't look anything like Empty, and the passport didn't have an exit visa anyway. He'd known from the start that if all else failed he knew where there was a passport which would not need an exit visa and would never be challenged … Sheikh Faisal's own. While he was at it, he'd taken his own for future use. The fact that Arab men dress much the same and cover their heads was one aspect of Saudi Arabian life that had helped Empty's plan. No one would interfere with a sheikh in a gold-edged cloak, especially an infirm, deaf one. The exclusivity of travelling first class had been a bonus. For all of this to work, he'd needed the unquestioning support of Amira and Kamal.

Empty looked up at Decko the Gecko. No, the name didn't work, and if they were going to spend a lot of time together, he would have to be renamed. Empty chose Paco. Paco the Gecko. That would have to do … at least it was a name.

He returned to his analysis of what had happened. Undoubtedly, booking the Jeddah-to-London flight in his own name, so ostentatiously on his credit card, had worked well; being trapped in the old airport during a dust storm had not.

"What would you like to drink?"

Empty snapped back to reality. "A margarita would be nice, but don't waste time dipping the glass in salt."

He would never change.

"Would sir like a paper umbrella and a cherry in his cocktail?"

"I've changed my mind. What shall I have, Paco? OK, I'll have a cold San Miguel from the fridge."

A couple of minutes later, Dawn brought the beer bottle, dripping with condensation, out onto the villa terrace, a pink paper umbrella projecting from the top.

Empty emerged from the bedroom into the dazzling Spanish sunlight. He scraped a heavy cast-iron chair across the red terrazzo tiles, put on some sunglasses and took a long drink from the bottle. "Beats that bloody cardamom crap which gives you nothing but …" he burped from the fizzy beer, "… wind."

Below him the children were playing among the oleander bushes with an overinflated Saudia jumbo. You had to feel sorry for the crew, whose experience must have been bumpy to say the least. Perhaps Otto, the inflatable autopilot in *Airplane!*, was in charge?

It was a Saudia TriStar, not a 747, that Empty had left in Geneva a week earlier during the forty-five-minute stopover which allowed rich Arabs to disembark for occasional visits to their Swiss bankers. Dawn and the kids had been waiting there for him since their hurried departure from high-rise High Wycombe. Having an idiot for a father had not prepared them for his arrival dressed as an Arab sheikh driving a limited-edition BMW 745i. It only had 2,360 kilometres on the clock, having previously never left the city limits of Geneva. Sheikh Faisal bought at least one new car every month so the BMW was probably high on his list for replacement; he just wouldn't have anything to trade in now. He had told Empty to use it the next time that he found himself in Geneva. All he had to do was tell the doorman at the Hotel Royal Continental … so Empty had.

Disposal of the car had not featured high on his plan. As he sipped his beer on the patio of his brother's villa, it was beneath his feet in the garage, unceremoniously hidden under two orange nylon sheets with a couple of broken sunbeds, a rusting Martini umbrella and a mattock for company. It was hardly the underground car park of the Hotel Royal Continental in Geneva. It would not be missed for a few weeks (if not months), but Empty wanted to get rid of it; five thousand pounds would be better than nothing.

He had devised a couple of oblique conversation pieces to explain its provenance but in the end they were not needed. At Casa Ronaldo the previous evening he had walked up to the bar through tables heaving with the British criminal underworld. How many Great Train Robbers were there? With deep brown suntans and the chain-smoking of filterless cigarettes, it was far more likely that cancer would get them before Scotland Yard did. There were even black blotches appearing on the serrano hams hanging from hooks on the ceiling. Loud, open-necked, short-sleeved shirts on thickset bodies revealed enough gold chains to anchor a frigate and Piaget watches with more movements than Schubert's life's work.

A delicate inquiry from Ronaldo (who came from Romford) about the difficulty of not having the necessary paperwork for the car had led five minutes later to several Brandy Alexanders at a table sat next to one of several ladies who all appeared to be called Doreen. She had a husky voice that could have stripped the ratchets off a funicular railway, probably caused by drinking what looked and smelled like agricultural diesel. Jacko – or, perhaps, Jack O. – who was her husband, soon offered 7,500 pounds in 'potatoes' for the car, unseen; he would pick it up in a couple of days.

"The thing is, you gotta keep hot metal moving." Jacko had offered free advice.

"As any foundry worker will tell you," Empty had said.

"So how many of these BMWs can you get, Michael?"

Later that week, 'Michael' and his family would move off down the coast to begin a new life in Fuengirola. With a villa bought for cash, and an old SEAT car, he would start a swimming-pool and irrigation business. He couldn't leave his brother's villa for a short while because he needed to wait

313

for the packages to arrive at the local post office. These were padded envelopes he had posted in Riyadh that may have contained scorpions; or, on the other hand, they may have contained wads of fifty-pound notes or large, ornate cheques.

"The kids need to go to bed," Empty suggested quietly.

"OK, kids, I've got a surprise for you up here!" Dawn was leaning over the balcony wall.

The children scampered up the tile stairs in huge anticipation.

"It's bedtime!" She grabbed them both to prevent them escaping.

"Aw, Mum, you lied to us!" they screamed in unison.

And we're going somewhere beginning with 'F', she thought to herself.

* * *

As Empty sipped his San Miguel *con parasol plastico* (Dawn's first attempt at Spanish), it was 2030 Zulu Time. Why the British Army should refer to Greenwich Mean Time as 'Zulu Time' is a mystery, not least to black Africans from Durban. However, twenty hours earlier at 0300 Zulu Time, Major General Jeremy Moore had signed the surrender of the Falklands in the Secretariat Building in Port Stanley. Brigadier General Mario Menéndez, whom the Argentinians refer to as the eighth Military Governor of the Malvinas, was probably also confused because it was 9.30pm in the Falklands; one of the few things upon which the British locals and Argentinians could agree. Just to complicate matters further, the British did not like the idea that the surrender might be signed on two separate days, i.e. at 9.30pm on the 14th June 1982 local time and 12.30am on the 15th June 1982 Greenwich Mean Time, so they metaphorically turned the clocks back to 8.59pm local time and 11.59pm in London.

If Empty had popped down to Casa Ronaldo for his evening beer, he would have seen the spontaneous outbursts of patriotism among the expat community watching the news of the Falklands on a television hanging high over the bar amongst the over-smoked hams. Insensitive to their Spanish friends who were present, these Londoners living in Cockfosters (as the Costas were known) sang 'God Save the Queen' and jeered every time an Argentinian appeared on screen. They saw themselves as British Bulldogs, although most had Dobermanns or Rottweilers. They waved their Union Jack-tattooed arms in the air in a display of patriotism that was only skin deep.

* * *

Someone else with a warped sense of patriotism was occupying a cell at Hereford Police Station on the 15th June 1982. Geoffrey Prime's indiscretions were still not public knowledge, and he had yet to confess to any. Detective Chief Superintendent David Cole, the senior investigating detective, was thinking through the alternatives by which Prime could be kept in custody without an application being made in open court, which would alert the media.

At lunchtime, DCS Cole was informed that he would be expected to attend a meeting in the Chief Constable's office later that day. At 5.30pm, the Director of Public Prosecutions, Sir Thomas Hetherington, stepped out of his car in Hereford to speak with the Chief Constable. It was made clear just how sensitive the interviews with Prime would be, given how long he had probably spied for the Russians.

In London, Sir Cecil was reasonably confident that Prime could not have had access to anything involving Project Canute. They had all been so careful to keep everything out of the system wherever possible, but you never knew, and at the beginning they had been less careful until the initial successes occurred.

Sir Cecil and his staff had the additional problem that neither Detective Chief Inspector Peter Picken nor DCS Cole was cleared to a sufficiently high level of security classification to hear Prime's confession. This was organised within a week, and on the 26th June 1982, Geoffrey Arthur Prime admitted to betraying his country to the Russians for fourteen years. He never mentioned Project Canute.

* * *

It was seventeen years later, on the 14th June 1999, that Randall paid his visit to Sir Cecil at his Cotswold home. It was the anniversary of the Falklands surrender, but was the relevance lost on Randall? This was more than likely. Randall had one task, and that was to find out why Robin Mills had cryptically suggested that he visit Sir Cecil. As the older man meandered from Riyadh to Goose Green and from Trabzon to Cheltenham, Randall fought to keep him on track. Had Robin thought that Cecil was insane? Disgruntled? Or that he knew something that they shared exclusively in a very small group?

"Lord Mallow, now he was a good chap."

"I'm sorry, who?"

"The Earl of Mallow and Blackwater."

"Oh yes," Randall replied, so as to avoid breaking the flow of the conversation.

"Good chap … well, he had a couple of misdemeanours … well, Miss Philippines, actually, wasn't it? Headed up the Falklands Liaison Unit; good Spanish speaker. He helped us to re-establish relations, you know, especially after the *Belgrano* … helped to pour oil on the waters."

That's the sort of insensitive thing that Robin would have said as well, Randall thought to himself. "What happened to that Tanner chap, Cecil?"

"No idea. Nothing, I should think."

"And the *Ikiz* cargo?"

"We got our wires a bit crossed there. Do computers still have wires? It was drugs, anyway. The Saudis sorted it out a bit sharpish. They were very grateful. Islam's a bit strict on such matters. Quite right, too."

"They didn't pursue Tanner?" Randall was not sure that this was getting him any nearer to anywhere important.

"No. All part of the deal, I think."

"And Tanner was Mannington's one and only spy?"

Sir Cecil looked up at Randall with a wry smile. "Mannington? That's the trouble when you put a lot of very bright people together … they *will* do stupid things."

There was a pause as a blackbird shrieked and clattered into the ivy on the opposite wall of the garden.

Inside the lounge, Sir Cecil continued. "They were right in one regard. Computers took over. That's why we set up the backup unit in London. Can't have all your eggheads in one basket, eh?"

Randall had been enormously patient. He had allowed himself to be patronised, diverted and generally taken around

317

the houses. Sir Cecil would have been flattered if he had known how very senior a position Randall occupied. He was the Deputy Director, which indicated how seriously Robin's swansong was being considered.

"Pennington got his job back?"

"Yes. No problem. Hit the old glass ceiling on the career front, but that didn't bother him. He was an Arabist through and through. Ran off with his secretary, I seem to remember. In general, Randall, woman problems can be dealt with. It's the young boys that are the career-killers. I expect that the problems got worse with all these grammar-school types now in the Service. They look at their frumpy wives and two spotty offspring at age forty only to decide that they are queer. At least at public school you know if you're queer by the time you go up to Oxbridge."

What was he talking about? *This may take another visit*, Randall thought to himself. How long would Cecil last? Perhaps the secret would be buried with him?

That thought reminded Randall that Sir Cecil had mentioned a Russian funeral on this date. Did this connect with the elusive Project Canute? "Delicate times in Russia, I hear?" He thew out some groundbait.

"Very unstable. If only Gorbachev could have lasted another couple of years." For the first time, there was genuine sadness in Sir Cecil's eyes.

"You mentioned a funeral?"

"Oh, nothing really," was the understatement to end them all.

Sir Cecil collected up the teacups. He had spent fifteen years engineering it so that Gorbachev or one of two other possible candidates would become President. Not even Gorbachev himself would know how his path had been cleared. The important funeral in Novosibirsk had followed the 'natural' death of Gorbachev's last main competition for the presidency. The man, like others before him, had been compromised by leaked false information that had led the KGB to take a more-than-active interest. From his time as First Secretary of the regional Communist Party in 1970, Gorbachev had been monitored by Cecil and the path around him cleared. Never would Sir Cecil or the other five men have imagined that their actions over all of those years would lead to the collapse of the USSR and the break-up of Eastern Europe. They had merely hoped that they could get a more liberal man into the presidency; one, it turned out some years later, Thatcher could 'do business with', to use her phrase. She never knew what Sir Cecil had achieved. He had, indeed, held back the tide, unlike Canute.

Now was not the time to reveal all of this, when it would cause an enormous political storm and might lead to a resurgence of the old Soviet Union under a reinvigorated Russia. Yeltsin was an embarrassing interlude that risked all of Sir Cecil's work. Soon he would be gone, surely? Cecil hoped that the Service was actively preparing the next person, but he doubted it. Perhaps in fifty years the story could be told. It would be a shame for it to be lost to posterity.

"Randall, I know the purpose of your visit and you can rest assured that I will take all of my secrets to the grave in St. John's Churchyard here in the village." Sir Cecil was choosing his words carefully.

A few minutes later, he showed his visitor to the door. The official chat was over.

"Anything planned for the Millennium?" Randall asked.

"A few fireworks, I think."